CALIFORNIA BEAR

ALSO BY DUANE SWIERCZYNSKI

NOVELS

Secret Dead Men

The Wheelman

The Blonde

Severance Package

Expiration Date

Canary

Revolver

THE CHARLIE HARDIE SERIES

Fun & Games

Hell & Gone

Point & Shoot

SELECTED GRAPHIC NOVELS

Breakneck

John Carpenter's Tales of Science Fiction: Redhead

John Carpenter's Tales of Science Fiction: Civilians

SHORT FICTION

Lush and other tales of Boozy Mayhem

WITH JAMES PATTERSON

Lion & Lamb

The Guilty (Audible Original)

Zero Tolerance (Audible Original)

CALIFORNIA BEAR

A NOVEL

DUANE SWIERCZYNSKI

MULHOLLAND BOOKS

LITTLE, BROWN AND COMPANY

New York Boston London

Copyright © 2024 by Duane Swierczynski

Hachette Book Group supports the right to free expression and the value of copyright. The purpose of copyright is to encourage writers and artists to produce the creative works that enrich our culture.

The scanning, uploading, and distribution of this book without permission is a theft of the author's intellectual property. If you would like permission to use material from the book (other than for review purposes), please contact permissions@hbgusa.com. Thank you for your support of the author's rights.

Mulholland Books / Little, Brown and Company
Hachette Book Group
1290 Avenue of the Americas
New York
NY 10104

mulhollandbooks.com

First Edition: January 2024

Mulholland Books is an imprint of Little, Brown and Company, a division of Hachette Book Group, Inc. The Mulholland Books name and logo are trademarks of Hachette Book Group, Inc.

The publisher is not responsible for websites (or their content) that are not owned by the publisher.

The Hachette Speakers Bureau provides a wide range of authors for speaking events. To find out more, go to hachettespeakersbureau.com or email hachettespeakers@hbgusa.com.

Little, Brown and Company books may be purchased in bulk for business, educational, or promotional use. For information, please contact your local bookseller or the Hachette Book Group Special Markets Department at special.markets@hbgusa.com.

Interior book design by Marie Mundaca

ISBN 978-0-316-38297-7

LCCN is available at the Library of Congress

Printing 1, 2023

LSC-C

Printed in the United States of America

For the Daughter

It's every man's business to see justice done.

The Memoirs of Sherlock Holmes

Why him? Why now?

Common Hollywood producer note

WEDNESDAY, MAY 30, 2018

THE BEAR

The California Bear, a serial torturer-murderer who had eluded justice for close to four decades, wanted a cookie.

He really shouldn't. Not with the diabetes and all. And he knew his wife would kill him if she found out he raided her secret stash. But what was life without the little indulgences?

The man was seventy-two years old. Back when he was the Bear, he liked to bind his victims with ligatures found around their homes (extension cords, shoelaces, medical tubing) and beat them senseless with his meaty fists. But right now, all this man cared about was pushing aside the row of grease-flecked cookbooks on the top shelf over the fridge to gain access to the sweet, carb-laden motherlode: a family-size package of Nutter Butters — his wife's favorite.

She thought she was so goddamned clever. But the man could easily follow her line of thinking. For years she'd nagged him to dust off the top of the fridge. He never did, because who the hell ever looks up there? So she hid the Nutter Butters there, behind cookbooks he'd never crack because — and this is a quote — "the day you boil an egg for yourself is the day they name me Queen of Mars."

The California Bear used to delight in mauling his victims' flesh with everyday household objects, relishing the terror he imagined this would invoke years later whenever the survivors would encounter these everyday objects again. But right now, he was focused on rooting around the fridge top until he found his prize. His fingers found the wrapping and he heard the crinkle. *Yes.* He pulled out the package and peeled open the top. The peanut-buttery scent was like mainlining his childhood. The man commanded himself to take just one. Fine, two. No more than four. He was a man used to keeping his impulses in check.

One of these days...

As he chewed, he toyed with the idea of lacing the remaining Nutter Butters with rat poison. See how the Queen of Mars would like that. Her throat seizing as her cow eyes registered all the dust on the fridge top. Dead little flecks of *them.* But like all his death fantasies involving his wife of thirty-four years, this would come to naught. The fun was the fantasy; the actual doing of the Thing would be counterproductive.

One of these days I'm going to...

Even though he'd eaten five — okay, six — cookies, his hunger remained. As the Bear, he had gotten away with dozens of horrors spanning four decades thanks to this highly disciplined restraint. But now the man was overcome with a great hunger inside him that couldn't be satisfied by mere enriched flour and corn syrup solids. He realized that now; he'd been denying it for way too long.

One of these days I'm going to cut you into little pieces.

The man left the house through the back door and lumbered into his detached garage. It was well after midnight; he would have the privacy he craved.

Once inside, he shed his sweatshirt, followed by his damp T-shirt. He carefully draped both over the Weber kettle grill pushed up against the wall. The man heaved a dozen heavy boxes until the trunk was revealed. For a minute, he forgot what he was looking for, what he was doing out here. But then it came back to him, like a tap on the shoulder. *Remember who you fucking are.*

Growing excited now, he fumbled with the tiny key on his chain. Slipped it into the lock and opened his chest of treasures. So many things to choose from. The keychain with the rubber frog. The white-gold wedding band looped through a chain. The Lady Remington. The cheap plastic toy soldier pointing his rifle at an unseen enemy. Best of all, a plastic baggie stuffed with colorful plastic alphabet fridge magnets.

Current events had brought this all back in a real way. Planning, dreaming, storytelling, reminiscing...all those forces brought him here, into this garage, searching for tangible pieces of his former self. Was this actually him, once upon a time, or was it just an extremely vivid dream that he never managed to shake? More importantly: Could he become the Bear again?

The man rummaged through the trunk until he found what he was really looking for. He didn't see them at first. He *felt* them cross his calloused fingertips. The metal claws, still sharp enough to draw blood.

THE GIRL DETECTIVE

This was a serious jam — perhaps her worst ever. Trapped in a window-less room, with no clear understanding of when she might be able to leave, or even why she was here . . . though she had her suspicions.

It was 4 a.m. on a Wednesday and she was utterly exhausted. Her brain felt lost in a thick marine-layer fog that had taken up residence in her skull. Which was unfortunate because her final English paper was due in just two days. If she blew the deadline, she might never make it to sophomore year. And as usual, she'd settled on a topic that was both ambitious and probably impossible:

She'd promised her English teacher she'd solve a murder.

Fortunately, she'd brought along her research materials. A few weeks ago, her uncle bought an armful of old mystery novels from the Iliad Bookshop in North Hollywood. His big idea was that he'd find some old detective story that just so happened to be in the public domain (meaning: free) so he could take (steal) the plot and modernize it for a screenplay. This idea was quickly forgotten, like so many of her uncle's harebrained ideas. But those writers — Agatha Christie, Arthur Conan Doyle, Dorothy Sayers, and Wilkie Collins — could teach her everything she needed to know about solving a murder.

So the Girl Detective had tucked the books under her arm and trans-ported them to her bedroom. And in turn, they transported her, at a time when she needed escape the most.

She hadn't been feeling well and was nervous about telling her aunt and uncle. Often it felt like even the whisper of bad news sent them both into a spiral of anxiety and panic.

Friends told her: just eat a fucking cheeseburger already. All she needed was a little iron in her blood. And while it was true, the Girl Detective had been a vegetarian for four years now, she knew that wasn't the answer. There was something else going on.

All this drama came to a head when her uncle offered to throw a cookout for the Girl Detective and her school friends one Thursday evening—mostly to blow off some steam before finals. Their apartment complex had a decent pool and a massive outdoor grill. The Girl Detective was chilling on one of the overstuffed wicker couches, waiting for her vegan hot dog to be finished...and the next thing she knew, it was an hour later. She had passed out. Worse yet, her bestie, Violet, said it had taken a few minutes to fully wake her.

Her aunt tried to make a doctor's appointment the very next day, but there was nothing available until the day after Memorial Day. The Girl Detective assured her aunt she'd be fine; it was just freshman-year burnout. At this point she was also trying to believe the lie that it was merely a lack of iron in her blood. Maybe Uncle Louis would grill her a medium-rare steak.

Saturday: Her aunt and uncle thought a trip to the Broad Art Museum would perk her up. She loved art museums, right? Dear Reader, she did not. The day was a slog, and she spent most of it worried about her final English paper. You know, the one where she had to solve a murder.

Sunday: Oof.

Monday: On Memorial Day her uncle tried to cheer her up with another cookout, but all she wanted to do was nap.

Tuesday: Finally, a visit to the doc, who sent the Girl Detective to St. Joseph's for bloodwork to see what was up with her being tired all the time. On the way to the hospital they found themselves following the pink Corvette driven by Angelyne. Which cracked up the Girl Detective. In LA, Angelyne was famous for being famous. No movie credits, no hit songs, no nothing. Decades ago she'd lucked into buying primo billboard space (to promote her nonexistent career) and somehow horse-traded that primo space into multiple billboards. Soon, a legend was born. Lucky denizens would spot her tooling around LA in her trademark neon-pink sports car. And there she was, idling directly in front of them, a neon-pink omen of California doom. The hospital drew blood and told her she just needed rest and (drum roll, please) some iron. But when the needle-stick site blew up like a balloon—a hematoma, she later learned—serious trouble was a certainty. She didn't want to deal with any of it. Especially on a school night.

Which brought her to her current predicament. At crazy o'clock this morning, her aunt received a panicked voicemail from the doc: *Get that girl to Children's Hospital LA on the double.* And now here lies the Girl Detective, in a glass-and-metal cell, waiting for the (sure-to-be) bad news. They don't rush you to the hospital for shits and giggles.

But she didn't want to think about that right now.

Instead she wanted to focus on the murder she had to solve.

It was technically a cold case, from just two years ago. A local real estate tycoon had been run over and killed inside an underground Burbank garage. Two witnesses saw the make and model of the car as well as a partial plate. That was enough to arrest someone for the hit-and-run, but the conviction didn't stick, thanks to a technicality. So, did their suspect do the crime, or did someone else get away with it? That possibility was what fascinated the Girl Detective. Maybe someone did this and just . . . walked. And they were out there, living their best life, not a care in the world.

Not if the Girl Detective could help it.

At first her English teacher, Mr. Wisher, was a little taken aback by her proposal for her final paper. He had been expecting what—the millionth essay extolling the virtues of freakin' *In Cold Blood?* How does a murder investigation qualify as a work of literature? But the Girl Detective played it smart. She knew Wisher was a big Tom Wolfe and Hunter S. Thompson fan, so she framed her paper as a New Journalism take on a crime that happened in her backyard. Shockingly, he bought it! Which was handy because the Girl Detective was going to pursue this investigation regardless.

She had the case file in her bag, along with many articles about California hit-and-run laws as well as background pieces on the real estate tycoon—a man named Julian Church. To know the crime, you must first know the victim. Yes, she tumbled down a rabbit hole of research. Yes, she should have stopped the research (which was the most fun part) and started the actual writing of the paper weeks ago. The Girl Detective had no defense other than she worked best under pressure.

She was lost in murder thoughts when the door opened with a loud, whiny creak. Someone needed to WD-40 that, stat. Her aunt and uncle and a man she presumed to be a doctor stepped into the room. She quickly closed the file before they could see.

"Hi, honey," her aunt Reese said.

Her inner Sherlock ignored the "honey." Instead she scanned for the telling details, the ones Aunt Reese was desperately trying to hide. The puffiness around their eyes, the lingering sniffles. The forced smiles on their faces, expressions completely at odds with being at a hospital at 4 a.m.

So before they told her what the doctor had said just a few minutes ago, the Girl Detective already knew. This was not something like a flu or a case of low iron levels in your blood. This was a moment most human beings dreaded, despite having seen it hundreds of times in movies and TV shows. This was the Moment You Hear Incredibly Dire News.

The doctor told her the dire news.

The Girl Detective looked at him and straight up asked: "Am I going to die?"

"KILLER"

Just after 5 a.m., ex-con Jack "Killer" Queen shuffled over to the motel fridge, opened the door, and drained an entire liter of bottled spring water. He took his time, enjoying the feeling of cool refrigerated air washing over his bare legs. Nobody telling him to hurry up, move it along now, no dawdling.

The restaurant below the motel didn't open until seven. Jack decided to walk down to the beach, stick his feet in the ocean, maybe look up at the fading stars. When was the last time he'd seen them? So long ago that someone else was president.

Making it to the beach wasn't as easy as he'd thought. There was a six-lane highway blocking his path and metal guard rails up the middle. After some wandering about like an idiot, Jack finally spotted a traffic light about fifty yards to the right of the roadhouse. But there was no pedestrian path. Even at this early hour traffic was constant in both directions. What, were people supposed to just stand here and squint at the ocean?

After a while Jack discovered a staircase that looked like it led down to a subway platform. Instead it was a pedestrian tunnel that burrowed under the six-lane road. The tunnel was dark and smelled like piss and salt.

Well, what choice did Jack have, if he wanted to step into the Pacific?

Halfway through the tunnel he started having those bad feelings again, as if the miraculous reversal of these past few months were nothing more than a dream, as if he were still inside, and he'd reach out and feel the concrete wall again and hear the rusty springs groan beneath his weight.

The temptation to turn back was strong. His heart raced. The animal part of his brain screamed this was a trap. *Run. Run away now.* But the perverse part of his brain — Jack liked to think this was his genuine self — forced him to keep going anyway. So what if it was a trap? If he wasn't fooled by this one, it'd be another one. Might as well get it over with.

Soon Jack found a set of stairs leading up to the dimly lit beach. Out in the darkness the waves smashed onto a surf he couldn't see.

He sat down on the sand and waited for God to turn up the dimmer switch.

When he saw the first glimmer of pink on the horizon, he wept. He wasn't exactly sure why. But he knew it had been years since he'd allowed himself to feel so intensely.

A strange thing, bottling up the tears for so long. But it was a matter of survival.

During the trial he had still been in a state of shock. He listened to his attorneys. His attorneys told him how to feel and what to project to the jury. When things didn't go his way, he clamped down on his emotions. You never want to show weakness behind bars, because that would mean certain death. He kept on clamping down until just yesterday, when he was finally released. Only now could he feel.

He was surprised by the power of his grief. It was almost like a seizure, the way it wracked his body. For a while he thought he might be permanently deranged by grief. He thought he might keep crying forever, that his tears would overwhelm the Pacific and kill a lot of people on the other side of the ocean.

But then the sun finished climbing its way into the sky, and pink turned to blue. Jack clamped it down again and felt the cool breeze off the water, the spray on his face. The Pacific seemed to tell him: *Your tears are nothing. I've been collecting them from your kind for millennia.*

A while later he started back toward the roadhouse. Only then did it occur to Jack that he was wearing skivvies and nothing else.

He also had no idea what time it was. He didn't own a watch. The one Jack used to wear was still locked up in Evidence somewhere.

On the way back Jack skipped the tunnel and decided to take his chances with the road, which turned out to be the Pacific Coast Highway. Now that he could see properly, there was a way to make it across if you timed the cars making the left turn from Entrada Drive.

Jack didn't see the roadhouse very clearly last night since they'd arrived so late. But now in the bright sun it revealed itself as bright green and absurd. Plaster dinosaurs and vampires and pirates and mummies and oversize insects lined the roof, as if gathered on the two-story building for a cocktail party. If you gave a five-year-old a shoebox and asked him to design a motel, this was pretty much what they'd come up with.

He didn't mind it. He couldn't wait to show his daughter in a few days.

As Jack walked across the parking lot, he could hear the 1940s swing music they piped over the loudspeakers all day. Last night, when he checked in and heard Artie Shaw's "Begin the Beguine," he thought that some old dude or young hipster had seized control of the jukebox. But now he was hearing Woody Herman's "Woodchopper's Ball."

Jack smiled. Matilda would appreciate the swing tunes. She was a modern teenager but a lover of all things retro. Maybe he could bring her down here later this week, when she was back from her school trip and his business with Hightower was over.

The bottom floor of Patrick's Roadhouse was all restaurant; the top floor was a series of "cozy" private rooms. One of them was Jack's—for the time being anyway. He went around back and walked up the creaky wooden steps. Once inside, he changed into his only set of clothes: a navy-blue suit they gave him at the prison gates.

Cato Hightower's door was ajar. Jack pushed it open with his fingertips and found the retired cop in his boxers, smoking a joint. Without even looking, Hightower held it out to Jack.

"It's legal now. Go ahead, enjoy yourself."

Jack dismissed the idea with a wave. "Never smoked it before. Can't see a reason to start now."

"That is *exactly* the reason to start. This shit is wasted on teenagers! They don't have fully formed minds, so what's there to expand? Middle-aged guys like you and me, we're perfect for the wacky weed."

Hightower was about as middle-aged as Jack was a member of a boy band. The man's thinning hair was spread over his skull in a vain attempt at full coverage. This fooled no one.

"No, I'm good."

"You telling me as a former jazz musician, you never got high? I'm calling bullshit on that. All you guys smoke reefer."

"Nah. Booze was my thing. As you may recall from the circumstances of my . . . arrest."

"Huh," Hightower said, as if the idea had never occurred to him. "Anyway, got some papers for you to sign, then we can go out and have some fun."

Hightower's room was identical to Jack's but in reverse. Same tiny kitchenette, same narrow bed, same beach art. Only this room had boxes all over the place. The floor was covered in them—overstuffed cardboard boxes with imitation wood grain, all with varying degrees of mildew and yellowing.

Hightower also had great thick lumps of clothes covering his bed, raising the question of where he'd slept last night.

But the real head-scratchers were the three ladies in the room with him. Topless, with flowing hair and stained-glass vaginas.

"What's the deal with these things?" Jack asked.

"Jack, meet the Weird Sisters. Weird Sisters, this is Jack."

"They're weird all right. Where'd they come from?"

"Had 'em commissioned from a metallurgist up in Ojai. The wife, though, doesn't quite appreciate their beauty. She's not a fine art person."

The Sisters were made of wrought iron twisted into curvy, seductive female shapes, detailed down to the pointy metal nipples.

"Can't imagine why."

"They were supposed to go on the deck at our place up in Port Hueneme," Hightower said. "We're still, ah, negotiating that point."

"Speaking of...I thought that's where I'd be crashing until Matilda was back home. Your place in Port Hueneme, I mean. I hate the idea of you shelling out for two rooms down here by the beach."

"The wife's juggling a few work deadlines, which means she's not exactly going to be feeling social. I thought we'd kick back for a few days. What better way to make plans for the future than to relax near the bosom of the Pacific Ocean? Besides, the rooms come with free breakfast. Are you hungry? Because I'm fucking starving."

Jack gestured to the Weird Sisters. "They gonna join us?"

Hightower stubbed out the joint in a stone ashtray, then plucked an impossibly loud Hawaiian shirt from the pile on his bed and pulled it over his bulky torso.

"Nah. They're watching their figures."

THE BEAR

Look at that skinny harlot dance! Not a care in the world. Framed by her picture window, as if she were a starlet on a private movie screen.

Back in the old days, the Bear would do his scouting in the daylight hours. So that's what the man did now. Nobody would give a second glance to an old man out for a leisurely stroll around Los Feliz on a hot and sunny Wednesday afternoon. Nobody in this town gave old men a second glance at all. In some ways Los Feliz had changed a great deal since his first trips here. Rife with petty crime in the late seventies, the neighborhood was more or less gentrified these days.

But this little slut in the window brought him back to that hazy sunbaked decade, when women looked and acted exactly like this. She was a living throwback, wearing shorts that were once denim jeans, the legs cut off so high that he could practically make out the outline of her vulva. She wore nothing else but a bra. It was as if she were performing a private dance for him, or whoever happened to be walking by.

Incredible.

He had been watching her for several days now to learn her routine. She had no husband, several boyfriends (apparently), and no visible means of support. Stealing mail had revealed little in terms of her financial life. No utility bills, and phone bills were a thing of the past. The catalogs were addressed to another — most likely previous — resident.

The man reached into his pocket and felt the handle of the vintage

15

razor blade. He was instantly transported back in time to this very house — a two-story single-bedroom on Rodney Drive.

Back then, the man hadn't put much thought into it. He'd followed an intoxicated woman here from a dive bar on Hillhurst after failing to work up the courage to talk to her. If that had been the era of smartphones, maybe he would have surreptitiously snapped a photo or three, just to have something to make sure she stayed in his memory bank. She was that fucking beautiful. Instead, he broke inside and terrorized and murdered her and took a souvenir before he left. In this case, the Lady Remington. It had been perched on the edge of the bathroom sink.

12 JULY '80 — that was what he'd scrawled on the side of the razor's handle. Followed by LF — RD.

Los Feliz, Rodney Drive.

A potential nightmare if a prosecutor ever got their hands on these souvenirs. But the man was glad he'd saved them all, especially now that it was so important that he remember *exactly* where and when these objects were acquired. These tangible relics were a direct hotline to the past. They were bringing back the Bear in him.

Now, in the present, the harlot had disappeared from her window. For a moment the man was confused, wondering if he'd just hallucinated her little dance . . .

But no. There she was, on her porch. She'd dressed herself in something slightly more appropriate. A thin hoodie shrouded her torso, and the denim cutoffs had been replaced by equally immodest running shorts. She stretched in the sun, this way and that, and then hopped off her porch and began walking with great purpose in his direction. This gave him a small jolt. Had she spotted him looking at her? Was she about to confront him?

When the lithe slut jogged straight past him, the man knew his worry was for nothing. She paid no attention, didn't even make eye contact. The elderly may as well not exist.

The man turned and followed, quickening his pace to match hers. She was power walking toward Hillhurst, toward that same dive bar where he'd found his first victim, as if time were rewinding all the way now. Halfway up the long block, however, the man's heart thundered in his chest, urging him to slow down. Sweat trickled down his back, and little electric sparks ignited in his fingertips. The man stopped and caught his breath. It was fine. There was no need to follow her now; that wasn't part of the plan anyway.

No, for this to work, she had to be home, in one of her most unguarded and vulnerable moments. And it had to be night. Always the night. Because even though everyone used to call him the California Bear, he thought of himself as the Midnight Man. He made a mental note to dig his Walkman out of the storage locker for his next scouting mission.

THE GIRL DETECTIVE

The Girl Detective's to-do list was officially out of control. In addition to her overdue English paper / murder investigation, there were now blood transfusions, a slow drip of platelets, and the specter of chemotherapy looming. It was all too much. All because of the l-word.

This was a left hook completely out of nowhere. Leukeme-*what*, now? This was a whole new villain to face, as if Professor Moriarty had been lurking in her bloodstream this entire time, just waiting for the right moment to pounce. Grudgingly, the Girl Detective put away the files relating to the Case of the Real Estate Tycoon and opened Google on her phone to check on all the stuff the doctor had told her aunt Reese and uncle Louis.

There was a brief moment there when the Girl Detective tried to rationalize the situation, telling herself: *Hey, this isn't the end of the world. Lots of people deal with leukemia. Maybe I can even receive treatment as an outpatient.* This, she quickly realized, was folly.

For one thing, there were apparently two kinds of leukemia — the treatable kind, and the other kind. The Girl Detective had the other kind (naturally). Both required chemotherapy, so there was no getting out of that. But the odds of surviving were quite different. This was not welcome news.

For *another* thing: the Girl Detective hadn't realized how close she had been to actual death. Her blood numbers were out of control, with white blood cells all over the place. When they stuck her with that needle yesterday (and she'd suffered that gnarly hematoma), she could have easily bled out. Which would have been the worst ending ever. Hence the urgency to bring her into the hospital early this morning.

So now her aunt and uncle were spreading the word on social media about blood and platelet donations. The Girl Detective was essentially a vampire now, requiring a constant stream of the red stuff (vintage: O positive) and the gross yellow stuff (platelets, which looked like chunky urine). The hospital did what they could, but supplies often ran low and depended upon the kindness of donors.

On top of all that, there was a series of tests and procedures to turn her body into a more efficient vampire. The most invasive of these procedures: the installation of a PICC line (a "peripherally inserted central catheter," she'd learned), which was essentially a freeway straight to her heart. This had to be put in right away, which made the Girl Detective feel like she was already on that freeway, hurtling toward a destination she never wanted to visit. Oh, and the spinal tap wouldn't be much fun either.

There was a moment when she was placed in her new room — her home for the foreseeable future — when she thought she might lose her mind completely. There were too many people in her face, wanting to do all kinds of things to her body, with Aunt Reese and Uncle Louis trying to keep up with the flurry of medical forms and releases and updates. The Girl Detective wanted to call a huge time-out and send everyone back to their corners.

This wasn't possible, so she did the next best thing.

"Aunt Reese?"

"Yes, honey."

"I hate to ask, but my throat is sore. Would it be possible for you to go to the cafeteria and find something cold, like a Popsicle? Or maybe ice cream?"

Aunt Reese nodded but clearly the request threw her into a new tailspin, asking the closest nurse if the Girl Detective was allowed to have a Popsicle or ice cream, and if so, what kind, and so on. This played out for a while.

But the Girl Detective knew it would pay off. Her request was calculated to remove Aunt Reese from the room for a short period of time. And surely Uncle Louis would follow, because he was still weirded out by being a surrogate parent. There was no way he'd sit here and sign forms and listen to even more dire news by himself.

"I'd go downstairs to the cafeteria myself," the Girl Detective said, "but..."

And with that, she lamely gestured at the IV line running into her arm, which would soon be replaced by a line running right into her chest. She didn't break out the full sad eyes and pouty lip; she let the medical gear do that work for her.

"No, of course, sweetie," Aunt Reese said. "What flavor?"

"Oh, anything, as long as it's cold."

And she truly didn't care. Her throat was not sore (yet). Her objective was to send Aunt Reese and Uncle Louis on a mission so that they could take a deep breath and get a grip on what was happening.

And while they were gone, the Girl Detective could finally weep. She owed herself that much. This day had already been a lot, and it was barely 9 a.m. She cried for herself, and she cried for her mother.

She felt vaguely guilty about bothering the ghost of her mother with grief and worry all the time. (The late Mrs. Queen had raised a stronger woman than that, hadn't she?) But she could also hear her mother saying, *Stop it. This is why I'm here.* Of course, that last part was a kind of lie, because she *wasn't* here. And then the Girl Detective would cry even harder.

Okay. Enough tears. Rationally, the Girl Detective knew she couldn't cure her leukemia. At least, not without proper funding and a lot of research. So why waste brain power on that? Better to stick to something she *could* do.

She needed to solve this case by Friday, when her father would be getting out of prison.

"KILLER"

Breakfast was included with the price of the room so long as you didn't spend more than $18. The menu was loaded with endless varieties of omelets and egg-based dishes; each happened to cost $17.99.

"I'm fond of the breakfast burrito," Hightower said. "Thing's the size of a colon."

Jack went with a diced-ham and green pepper omelet named after a celebrity he'd never heard of, paired with tomato juice that came in a glass so skinny and tall it looked like part of a science experiment. Hightower ordered the breakfast colon along with a Diet Coke, which was served in a plastic mug the size of a quart of paint.

"The servings are generous here," Hightower said, somewhat ominously.

While they waited for their food to arrive, Jack listened to the swing music (Glenn Miller's "In the Mood") and scanned the room. Patrick's appeared to have begun its life as a modest dining car next to a gas station on the PCH. But then it mutated, adding a large dining room off to the right, the small apartments above, and then finally dinosaurs and monsters. Jack and Hightower had been seated in the dining room, where the décor was homey, in a garage sale kind of way. Behind Hightower, pushed up against the wall, was a massive throne reserved for the thirty-eighth governor of California: Arnold Alois Schwarzenegger.

Jack noticed that Hightower kept looking at him, as if waiting for the ex-con to say something. Jack took the hint.

"Thank you again for everything you've done for me."

"You don't have to thank me," Hightower replied. But he said it in a way that implied Jack should continue thanking him for all his hard work.

"I'm serious. You spent a long time fighting for me. I can't thank you enough."

"It's nothing."

"It . . . is a big deal. You could be on a beach somewhere. Instead, you're working these cases."

Hightower smiled. "Beach is right out there."

Before Jack could say "you know what I mean," the food arrived. Hightower had not been joking. His breakfast burrito looked pregnant with six other burritos. Jack's celebrity omelet was as thick as a Gideon Bible.

"We're not going to have to eat until supper," Hightower said with great delight.

They ate in near silence. There was really no choice. A breakfast plate this vast required one's full attention. The forking, the knifing, the lifting, the chewing, the swallowing. When they finished, it was like the two of them had served a tour of duty together. Jack's heart beat faster just to process everything. Hightower leaned back in his wooden chair to the groaning point. Tomorrow, Jack decided, he'd order the fruit plate.

"How was your first full meal as a free man in two years?"

"Best omelet I've ever had."

"You gotta try some of the others. Be adventurous. Don't be afraid of the hot stuff. Unless you've got a weak stomach."

"I'm practically a goat. Prison food prepares you for anything."

Hightower laughed. "I hear you, buddy. I've had my share of institutional meals. I regret every single one of them."

"I was serious earlier. Tell me why you did this. What's in it for you?"

"I told you when we first met. I wanted to do some good."

"Come on. There must be something else."

The ex-cop grinned. "As a buddy of mine once said, it is an immodest thing to talk about yourself. But then again, modesty has never been my strong suit."

Hightower explained that he had been an ex-cop longer than he'd been a cop. He was proud of saying that, for some reason. He never drew a gun. Never threw a punch, even. He was one of those lucky cops who put in his twenty years without so much as a sprained ankle.

"And that bugged the shit out of me."

Twenty years, Hightower continued, and for what? Did he make the world a better place? Did he change lives? Fuck if he knew. It all just felt so useless. So one day in his early retirement, Hightower read a *Los Angeles Times* story about a guy who'd been sent up for a murder he didn't commit. A retired cop worked thirty years to prove this man's innocence, reinvestigating the case and petitioning for new DNA tests and appealing all the way up to the governor's office.

"That story was an electric shock," Hightower said. "All of a sudden I realized — *that's* what I want to do with my life."

"And somehow you found me."

"Well," Hightower explained, "no use saving a life that can't enjoy living."

"What do you mean?"

"That ex-cop and ex-con from the *LA Times* story? They died, like . . . *months* later. Prostate cancer for the cop. The other one had a stroke. I mean, both were in their eighties by the time the case was resolved. On the bright side, the ex-con had no heirs, so the state saved itself millions in that wrongful conviction suit."

"That's insane."

"Life will always find a way to fuck you."

The bill arrived, which came to pretty much their drinks plus tip. Hightower insisted on covering that too. Which was good because Jack only had two hundred bucks in gate money.

"Let's go get hammered," Hightower said.

At this point it was not even noon. Jack was pretty sure Hightower was as baked as a potato.

"Didn't you, uh, say I had papers to sign?"

"We can do that tomorrow. Jack, you've just been sprung from the Gray Bar Hotel! When's the last time you had a drink? And I don't mean that pruno shit the cons brew up in their toilets. Please don't tell me you drank that shit."

"I did not," Jack said, "drink that shit."

"So what's your poison? You were a whiskey man, as I recall."

Jack flashed back to his trial, the DA's office making a big deal about the brand. Knob Creek. *Well, aren't we a fancy killer.*

"I don't think this is a good idea."

"Do you have something else in mind? I can't do whores or hard drugs. For one I'm happily married, and for two I'm a former agent of the law, so I'm not getting into anything illegal."

"That's not what I meant."

"What then?"

"I was hoping to . . . you know, start looking for a job. Reenter society and all that. I didn't presume I'd be playing gigs again, but I'd like to find something to pay the bills. So I can take care of my daughter. Who I'll be seeing in two short days."

Storm clouds rolled over Hightower's face. Then he furrowed his brow, just in case Jack didn't get it the first time. He opened his mouth, closed it, then opened it again.

"Listen, Jack. That's a battle we're not going to fight today. Today, and tonight, we're going to get shit-faced. And then tomorrow morning we'll pour our sore asses back into these uncomfortable wooden seats, order ourselves an epic hangover breakfast, and then we'll start drawing up plans for your future. How does that sound?"

"I also need to hit a mall or something. I don't want to be stuck wearing this old suit all the time."

"Sure thing, buddy. *After* we celebrate."

"Mall first, celebrate later?"

Hightower slapped the table. "No further questions, Your Honor. Let's get soused."

THE GIRL DETECTIVE

This whole "fighting death" thing was exhausting, and seriously getting in the way of her real work.

The constant flow of blood and platelets was one thing, but what they don't tell you about hospitals is how you're interrupted all the time. Blood pressure and temperature checks. An introduction from this specialist and that pediatrician and someone in charge of "Child Life" (which sort of cracked her up, considering the mission at hand was preventing Child Death) and a dizzying array of nurses. Some of them were cool, but even the cool ones had a knack for interrupting her train of thought.

As much as the Girl Detective hated being a cliché, her only option was to bury herself in her phone for a while and allow the chaos to continue to swirl around her.

She messaged her best friend, Violet, who would be at lunch right around now. So weird to think that in some alternate universe — the one where she wasn't doing battle with the l-word — she'd be right there with her, stealing fries from their friends and conspiring to trade her way to a second dessert.

What up, V, she thumbed.

M!!! Are you still at the hospital

Yep just living my best life

You think you'll be back in school tomorrow???

The Girl Detective didn't want to drop the leukemia bomb on her bestie. Not just yet. Certainly not in a text. That would be cruel and confusing for Violet. Better to do it in person at some point. For the time being, she would tell Violet that her blood numbers were low, and they were giving her transfusions to help. Technically, not a lie.

Probably not they want me to rest :(

Violet was also a worrier, and a bit of a gossip, and if the Girl Detective told her the truth, the news would spread among the freshman class in a nanosecond. There was very little she could control at this point; at least she could control that.

Last day of school is Friday! Are you going to miss that?

Considering Friday would be her first day of chemo . . . yeah, chances were excellent that her days as a freshman were officially over. She'd file her papers through the school server, and boom, she'd be a sophomore. If, heh heh, she lived long enough . . .

Maybe it was too soon for those kinds of jokes. The Girl Detective wasn't sure. Mostly, she was still numb with shock and hanging on to a tiny filament of hope that this was just a dream and she would wake up in a second and be back to her usual tired self.

We'll see, she thumbed. Then, wishing very much to change the topic: Hey, can you do me a favor?

Anything!!!

(Violet really had a thing for multiples of punctuation. At some point, the Girl Detective was going to have to wean her off that.)

The Girl Detective told Violet exactly what she needed from the Burbank Public Library. Violet agreed to stop there after school and take photos of what she found. Which was a relief, because the Girl Detective had no idea how she'd be able to do that kind of research from the confines of her torture rack (i.e., her hospital bed).

The end of lunch period was close at hand, which the Girl Detective had counted on — she never liked awkward goodbyes, especially when she was hiding something. Violet went off to English class. The Girl Detective desperately wished to be heading there too.

All this communication left her exhausted. Maybe she should rest, like the doctors — and nurses, and specialists — kept telling her.

But as she closed her eyes, the Girl Detective overheard her aunt and uncle fighting in the hallway over something. Not something; it had to be about *her*. But she couldn't piece together all the words. Something about "literally *today*" and "you're such a selfish prick" and "why did you lie?" This was nothing new. Reese and Louis had two anxiety-inducing careers—hers, selling real estate; his, trying to become the next Quentin Tarantino. They would routinely fight and then declare a cease-fire, and then it would be a weird cold war of forced politeness until they started fighting all over again. The Girl Detective had no idea why they stayed together. Adults were weird.

But their strange relationship was a mystery for another day. She had her immediate family—what was left of it, anyway—to figure out.

For three months now she'd known that her father would soon be released from prison, which put a strange kind of deadline pressure on her. The Girl Detective had assumed her new reality (life without her parents, living with Reese and Louis) would be a jail term until she turned eighteen and could legally strike out on her own. She imagined that one day she'd have that long-dreaded conversation with her father—something along the lines of *What the hell were you thinking, Padre?*—but not until she was well into adulthood and had years of processing (and possibly therapy) behind her. The Girl Detective certainly didn't expect to be doing this... well, *now*.

And when the Girl Detective looked him in the eyes in a couple of days, she would ask him the question she'd been too young (and frightened) to ask at the time of his trial:

Did you do it?

To *truly* believe him, however, and repair their fractured relationship, the Girl Detective would have to discover the truth for herself.

"KILLER"

Hightower started his personal drinking party at Venice Beach's famous Sidewalk Cafe, which was originally an offshoot of the independent bookstore next door. Over the years the café took on a life of its own, and now the bookstore was the afterthought. Jack made a mental note to pop in there later, maybe find something motivational to read. Something like *So You've Been in Prison and Need to Get Your Shit Together.*

They sat at the bar inside, and Hightower suggested they skip the foreplay of a couple of beers and opt for whiskey shots.

"No, I'm good," Jack said.

"Come on," Hightower responded, a tone of petulance in his voice. "You're not going to have me drink alone, are you?"

"You won't be drinking alone. I'll be right next to you, watching you."

"Fine. At least have a beer."

"No."

"No means yes," Hightower said, "and a restraining order means no. Bartender, two shots of Jack with Dos Equis chasers. And lime. That beer's gotta have lime."

"Seriously . . . Hightower. *No.* I can't do that anymore."

Jack had been cold sober for two years now. Not by choice. He would have stayed drunk throughout his prison term if he could have. He used to have what people called a high tolerance. But all that was gone now. His brain and liver were reborn virgins. And now that he had achieved that status, he wasn't about to fuck it up again.

"You say *no*," Hightower said, "and I hear no . . . strovia."

"You're not saying that word right."

"After a few, it won't matter."

Jack ordered and proceeded to nurse a Diet Coke with a slice of lemon. Hightower shrugged and downed both shots, both beers.

Outside the Sidewalk Cafe, directly across Ocean Front Walk, sat a weathered black grand piano, looking as if it had been blown off the deck of some cruise ship out on the Pacific. The piano's placement turned out to be intentional. Jack noticed a scruffy-looking man in his fifties or sixties sit down at the keys and begin to play an astonishing series of classical pieces, much to the delight of tourists and beachgoers. After about an hour of playing for tips, the scruffy-looking man closed the lid on his instrument, then shuffled off.

Jack stared at the piano for a long time, trying to lose himself in the past. But invisible waves kept dragging him back to this awful present.

Hightower, meanwhile, was having a grand old time. He noticed a barback hauling a bucket of ice toward the sink. The barback, who looked to be in his sixties and junkie thin, noticed Hightower noticing.

"How's your day going, sir?"

"Excellent," Hightower said. "How about you, brother?"

The barback dumped the ice, then pondered the question a moment. "I woke up yesterday morning with a big jar of pennies, nickels, and dimes. You know, one of those glass jugs, filled halfway to the top."

"I know what you mean."

"I counted it," the barback said, "and realized I was down to my last five bucks. All that I owned in the world. I had to make a change. I had to go on an *adventure*."

"I hear you, man. You had change, but you needed change."

"That's exactly what I'm saying! So I set out that day, and I ended up here. How do you like that?"

Hightower slapped the bar top. "Congrats, my friend. This your first day on the job?"

"It's my second, technically."

"Well, let me buy you a drink."

"Uh-uh, sir, no, thank you. Having a drink is how I ended up with nothing but a jugful of pennies, nickels, and dimes."

Hightower leaned in close to Jack. "Aren't you glad we had that big breakfast?"

Hightower dragged Jack to another bar a few blocks away, next to a giant mural of *Touch of Evil* someone had slapped up on the side of a turn-of-the-century building. The ex-cop had more shots. The ex-cop had more beers. Jack got tired of Diet Coke and switched over to bottles of Topo Chico mineral water with lime. At one point somebody put the Bee Gees' "Every Christian Lion Hearted Man Will Show You" on the jukebox, which was just weird. The sun vanished. Jack thought a lot about that *Touch of Evil* mural. It seemed to be mocking him. The more Hightower laughed and smiled, the more Jack wanted to walk out of the bar and head directly into the ocean, allowing the waves to wash over him, muffling the sound. He ended up going as far as the beach.

What was he going to say to Matilda when he saw her? When Jack was sent away to prison, he prayed she wouldn't ask him the Big Question directly, because he vowed to never lie to her. She had been only twelve at the time, and still very much in shock from the sudden loss of her mother. But Matilda asked with her eyes, every time he saw her. Back then Jack was too much of a coward to answer her directly because he thought that would destroy their relationship forever. With one parent gone, Jack was supposed to be the one to grow the fuck up and take care of her, not lash out like some angry toddler because life didn't turn out the way he thought it should.

Could he possibly tell her the truth?

Could he tell *anyone*?

After a long while, an extremely intoxicated Hightower came rambling out onto the sand and semi-gracefully collapsed next to Jack. He moaned, he let out a belch, and he moaned again. Then he started laughing, before he abruptly stopped.

"Hightower," Jack said.

"Yeah, free man. What's up?"

"I gotta get something off my chest."

"You shouldn't use the word 'got.' It's one of those empty placeholder words."

"Seriously. I need to tell you something."

"Anything, my brother."

"Brother?"

"It's an expression. Go on. Lay it on me."

"You're not going to like this. Like, at all."

"Try me."

"I'm serious."

"And I'm Roebuck."

"What?"

"Never mind. Go ahead. Let me have it."

Jack looked into the ex-cop's eyes. "I did it."

Hightower's brow furrowed. "Come again?"

"I don't mean to cast aspersions on all your detective work, or whatever paint-chip bullshit you pulled out of your ass. The last thing I want to do is insult you."

"No insult taken."

"But I did it."

"Did what?"

"Did . . . it."

"You're going to have to be more specific."

"For fuck's sake, Hightower . . . I actually killed the guy they say I killed. I got drunk and heard where he was, and I ran him over with my car."

"Yeah," Hightower replied. "Of course you did. What, do you think I'm an idiot?"

THE BEAR

Near midnight he drove to the Silver Lake home to scope out the second house. There was a couple renting the place now. The man was faintly surprised to discover the couple wasn't the same race, and neither of them white. That was ... interesting. In the old days, he only stalked white people. This was not a message, or anything like that. Serial killers usually worked within their own ethnic group, and the man who used to be the California Bear supposed he was no different.

But the house was the house, and he had no control over who populated it now.

This neighborhood had also changed and would be a little trickier, though he supposed that was the point. The challenge of the re-creation—1981 versus 2018. To transport himself there, the man slipped the headphones over his ears and went back in time again.

He'd purchased one of the very first Sony Walkman models in 1981 and used it to psych himself up for his "nighttime patrols," as he called them. While his current Walkman was a slightly newer model, the man listened to his same favorite cassette tape, which was a mix loaded with 1970s "yacht rock," along with heavy doses of Pink Floyd and the James Gang.

His favorite Pink Floyd song was "One of These Days," which he first heard on their 1981 compilation album, *A Collection of Great Dance Songs*. He bought the LP for their hits "Money" and "Shine On You Crazy Diamond," but was pleasantly surprised at how much "One of These

Days" obsessed him. The repeating bass line seemed to anticipate Giorgio Moroder's disco noir soundtracks, and the song's only lyric drove the Bear wild:

One of these days I'm going to cut you into little pieces.

The Bear often caught himself gazing up at his own reflection and speaking the line exactly how it sounds in the recorded version — like an angry Muppet about to embark on a homicidal rampage.

One of these days I'm going to cut you into little pieces.

Driving around LA, catching his own eyes in the rearview:

One of these days I'm going to cut you into little pieces.

The Bear's all-time *favorite* song, however, was the James Gang's "Midnight Man," which took on deeper levels of meaning the more he listened to it. He was the Midnight Man made flesh. The press may have given him the vaguely insulting moniker of the California Bear, a lazy association with the burly beast on the state flag, but in his big thudding heart, he'd always been the Midnight Man.

At first it started out as long drives around Hollywood, following the major streets. He didn't know the place at all, despite growing up just a few miles away. The decadent Hollywood Hills always felt like an impenetrable buffer zone standing between bland suburbia and the Hollywood neighborhoods where all the cool people lived.

The first time the Bear broke into a house, he was thirty-two years old. He'd spent five years on the force and was restless living at home with his mother. Same house he lived in now with the Queen of Mars, in fact; he'd inherited the oversize bungalow when his mother passed away. But back then he had no wife, no girlfriend, no prospects along those lines. He didn't have much in the way of hobbies. Mom didn't expect rent or money for groceries. (He forced her to accept some money anyway.) The rest of his paycheck went into his car — a hardtop '78 Plymouth 'Cuda. He felt his stocky frame was a bit too large for this sleek monster. Like a Bear riding in the belly of a great white. But he liked the looks it earned him on the freeway. He'd worked LA long enough to know that your ride defined you.

So he started taking drives that spring — 1978. Down the Cahuenga Pass, up and down Hollywood Boulevard until it was boring, then Sunset until the same. Sure, there were whores galore, but that didn't interest him. He started pushing out to the neighborhoods around Hollywood: Los Feliz and Silver Lake and Echo Park.

The Bear's MO back then was the same: find some diner or dive bar and scope out the scene. He'd always order a hamburger (hard to fuck that up) and a bottle of beer, usually Miller High Life. He'd get to know the neighborhood by studying the patrons. They would, in turn, instantly peg him as a cop, even when he started growing his hair a little longer later that summer.

By midsummer he was working vice and his hair was even longer. He was letting his beard grow in a little too. He was hoisting iron and swilling High Life and listening to Deep Purple. By late summer he was breaking into houses on a regular basis.

This house here in Silver Lake, however, was the location of his second murder. This would have been the fall of 1981. He followed a drunk woman all the way home from a bar down on Sunset. The Bear found the back door unlocked and crept through the lower level. Upstairs, he heard a blistering argument. A male voice, much to his surprise, and the voice of the beautiful drunk woman. And then the argument faded, and soon they were fucking.

Which filled the Bear with all kinds of feelings. He wasn't sure what to do with them. Who was this rude jerk who could yell at a beautiful creature like this, then turn around and defile her? *They needed to be taught how to behave...*

Now, in the present, the man watched the new occupants through the lighted windows. They were curled up together on a midcentury sofa staring up at one of the living room's massive walls. From his vantage point, the man couldn't see exactly what they were watching. Cuddling, or playing with each other's fun parts?

The man carefully made his way to the same back door that he'd used in 1981. As far as he could tell, nothing had changed — even the doorknob and lock appeared to be the home's originals. He slipped on the mask and glove *and became the Bear again.* It was that simple, and it felt like no time had passed at all. The Bear reached out with a gloved hand and tried the knob. *It was open...*

The thick wooden door, however, made a piercing creak as it swung into the kitchen on its hinges.

"Hello?" A male voice, unsure, groggy, called out from the interior of the home. "Someone out there?" A shadowy figure, backlit by the projected images, appeared in the doorway leading to the living room.

The Bear, in his furry mask, *growled* at him.

"Holy fucking shit!"

The Bear turned, quickly skulked out the way he came in, ignoring the excited cries coming from the house, pulling off his mask and clawed glove, tucking away his headphones, and letting gravity speed him down the hill to where he'd parked his car. Maybe it had been too much, too soon.

But make no mistake — next time, the California Bear was going to cut *someone* into little pieces.

THURSDAY, MAY 31, 2018

"KILLER"

The next morning Jack made the same predawn trek to the beach. Only this time he wore a T-shirt and his suit pants, and he threw up twice on the sand. This wasn't a traditional hangover, because he hadn't been drinking. This was a stress hangover. He thought he'd feel better after, and that maybe some of the anxiety would fade. He was wrong.

Jack watched the waves, pondering his next move.

Hightower's next move was obvious. He was going to babysit Jack's guilty ass until payday and then take his cut.

Over the many months Hightower worked to exonerate Jack, he also worked with an attorney pal to petition the state of California for a wrongful conviction settlement. The standard in the state was $100 per day of incarceration, which in Jack's case came out to roughly 73 grand. Not exactly a killing.

But for Hightower, 73K would be a decent payday in exchange for a few months of patience and paperwork. Jack had the feeling that when the check arrived, Hightower would make him sign it over in exchange for his silence. Jack supposed if he refused, Hightower could tell the governor *whoops, my bad* and Jack would be sent back to lockup. What sane free man would choose that option? Perhaps this (maybe) sane free man, Jack thought.

No. Screw that. Jack would be damned if he was going to let this motherfucker get away with this. And he wasn't going to let him steal his future with his daughter.

After returning to his room and pulling on the rest of the clothes he owned, Jack took a deep breath and nudged open Hightower's door with his knee.

"Hey, man..."

Hightower was nowhere in sight.

Hightower's stuff was still scattered all the hell over the place, guarded by the Weird Sisters, none of whom had bothered to put on a shirt since the last time Jack saw them. For an ex-cop, Hightower didn't give much of a shit about security. Anybody could just walk in here and nose through his files. Or try on one of his ugly button-down shirts.

Jack decided to wait. There was nothing in his room to occupy his attention other than a battered Michael Connelly paperback somebody had left behind. And maybe he should save that for the bus ride back to prison.

Instead he nosed through some of Hightower's file boxes. Jack flipped off a lid at random, fingered through the dusty folders. Repeat. After a while, it became clear that these were random cases from the past three or four decades. Homicides, mostly. Seriously grisly homicides. Where did Hightower find this stuff? Could you buy this morbid crap on eBay? Maybe he had the JFK assassination files somewhere around here too.

"Find anything good?"

Jack almost jumped out of his old suit. He turned to see Hightower's frame filling the open doorway. He had a smile on his face like he'd caught Jack eating the next-to-last slice of cake while defiling his wife — who was eating the last slice.

"Just looking for some bathroom reading."

"Eye-opening stuff, isn't it."

"You have some real monsters in these files."

Hightower beamed. "See, you get it already. I'm impressed."

"Get what?"

"Sorry to leave you to your own devices. I had to go take care of something back at the house up in Port Hueneme. Otherwise the wife would be up my ass all day."

Hightower remained there in the doorway as if Jack were about to make a break for it. And sure, Jack was tempted. But he figured it'd be better to talk things through, see where he stood.

"Look, man," Jack said, "we gotta talk."

"Agreed. But first, breakfast."

Jack's brain wanted to disagree, but his rumbling stomach told it to shut the hell up. Whatever was going to happen, better to get it over with. He just had to stall the inevitable until tomorrow, when Matilda would be back home from her trip and he could hold her in his arms again. Only that would make this all worth it.

THE GIRL DETECTIVE

When she woke up this morning, the Girl Detective decided to focus on a single aspect of her murder case: the car paint.

When you strike a human being with, say, a moving vehicle, the encounter leaves traces behind. On the human being, those traces would tend to be nasty and obvious and could be collected for forensic experts. On the vehicle, not so much — and you could easily scrub, buff, or repaint the evidence away.

In her father's trial, it all came down to the paint — the one piece of physical evidence linking the victim with the defendant's vehicle. After all, witnesses' memories could be compromised, faulty, or just plain wrong. But science doesn't lie.

At the trial, an expert testified that he was "reasonably sure" the paint from the victim matched the type of paint from her dad's car. (The same vehicle she had fantasized about driving someday — she called it his "midlife crisis whip.") Six months ago, that same expert was publicly exposed as a fraud (and a cokehead). Many cases were called into question, including her father's. This was when the old-guy ex-cop — Hightower — popped up and took on the case pro bono. Well, duh. All the heavy lifting had already been done. Hightower just had to hang in there to help with the paperwork.

But the Girl Detective wanted to do the work herself and reach her own conclusions.

Violet had come through for her — dropping stuff off at her aunt and uncle's apartment. Her aunt assumed it was homework. If she'd looked closer, she'd have found journals such as *The Journal of Raman Spectroscopy*, which published Patrick Buzzini and Edward Suzuki's October 2015 classic, "Forensic Applications of Raman Spectroscopy for the in situ Analyses of Pigments and Dyes in Ink and Paint Evidence."

The best thing about Violet was that she never questioned the Girl Detective's somewhat strange research requests. She was her Watson, her Captain Hastings, her Archie Goodwin.

The best thing about the Girl Detective (if she did say so herself) was that she was very skilled at taking a dry, scientific piece and wringing the useful nuggets of info from its desiccated shell.

And she was beginning to unpack it in her mind when there was yet another interruption—the nurse, coming to take her downstairs to have the PICC line installed. You know: the drug freeway to her heart.

"Can I have just another half hour?" she pleaded to Meghan, the nurse. "I'm working on a key part of my English paper."

"I wish I could make that happen," Meghan said. "But they're waiting for you down in the basement torture chamber."

"Well, that doesn't sound ominous at all."

"It's a very nice torture chamber! And the staff is great. Especially Nancy, the anesthesiologist. We're buds. She'll take good care of you."

"Hmm. Would a bribe buy me a few more minutes with my homework?"

Meghan—who was one of the good ones on the oncology floor—fought back a smile. "Exactly what kind of bribe are we talking?"

"Oh, I'm only talking about the best bribe ever. Not just for you, but the entire nurses' station."

"Keep going," Meghan said, but began the preparations for transporting the Girl Detective and her massive bed through the halls and elevators of CHLA until they reached the sterile room where they would turn her into a cyborg.

This meant the bribe would *not* prevent her from being transported down to the hospital's subterranean torture chamber, of course. But that was okay. The Girl Detective never thought it would. She was merely laying the groundwork for future favors, trying to ascertain what might turn Nurse Meghan's head.

"I'll give you a hint," the Girl Detective said. "It comes in a pink box. Usually in multiples. And if the place is good, they'll thrown in a thirteenth."

"I think I know what you mean," Meghan replied. "And that is an excellent bribe, especially for nurses."

"I'm prepared to go as high as two boxes."

"You really are desperate to keep working on your paper, aren't you?"

"You have no idea."

"Sadly, I'm not allowed to take a bribe," Meghan said, "when it comes to patient safety."

"What I'm hearing is, you're open to bribes when it comes to other things."

Meghan wiggled her eyebrows suggestively. The Girl Detective couldn't help but smile.

"Are your aunt and uncle coming soon?" Meghan asked. "I thought they'd be here to see you off."

"Well, thanks to my current situation," the Girl Detective explained, waving her arms to take in the hospital room, the IVs, the monitors, all of it, "they have some things to sort out at home. So I told them not to rush back."

"That's very considerate of you.

"I can go as high as three pink boxes?"

"Okay, now I'm seriously considering it. But tell you what. When you wake up from the procedure, I'll be there with a little bribe of my own."

"A bribe for me? Interesting. What kind of services or favors are you hoping to procure?"

"No specific favor. I just want to be your bud. You seem cool."

"I don't know if that's such a wise move," said the Girl Detective. "Why invest the bribe in a friend who may have an expiration date?"

Meghan's initial reaction was an astonished laugh—the kind you stifle at a comedy show when the person on stage has said something beyond the pale—and a quick wilting of that laugh, because the joke might be (sort of) true. The nurse tossed a warming blanket over the Girl Detective's head.

"Come on, we're running late. On the way down you can tell me what kind of doughnut you'd like."

"You've got a deal," the Girl Detective said, her voice muffled under the blanket.

"KILLER"

Jack went with another omelet named after yet another celebrity. This version had bacon, caramelized onion, sharp cheddar, tomato, and avocado. Hightower had another of his beloved atomic monster-size breakfast burritos. They ate in silence and then regarded each other from across the table. It was a Mexican standoff. Jack refused to go first, out of sheer stubbornness. Cops, however, were expert at shutting up and letting the other guy talk himself into trouble. Jack realized they might be here all morning.

The tension was broken when the guy brought the check. Hightower paid for the drinks and tip, then said, "Let's go see the guy."

Jack barely understood the statement. He just went with the flow. They were on the road a good ten minutes before Jack was able to formulate a question.

"Uh, what guy?"

"He's up in Studio City. About an hour away, in this traffic. Everything's an hour away in LA."

"I know, Hightower. I used to live here. What I don't know is . . . who the fuck is this guy you're talking about? Does he have something to do with my paperwork?"

Hightower glanced over at Jack and smiled. "You're going to like this one *a lot*."

"I don't even know what *this* is."

Jack knew these freeways, of course. The PCH took them to the 10, which in turn led the way to the 405 up through the Sepulveda Pass. This was the way he used to drive his family to the beach in another lifetime. But as they started to merge onto the 405, Hightower muttered, "This fucking guy."

Jack turned around. There was a white Audi—or some other status symbol on wheels—rocketing toward them at an obscene speed, headlights blinking angrily.

"Guess we're not driving fast enough for this asshole," Hightower said, devilish gleam in his eye. "Watch this."

The Audi accelerated until it was seconds away from rear-ending Hightower's Honda Accord...then zoomed into the next lane. But Hightower anticipated this and changed lanes at pretty much the same time. The Audi had no choice but to stomp on his brakes. In a duel between a $130,000 car and a $17,000 sedan (used), one side had far more to lose. The Audi shimmied and skidded as it tried to stay on the road.

"Eat my ass!" Hightower shouted.

The Audi stabilized, then moved one lane over. But Hightower anticipated this, too, and matched his move, blocking him. The Audi laid into his horn like he was warning California of an incoming missile attack. Hightower grinned.

"And check my prostate while you're back there!"

Jack's hands were clamped on the dash. "How about we *don't* die on the freeway this morning."

"Aah...I could do this all day." The man was positively gleeful.

"Please don't."

"You're no fun."

Hightower allowed the Audi to pass but raised a one-finger salute to send it off. Jack caught a glimpse of the enraged driver as the Audi blazed by. She was kind of beautiful, even with the veins popping out of the sides of her slender neck.

"People complain about the freeways," Hightower said, "but it's the best free show in town."

They drove past a steep hillside that was completely charred. A couple of times a year God tries to set LA on fire, but the inhabitants stubbornly fight back with chemicals and money. One of these years he'll make it work. Light the whole works up.

After winding down Coldwater Canyon, Hightower hung a left on a quiet residential street. Leafy. Generous yards. Jack always wondered who could afford to live in places like this. Rent was climbing out of control even before he went to prison. He had no idea what kind of market he was facing now, what kind of place he'd be able to find. If they even rented apartments to ex-cons.

Hightower slowed way down. "If we're lucky we'll catch him outside."

"Who the hell are we talking about? Why are you being so cryptic?"

"Cryptic," he said with slow appreciation. "Yeah, I like that. Completely forgot that was a word. I'm going to have to work it into the rotation."

Hightower pulled the car to the side of the street, then slowly inched back and forth until he found just the right spot. He pointed to an old man walking across his front lawn on the other side of the street.

"He's right over there," Hightower said.

"Who am I looking at?" Jack replied.

"Take a closer look. This is going to blow your mind."

Jack was already tired of this. "Jesus," he muttered.

"No, not Jesus. Christopher Albin Dixon. The California Bear himself."

"Is that supposed to mean something?"

"How have you not heard of this guy?" Hightower asked. "Okay, maybe his star has faded a little, but for a long time he was right up there with the Hillside Strangler, the Original Night Stalker, the Grim Sleeper, and that Ramirez freak."

"Sorry. I'm not up on my freaks." Which was the truth. His late wife used to follow all the true crime stuff, but not Jack. He didn't want any of those morbid details in his brain. Not when it could be full of actual useful information, such as the session players on every Blue Note album released in the 1950s.

"Dixon is not a freak, he's ex-LAPD," Hightower said. "But from another generation. A real old-timer."

"In other words, like you," Jack said.

Hightower shot him a look. "Point is, the California Bear raped and murdered at least eight women between 1978 and 1984 and terrorized twenty-six others. He used his smart cop brain to case houses and target his victims and destroy all traces of forensic evidence. Nobody knew who he was. And then one day he stopped. No one has any idea *why*."

"And that old dude is this California Bear?"

The old dude in question was currently struggling to unravel a hose from a spinning metal rack mounted on the side of his house. He had a large frame, but his clothes still looked baggy on him.

"He lost some weight since he retired," Hightower said. "I'll bet the wife has him on a strict diet."

"The ex–serial killer is married?"

Hightower ignored the question as if it were absurd. "Don't let him fool you. I think he plays up the weak act in front of his neighbors, hoping for some unpaid labor."

"I know I'm going to regret asking this, but why isn't this super-famous serial killer in jail?"

"Because he was never brought to trial. Or even arrested, for that matter."

Jack turned toward Hightower. "So how do you know he did it?"

"I know," Hightower said. "Just like I know *you* did it."

"Jesus Christ."

"No . . . Christopher Albin Dixon. That's the Bear's real name."

"Again . . . what's your proof?"

"It's kind of an open secret around the LAPD."

"Wait a minute. You're claiming that the entire department not only knows this guy was a serial killer, but they're fine with him running loose around the San Fernando Valley?"

"I didn't say the entire department knew. Okay, fine, it was more like one guy...but he was an unimpeachable source. He kind of took me under his wing his last few years on the job and we stayed in touch. He was always good for a whiskey or five...well, until his stroke last year. God rest his crazy ass."

"Great. Your iron-clad proof is gossip from a dead, drunk retiree."

"Hey. Show some respect."

"It's not *proof,* Hightower."

"My pal was on the job at the same time as Dixon and always had his suspicions but could never nail down any hard evidence. And no, wiseass, I'm not basing this on gossip. I have solid physical evidence that the old dude on that lawn butchered eight women."

"What's your evidence?"

"We'll get to that. But first, let me lay it all out for you."

Hightower put the car in drive and continued down the street.

THE BEAR

The California Bear pulled the flip phone out of his jeans pocket and thumbed a number.

"Yeah. Cubby. It's me. Got a plate for you to run off some shitty Honda Accord."

After ending the call, the Bear wondered what that could have been about. Most likely some real estate speculator, wondering if old people lived in this house and how close they might be to death. Maybe they were lost tourists thinking they'd spotted a down-on-his-luck celebrity in the wild. Boy, would they be in for a rude treat if they learned the truth.

The Bear ambled his way down the alley on the side of his house toward his detached garage.

He referred to it as "the garage," even thought it had never housed a vehicle, nor had it been built for such a purpose. "Pool house" might be slightly more accurate, although it was never used as one. The previous owners had built this structure sometime in the 1960s after they'd covered up the in-ground pool with thick pieces of plywood. Most people would have had the damn thing filled in with dirt, but not the previous owners. Maybe they thought they'd have the money to resurrect the pool someday. The structure, he supposed, was meant to keep the rare rainstorm off the plywood. God knows what they had used it for—actual guests? Storage? Kinky sex games they wanted to keep out of the house proper? Didn't matter. For the Bear, the structure was a huge selling point. The house had no basement, so he was giddy at the idea of using the not-quite-a-garage to store all his things.

The Queen of Mars wasn't crazy about it, but what could she do?

The Bear had equipped his space with the usual creature comforts — couch, mini-fridge, stereo system. None of it was new. Well, the mini-fridge was a purchase from ten years ago, but only because the compressor in the primitive model he'd hung on to since the mid-1970s finally gave up and sputtered out. It would cost more to replace than buy a newer model, so the answer was obvious. Still, the Bear missed that old fridge.

He pulled a can of Mug root beer from its replacement. He drained half the can before closing the mini-fridge door, then on impulse grabbed a second one. Whatever. The Queen of Mars would never know, unless she was sneaking in here to count cans of fucking soda.

One of these days . . .

But the real reason the Bear loved his not-exactly-a-garage? Why, the very thing that had happened this morning, with those two idiots in the Honda Accord.

Over the decades, the Bear had secretly worried that someone would eventually come knocking on his door. His identity was a secret, but possibly not an airtight one. People sometimes put things together. And the Bear had to be prepared for such a situation. So he spent a long time dreaming up ways to discourage any curious visitors. A lot of that planning involved the use of the secret pool beneath his not-exactly-a-garage.

After a few minutes the Bear's phone chirped. Cubby, naturally. Who else would be calling him in the middle of the day? The wife handled everybody else.

"Hey," Cubby said. "The Accord is registered to an address in Port Hueneme."

"Port Hueneme?" the Bear repeated. "What are they, a couple of military guys who got lost? What the hell do they want with me?"

"No idea, chief. Want me to check them out?"

The Bear hesitated, but not because of the answer. The answer was obviously *yes*. All threats had to be identified as early as possible. Especially now, with his comeback imminent. The last thing he needed was these two jokers fucking everything up.

No, the Bear only hesitated because he was half-tempted to go "check them out" himself. All his recent trips down memory lane had stirred up a lot of old feelings. *Fun* feelings.

But a man had to recognize his limitations.

"Yeah, Cubby," the Bear said. "But call me when you're there. I'll walk you through it."

"KILLER"

Hightower drove them down Ventura Boulevard under a canopy of swaying palms. "I will have you know, I've given this a lot of thought. Like, years of planning."

"Well, that's a load off my mind."

Jack said that to defuse the tension, but it only seemed to annoy Hightower.

"I've been looking into wrongful conviction cases for over a decade now. And you know what I realized? What nobody else even considers? For every poor bastard who's sent up for a crime he didn't commit, there's some slick son of a bitch who gets away with it. And that's when it hit me. I want us to nail those sons of bitches."

"Now, by 'nail,' do you mean arrest them? Or something else entirely?"

Hightower frowned. "I didn't say anything about killing anybody. You're the one putting that out there into the universe."

"I'm not putting anything anywhere!" Jack protested. "And who said anything about killing? This is your crazy scheme."

"Wait, so now you think justice is crazy? I don't know, Jack. Worked out pretty well for you, seeing as you're tooling down Ventura Boulevard a free man."

"Stop. Go back a minute. I want you to define the word 'nail.'"

"You know. *Get* him."

"Get him *how*, exactly?"

"Punish him for the crimes he committed."

"You're going to have to be a little more specific."

"Am I, Jack?"

Ever since meeting Hightower a bunch of months ago Jack had considered him a strange kind of angel. Weird dude — idiosyncratic but well-meaning. A useful goofball. If Hightower was serious about devoting his spare time to springing him from prison, then Jack was all for it. But now that Jack was out in the real world with him, he realized he'd missed something important: Hightower was clearly a very troubled man.

"Can we stop talking about this now?" Jack said. "Because whatever you have in mind, count me out."

Poor Hightower seemed genuinely dickhurt. "After all I've done, you can't even do me the courtesy of hearing me out?"

Jack closed his eyes and shook his head, which Hightower took as an affirmation. He wound his way up to one of the Mulholland Drive overlooks. This one didn't offer a view of the Hollywood sign, or the Bowl, or even downtown off in the distance. This was one of the smaller ones, easy to pass by unless you knew where to look. This overlook offered up a breathtaking view of... the San Fernando Valley.

"Come on," Hightower said.

Jack followed as the ex-cop jogged across the two-lane mountain road and ambled up the dirt path to the overlook. A classic Trans Am rocketed behind them just after they cleared the road, honking its horn and generally being an asshole. Just a few seconds slower and they would have been roadkill.

Once he was up over the short mound of dirt, Jack skidded to a stop. He wasn't afraid of heights. He was, however, nervous about unfamiliar terrain. One false move and he could be tumbling down the side of a mountain.

And there was Hightower, presiding over the valley.

"You and I owe a karmic debt to the world," he said.

"Cool," Jack said.

"I'm serious. You owe a debt because" — he lowered his voice even though there was absolutely no one else within earshot — "well, you *killed a man*. And me, because I was a shitty, ineffectual cop for my entire career. I squandered the opportunities I'd been given. The two of us *owe* humanity something in return. This is how we're going to pay it back."

"How about a couple of shifts at a soup kitchen or a homeless shelter?"

"Our debts are way too large. We're talking people's *lives*. Generations forever altered by violence or cowardly inaction. This is our chance to help restore balance."

Jack wondered if he'd cribbed that from a single self-help book or a half dozen of them.

"Just to get this straight," Jack said, "you want us to be vigilantes."

"Ugh, I hate that word," Hightower said, twisting his face up into a scowl. "A vigilante is just some asshole with a gun or a tire iron looking for revenge or to get his sadistic rocks off. We're not like that. We just want to remove evil scumbags from society. Like a surgeon hacking away a tumor."

"I can't believe I'm telling a cop this, but isn't that what the justice system is for?"

"That's just it. The system failed! These assholes got away with it!"

The way Hightower seemed to be frothing at the mouth confirmed it. *This man was bonkers*. Yes, he did help spring Jack from prison. But he also had a brain filled with insane schemes that could land them both in prison, and that was something Jack could not afford to be part of. Jack had to find a polite exit that wouldn't raise the man's suspicions.

Thankfully, one instantly occurred to him.

"Buy me a cheeseburger and you can tell me whatever plans you like," Jack said. "There's a place called Patys down in Studio City, not too far from here."

Jack only knew about Patys because his daughter, Matilda, had mentioned it to him as a favorite old-school diner. And as a bonus, it was within walking distance of where she was living with her aunt and uncle.

"You're seriously hungry?" Hightower asked. "After that epic breakfast we had?"

"I'm making up for lost time."

"Let me just finish telling you our plan. You're going to love it."

"I think better on a full stomach."

"Yeah, me too. That's what the breakfast was for!"

"I think Patys serves beer."

A short while later, Jack and a slightly placated Hightower were sitting at an outdoor table at Patys. A slanted roof kept most of the sun off them. Still, Hightower started to grouse about the light in his eyes, at which point Jack reminded him that he'd spent twenty-two hours of every day over the past two years inside a dim, cramped cell. Hightower sighed, relented. Jack ordered a double cheeseburger deluxe he didn't want to eat. Hightower ordered two bottles of Dos Equis with lime.

"Okay," Hightower said, leaning forward over the table. "I'll give it to you straight. If we play this right, we could make a fuck ton of money."

"Interesting," Jack said, then took a for-show bite of his cheeseburger. He had to force it down his throat. "I thought you were in this for the justice."

Hightower took a long pull of his Dos Equis, smirked, then reached into his pocket. He pulled out a piece of paper that had been folded into quarters, then unfolded it as if he were revealing the Shroud of Turin. Hightower slid the paper toward Jack.

Even though Jack was capable of absorbing the material, Hightower felt the need to narrate anyway.

"That piece is from Deadline Hollywood," he said. "Some fancy-pants documentary chick just signed a deal to write and direct a streaming series about the California Bear."

"Yeah I'm seeing that..."

Not just some "fancy-pants documentary chick." This was cult documentary director Lasca Foster, in fact, and she'd signed a $450-million-dollar deal for the series (and a possible sequel). Which sounded like an absurd amount of money, Jack realized, but not if the director could deliver on what she promised in the pitch...

"But get this," Hightower continued. "Ms. Fancy Pants claims that by the end of the series, she'll be revealing the identity of the California Bear!"

A 40-YEAR-OLD COLD CASE FINALLY SOLVED! Read the Deadline piece.

"A forty-year-old cold case finally solved!" Hightower said. "And here's the thing. If Ms. Fancy Pants is telling the truth, that means Christopher Albin Dixon is cooperating."

"Well, that's a giant leap. How do you know that?"

"They're not going to risk a production like this without nailing down the life rights. And if Dixon's cooperating, then he sure as Shinola ain't cooperating for free."

That made some twisted sense to Jack. Unlike the rest of Hightower's plan.

"So your brilliant idea is to what...blackmail him for part of his money?"

"Blackmail?" Hightower exclaimed. "Hell no. Nobody said anything about blackmail. I just think if he wants to hang on to his sweet little streaming deal, he should have to pay handsomely for the privilege."

"That is the literal definition of blackmail."

Hightower slapped the table, rattling silverware and his two beer bottles. "Do you really think a monster like that should profit from torturing and killing women?"

"I think justice is going to sort itself out," Jack said. "I mean, he's not going to walk. Money won't do him much good in prison."

"Don't be naïve. He'll never serve a day! Asshole will be famous, and people will be throwing money at him. On top of the money he probably already has. And you're okay with this?"

"Maybe he's agreed to donate all profits to women's shelters."

Hightower opened his mouth and shook his head, as if he had no idea how to deal with someone so impossibly stupid. Jack, meanwhile, pretended to have a stomach twinge. In truth, he didn't have to pretend. His stomach was having none of this. "Hold that thought."

"You gotta be shitting me."

"Exactly."

Jack flagged down a passing waitress and asked about the location of the men's room. Inside, she told him. But that was just for Hightower's benefit. Jack walked through the crowded diner, turned left, and then exited through another set of doors, which led to Riverside Drive. And then he kept on walking.

THE BEAR

The California Bear lumbered out to his garage. Again, he stripped off his shirt. He always preferred doing physical things while bare-chested, even if the Queen of Mars didn't like it. *I don't want to see that,* she'd say. *Well, tough beans,* he wanted to tell her now. *You're going to be seeing a lot more of me in the days to come.*

He started playing Tetris with the boxes until he'd finally unearthed a rough third of the former pool. That should be enough. The Bear peeled back the artificial turf, then began the work of pulling up the heavy sections of plywood, which had splintered and partially rotted over the years. And then the heavier planks of wood beneath that layer, finally exposing the pool beneath.

The Bear paused to catch his breath and calm his thundering heart. But the effort had been worth it.

Time had faded the blue to nearly white, making it look like a mammoth six-foot-deep bathtub that nobody had bothered to clean in decades. Despite the wooden covering, all manner of dirt and desiccated insect husks had found their way down to this barren underworld.

There would be no need to clean it out because the chemicals he'd be dumping down there would eventually take care of everything.

Now it was time to go shopping, but the Bear knew he couldn't buy all the supplies in the same place. That would arouse too much suspicion; this old man wasn't *that* invisible. So that meant making separate trips to different hardware stores—a Home Depot here, a Lowe's there. All of that seemed exhausting, and he had better things to do with his time while waiting for Cubby to report back.

Fuck it, the Bear thought. *I'll just order it all on Amazon.* What, was Jeff Bezos going to show up and wag a finger at him? And if that happened, he'd push him into the pool too.

"KILLER"

Jack's relationship with his daughter fell into three phases. There was life before the Awful. There was life during the Awful. And finally, there was the past three months, an era that had yet to be defined.

The Awful was the two-year period spanning the death of his wife, his drunken revenge, and his trial and incarceration. They were both in shock at first and clung to each other like survivors of a shipwreck, lost and confused. Jack was determined to be her rock but soon felt the fissures in the stone and tried to seal them with booze. At first he told himself he could handle it all: be there for Matilda when she needed, but take the time to fall apart now and again. This turned out to be a fatal miscalculation.

When Jack went off to prison, Matilda would send cards and letters, probably encouraged by her aunt or possibly her teachers. Jack wrote back pretty much the moment he received them, rushing to get his replies in the mail. Only then would he take his time and reread them, savoring every line. Imagining her sweet self at a little writing desk with her colored pencils.

Soon came the time when she would visit Jack. His sister-in-law, Reese, tried to bring her as often as possible given her hectic work schedule. It was a long drive, though, and he didn't blame her for not making it every week. Life gets in the way. Those visits, though. They kept Jack alive.

But three months ago, the visits halted completely. Reese apologized, but there was nothing she could do — Matilda was going through *something,* possibly freshman-year burnout. Jack said he understood, but on some deeper level he really didn't. Maybe that was the age your kid started to pull away regardless of what you did. Or maybe that was just when she awakened to the idea that — oh shit, my father is a murderer. That phase nearly destroyed him. Why was he bothering to go on living?

In fact, if it weren't for Hightower showing up right about then, claiming that he knew Jack was innocent and could prove it, he might have gone off into a very dark place forever.

But when it started becoming clear that, *holy shit, I might actually be getting out of prison,* Jack tried writing her again. But — no replies. His sister-in-law even wrote him a terse letter along the lines of "Please don't. Not until you're sure. I don't want to get her hopes up."

Jack's daughter lived with Reese and her husband, Louis, at an apartment complex in Toluca Lake, within walking distance of Patys. As he approached the corner of Oak and Pass Avenue, he felt eyes on him. Hightower couldn't have figured out the ruse this quickly, could he?

Jack scanned the area, but the only person around was a young woman leaning against a bike rack across the street. Dark-red lipstick, hair pulled back in a severe tie, her slender frame covered with a black leather jacket, despite the heat. She *was* looking at Jack, but probably out of boredom and nothing else. She looked away a second later, then strolled off down Pass Avenue. LA was full of oddball characters. He needed to remember that. Not everyone knew who he was or what he'd done.

Jack approached a side gate and pressed a few random numbers and then the CALL button. A groggy stoner voice answered, even though it was almost noon. Jack mumbled something about forgetting his keys.

Nothing happened for a few seconds. Then the same groggy voice called him an asshole. The door buzzed. Jack slipped inside.

Reese and Louis's apartment number was forever burned into his memory from all those letters to the Daughter. Jack used to wonder what this place would look like. "Toluca Lake" always sounded exotic, but this place was a little more run-down than he would have liked. Only later would he realize this apartment complex was what they called "Toluca Lake–adjacent."

He knocked on their door, then stepped out of view of the peephole. The door opened a few inches. When his sleepy-eyed brother-in-law saw Jack, he did a double take. "Oh . . . *hey.*"

"Hey, Louis."

"What . . . what are you doing here?"

"I know Matilda's not back from her school trip until tomorrow, but if you and Reese are cool with it, I'd really love to crash here tonight."

"Oh. Uh . . ."

"Look, you'd be doing me a huge favor. The guy who helped with my case? The ex-cop? He's going through some things, and it's probably not a smart idea to stay with him."

Jack tried to avoid doing that thing where you look around someone to see who's inside, because that would be rude. But he totally looked around Louis to see who was inside. The apartment seemed cluttered. Granted, it had been two years (at least) since he had seen Reese and Louis's living space. But something felt off to him. And Louis's next words confirmed his suspicion.

"Did . . . Reese call you?"

"I feel like an idiot standing out here. Mind if I come in?"

"That's not a good idea. Can you, uh, come back tomorrow?"

"I literally have nowhere else to go. No money for a hotel. Nothing."

"You can go back to that ex-cop. I mean, that's who you were supposed to stay with."

"Did you hear what I said? Do you want me to beg or something? I just want to crash on your couch for one night until Matilda's back."

"Look, she won't be back for a while."

The cheap concrete floor felt like it dropped out from under Jack. "Why? Was the trip extended or something?"

"How about you come back later tonight when Reese is here?"

And with that, Louis began to timidly close the door. Jack pressed his hand against it, stopping it at the halfway mark.

"Louis, where is my daughter?"

"Please, just wait outside a second while I call my wife."

"No."

Jack pushed past Louis, spinning him a bit as their shoulders collided. "Hey!"

The apartment wasn't huge; it shouldn't be too tough to find his daughter's room. Reese and Louis didn't have any kids of their own. Jack opened the first door he came to and peered inside. It was dark. The walls were covered in posters of bands and celebrities he didn't recognize. Was this who his daughter was now?

Matilda's small room was spotless, in stark contrast to the chaos in the rest of the apartment. Bed made, sheets pulled tight, pillows and stuffed animals precisely arranged. Jack touched a flat table with girl stuff—brushes, makeup palettes, a light-up mirror—and his heart felt like it was ready to burst. This was the first tangible connection he'd had with her in so, so long. He checked her desk, curious about what she was working on these days. The surface was strangely empty, as if she'd used her arm to scoop everything into a bag or a trash can. Jack checked the trash can.

Inside was nothing but a wadded-up bundle of gauze, stained with blood, and medical tape stuck to the sides. What the hell was going on?

"C'mon, Jack," Louis said from the doorway. "You really should call Reese."

"Where is my daughter?"

"You're making this really difficult for me."

"Difficult for you?" Jack turned to face him. "I want to know where she is right fucking now."

Louis reached out to grab him . . .

Or did he? Maybe Louis reached out for a reassuring pat on the shoulder or something? In the moment, his intentions were unclear. But prison had rewired Jack Queen's nervous system. If someone reached their paw out in your general direction, they weren't trying to reassure you about anything.

And yeah, later Jack would admit he might have gone a little overboard when he bodychecked Louis into the hallway wall.

The man made a whimpering noise as all the air blasted out of his lungs. Jack let him slide down to the floor and went back into his daughter's room, slamming the door shut behind him. He needed a second to think. What did the blood mean? Was she experimenting with drugs, for God's sake? No. That wasn't Matilda, and even if it was, she'd do a much better job of hiding the evidence.

Jack opened the door to question Louis, but someone set his eyeballs on fire.

Jack was not the world's toughest fighter, but he knew how to land a punch. Take one too. He'd had a few fights inside, but nothing too devastating. Mostly guys trying to figure out how far they could push him. Jack was considered tall and burly and not worth it. His main advantage was an ability to read a situation. Intent. Focus. That sort of thing.

But take away Jack's eyes and that all goes out the window. He kind of went into berserker mode.

He almost felt bad for Louis.

Jack blind-slapped the canister of Mace out of Louis's hand — a lucky hit — then bodychecked him into the wall again. Louis yelled, then wriggled away and crab-scurried back up the hallway.

Jack had never particularly cared for Louis. Before he went inside, Louis Faltermeyer was just this dipshit LA guy who was too lazy to make it in the creative field and instead glommed on to his sister-in-law, who had a steady job. Little did Jack suspect Louis would become the surrogate father to his only child. Jack owed him a great deal, actually.

Jack made a mental note to thank him for all his help after he finished beating the living shit out of him.

Jack managed to grab hold of Louis out in the living room, catching a fistful of his T-shirt. It was enough. Jack yanked him backward. Louis yelped. Jack tackled him to the floor. There was a table in the way. It was not strong enough to support their combined body weight. In all the action movies, it would have been a glass table that shattered spectacularly. Instead it was a cheap Ikea-type thing that simply collapsed. Jack found Louis's head and grabbed some hair. Jack wanted to smash him into the table debris repeatedly.

But what good would that do? And with that, the berserker vanished.

Jack let him go and sat down on the floor. His nuclear-waste eyes saw the blurry form of Louis roll off the broken table.

"Where is she?" Jack said, as calmly as he could.

"Fuck you, you fucking animal. Why did they even let you out of jail?"

Another voice spoke out from the other side of the room.

"She's at Children's Hospital," Hightower said.

THE GIRL DETECTIVE

"Honey? Are you awake?"

If one more person honeys *me,* the Girl Detective thought, *I swear I'm going to personally install a PICC line inside their chest.* Without *anesthetic.*

Granted, it had only been an hour since her procedure and she was still feeling weird and woozy (and irritable) from the anesthetic. Nurse Meghan's pal Nancy had hooked her up with some potent shit. She could barely feel the newly installed freeway snaking its way through her chest and into her circulatory system. But annoyingly, she couldn't concentrate on a single thought for very long. And people continued to want to speak with her, ask her questions, interrupt her as she tried to swim back to the land of paint samples and Raman spectroscopy.

But this wasn't a random nurse bothering her now; it was her aunt Reese. She didn't deserve a wiseass response; she was also living through this nightmare.

"I'm up," the Girl Detective said. "I'm okay."

Aunt Reese sat on the edge of her hospital bed and reached out for her hand. She squeezed it. The Girl Detective squeezed back, already running through the possible worst-case scenarios. Did she have something worse than leukemia? Did she have super-leukemia? Was there a tsunami warning, and the LA Basin was about to be wiped out? (That actually would be welcome news.)

"It's about your father," Aunt Reese said.

"Did something happen with his parole?"

"No, honey. He's been paroled. But he's on his way here. Your uncle Louis tried to tell him that now wasn't the best time, but . . ."

"Wait — I thought he was coming home tomorrow."

"There was a miscommunication. He should be here soon. Are you okay with that?"

Was she? This threw her personal deadline straight out the hospital room window. There was no way she'd be able to solve this murder between this very second and soon. She should be panicked. Or angry. Or frustrated.

Instead, to the Girl Detective, it felt as if Nancy the Narcotics Queen had spiked her blood bag with the most potent painkiller on earth. Joy and relief instantly flooded her veins. Maybe this wasn't hell after all; maybe this was the world righting itself again. She wanted to cry so much — but she didn't want to freak out Aunt Reese.

But her dad! Her father!

He was finally coming for her.

"KILLER"

Hightower drove down the I-5. At least, Jack hoped he did. Jack couldn't see very well, despite having flushed his eyes out with handfuls of LA tap water. The slightest bit of sunlight stung like hell, even though he was wearing a pair of sunglasses he'd borrowed/stolen from Reese.

"Those are lady sunglasses, you know," Hightower said.

"I'm gender fluid," Jack said. "Why did you lie to me about Matilda?"

"Are you thirsty?"

"No."

Hightower pushed an aluminum can into Jack's hand anyway. It was very cold. A good idea, after all. Jack removed his lady sunglasses and pressed the can to his burning eyes until the cold became too intense. Come to think of it, maybe a cool sip of soda would help. Jack cracked the pull tab and took a drink. The soda tasted rancid. Brackish. Jack coughed some of it up, then squinted at the label.

"What the hell is this?"

"Chardonnay. Or are you more of a red kind of guy?"

"Why the . . . why the *fuck* are you giving me a can of wine?"

"Trust me, buddy, the way your day is going, you're going to need it."

"And when did they start putting wine in fucking cans?"

"They're from Trader Joe's. Pretty good, right? When you pulled a runner, I knew exactly where you were going. So I stopped in for a few refreshments. Figured you'd need them."

"Cut the shit, Hightower. Why didn't you tell me my daughter was sick?"

"I only found out yesterday morning! Look, it didn't seem like the right time to hit you with everything. I mean, you're fresh from the pokey. There's only so much stress you can handle. Which is why I thought we should go drinking."

"You are *such* a fucking asshole."

"And when I touched base with your sister-in-law yesterday, she didn't think it was such a good idea either. We agreed that a little white lie or two would help both of you adjust to . . . you know, things."

"*Asshole.*"

"Drink up."

"*Fucking* asshole."

By the time a half-blind Jack found the cup holder and dropped the can of wine into it, Hightower was taking the exit for Los Feliz Boulevard.

"And, look . . . for the record, your daughter didn't want you to know she was feeling sick. She swore Reese to secrecy until you were out of the slammer."

Jack was about to come up with a third variation of telling Hightower he was an asshole but then realized no; this sounded right. Such a selfless act was pure Matilda—not wanting to worry Reese and Louis, even when she was enduring a special hell of her own. This killed Jack. His daughter, carrying this horrible burden in secret. Which would also explain why Matilda had been so strange to Jack over the past three months.

Christ, now Jack was the one who felt like the *total fucking asshole.*

"Did you know Arthur Conan Doyle, the guy who created Sherlock Holmes, once freed an innocent man from prison?" Hightower asked.

Oh, here we go with more of Hightower's fucking crazy.

"You're just trying to change the subject."

"No, I'm talking about our case. And it's a true story! I read a piece about it the other day. Guy named Oscar Slater was accused of beating an old Scottish woman to death in her apartment. Now, Slater was no saint. He liked his whores; he liked to gamble. But he also wasn't in Glasgow at the time of the murder. He begged Conan Doyle to take the case, and after years of lobbying, Slater was finally freed in 1928."

"So you're comparing yourself to Sherlock Holmes."

"Please. But that's not the interesting thing. The interesting thing is that Conan Doyle ended up suing the guy."

"Really."

"Yeah, really. The courts gave Slater six grand in pounds or whatever, and Conan Doyle thought he deserved a piece of that. Slater disagreed. Conan Doyle called him ungrateful and foolish. They ended up settling for 250 bucks, or pounds or whatever. A month later, Conan Doyle was dead."

"Huh. It's almost as if you're trying to tell me something."

"What? No. I just thought it was interesting. Drink your wine."

"No wine. Just get me to the hospital and drop me out front."

"What? No way. I'm not leaving you alone in your hour of need."

"My sister-in-law says she'll meet me in the lobby for a visitors' badge."

"And one for me too?"

"I guess — but why do you want to come along? Aside from helping me in my, uh, hour of need?"

"Brother," Hightower said, "don't act like a stranger. Have I not been by your side this whole time? Why would I split now?"

Because I'm your meal ticket, Jack thought. *If you can't blackmail the serial killer, you still have my payday to look forward to.* But perhaps now wasn't the time to bring that up.

Hightower almost got into a fistfight with the security guard at the parking entrance. This was largely because Hightower had insisted on VIP parking at the top level — "this man's daughter is very sick!" But the guard wasn't buying it.

"Lots of people's kids are sick, man. There are spots down at the lower levels."

Jack fought the urge to jump out of the passenger seat and bolt straight into the lobby. But no. *Breathe. Keep it together. The Daughter needs you to keep it together now.*

The path down into the bowels of the hospital felt like a descent into visitors' parking at Dante's Inferno. Pale, dirty walls. The ass end of hundreds of cars. People shuffling around, carrying overnight bags, looking entirely lost, as if they didn't know what had just happened to them. Jack could empathize. The elevator ride up to the main lobby was a small eternity, with everyone jammed too close together. Even though they were rising back to surface level, it somehow felt like they were being lowered deeper into the abyss.

Hightower had to almost jog to keep up with Jack as he headed straight for the main reception desk. But then Jack suddenly stopped and froze.

"Whoa!" Hightower exclaimed. "What is it?"

"I can't go in empty-handed," Jack said. "It's been two years. Where's the gift shop?"

"Uh, I don't know. The last time I was inside Children's Hospital was the fifth of never, because the missus and I don't have kids, so — "

"You're absolutely useless."

"You're welcome."

THE GIRL DETECTIVE

She had to work hard to convince Aunt Reese that she didn't need help in the bathroom. She'd been managing quite fine for years now, thank you very much. She was almost fifteen.

But really, she just needed a minute to think.

The walls of the bathroom swam around her. The painkillers were still doing their thing, and yeah, she probably should have someone in here with her to make sure she didn't do a Splat the Cat on the tiled floor. She didn't want to look at her PICC line just yet, because that might make her feel worse.

The Girl Detective held on to the IV pole and focused on her breathing. She told herself: *You can do this.* The body is just a flesh puppet, but the brain is in charge. If Sherlock was able to solve all kinds of cases while blitzed out of his brain on cocaine, then she should be able to concentrate on this one little thing.

In this case, the one little thing was squirreling away her small stack of research files for her English paper. She couldn't risk her father seeing it, because that would lead to a whole lot of questions she didn't want to answer quite yet.

So where should she hide them? This wasn't her bedroom at Aunt Reese's place, which had an absurd number of hiding places. This was a room that was designed for maximum medical efficiency and minimum privacy. She also didn't want to tuck them away in a spot where she couldn't easily access them later. There was work to be done.

By the time she was back in her bed, the Girl Detective was starting to panic. Her heart racing seemed to have woken up her PICC line, because now she was horribly self-conscious of the hardware that had been installed in her chest.

But then a flash of inspiration hit her. Sometimes, the best hiding places were in plain sight, where no one's attention bothers to linger.

The Girl Detective was relieved her brain was still working, despite the drugs and tubes and low blood numbers and everything else her meat-sack body had endured. She had just finished tucking the last of the murder research away when he stepped partway into the hospital room, lingering in the doorway as if waiting for an invitation.

She looked up and smiled.

"Hello, Father."

"KILLER"

Jack had named his daughter after the heroine from Luc Besson's *Léon: The Professional* as well as the chorus from the Tom Waits song "Tom Traubert's Blues (Four Sheets to the Wind in Copenhagen)." Jack's wife let him have that one but always called her "Mattie." In person Jack would call her a variety of nicknames. In letters to her, it was always "Dear Waltzing Matilda." Probably silly, but it felt right. And sure, it stung a little when Matilda opted to use her mother's maiden name instead of their family name. But he understood. *Dad, I'm not going to start high school with everyone calling me Queen Matilda the Third.*

But now was not the time for proper names or cute nicknames. They would forever be Father and Daughter.

"Hello, Daughter," he said in response to her greeting. "How are you feeling?"

"I'm just here, living my best life."

"Can I get you anything?"

"That's the one good thing about this place," she said. "I push a little button, and someone brings it to me. After a while."

Reese, meanwhile, refused to look at Jack and instead focused her white-hot hate on poor Hightower. Jack felt bad for the crazy bastard. "I thought we had an understanding," Reese said under her breath, hoping Matilda wouldn't hear. But of course she did; Jack watched her cringe a little.

"We did!" Hightower said. "This is not my fault. Talk to your brother-in-law."

She drilled deeper into Hightower's eyes. "Can we speak out in the hall?" She made this suggestion the same way an umpire suggests to a batter that he's out.

After they left, Jack held Matilda's hand. The one unencumbered by an IV line.

"Tell me what's going on with you."

"You're going to want to pull up a chair, Padre."

Seems that while Jack was preparing to lie his ass off to the state of California and spring himself from prison, his daughter's bone marrow was going haywire, producing mutant white blood cells that, left unchecked, would kill her.

Now she was hooked up to an IV through two lines running out of her skinny right arm. She was surrounded by pillows. Which reminded Jack of the bag he was holding. "I brought you something." He reached into the bag and pulled out the stuffed mouse with the long tail that he'd purchased in the gift shop.

"You brought me a rat?"

"It's supposed to be a mouse."

"Well, it's definitely a rat, Dad. Did they sell these in the prison gift shop along with the shanks?"

"You don't have to keep it."

She took the rat and started to pet it anyway. Jack looked up at the IV bags, still processing this whole thing. None of this felt real. This was a cosmic joke or a nightmare.

"What are you getting in that thing? Looks sort of like urine."

"They're platelets. Whenever my count goes below seven, they give me a couple of bags. Also I'm sad to hear your urine is nuclear yellow and chunky. You might want to get that checked out."

They stared at each other for a moment, just soaking in the memory of each other's faces, before looking away. To an outside observer it might have sounded like she was giving her old man a hard time, but this was the warmest conversation they'd had in years. Jack and Matilda didn't go for mushy father-daughter stuff. They bantered. The fact that they were still bantering was a very good sign.

"Are you sure I can't get you anything?" Jack finally asked.

"I'm Gouda."

Translation: good.

"I didn't know, or I would have come right away."

"I'm glad they didn't tell you right away. You had enough on your mind, getting out of the Gray Bar Hotel and all."

"That doesn't matter. You shouldn't have been here alone."

"Aunt Reese is taking good care of me. Speaking of, why are you wearing her sunglasses?"

Jack lowered them to show Matilda the damage. "Your uncle Louis Maced me."

Matilda shook her head. "I'm not even going to ask."

Jack dug deep for something sincere and fatherly — that he would be here with her through this whole thing, no matter what. They'd figure it out together. But a nurse interrupted to take her blood pressure and temperature, and then it was time for a bathroom break. Jack excused himself and stepped out into the hallway. A nurse named Meghan directed him to a family lounge about thirty yards away, near the nurses' station. This was as good a place as any to let all of this soak in.

About a minute later he wished he hadn't. Because his sister-in-law, Reese, was already there and waiting to pounce.

"We need money."

Thankfully, Hightower had fucked off to parts unknown; Jack didn't want to have this conversation in front of him, of all people."

"For the treatments," Jack said.

"For *everything.* We don't have health insurance. We're barely making rent. We've coasted by without it until . . . well, yesterday."

"I have money. I mean, I *will* have money."

"The wrongful conviction money, I know. It'll be about eighty grand, right? How soon will you receive a check?"

"I have no idea. Hightower had me sign some papers yesterday..."

"Well, you need to get on that shit now. Because we need that money. Matilda needs that money."

Sometimes Reese looked so much like her twin sister it was like a dagger to his rib cage, taking his breath away, leaving him powerless.

"Reese, I'm not going anywhere. I'm going to do everything in my power to give Matilda what she needs."

"I appreciate the platitudes. But you're not understanding me, Jack. We need money *now*. Louis and I are barely hanging on, I work on commission and sales have been awful lately, and now with this..."

"I hear you. But I'm wearing everything I own. You just have to give me a little time."

"You have wine on your breath. Did you do some celebrating this morning? Did you have fun? And was that before or after you assaulted my husband?"

Jack knew the truth, but it wasn't worth explaining. Let her have that one. "What do you want me to do?"

"I don't know, Jack. You're a criminal. Go out and do something criminal to make money."

THE GIRL DETECTIVE

With her father out of the room, the Girl Detective realized she was going to need a much better hiding place for the murder files she'd smuggled into the children's hospital.

Hiding them in plain sight (her brilliant idea from just a few minutes ago) wasn't going to cut it for the long term. That had been the drugs talking. Her father would most likely be spending many hours here in this room. Like most human beings, he'd grow bored. He'd start poking around, checking out the room as if it were a vacation rental. And eventually, he'd find the paint report and the case file and her notes and holy God would that be a disaster.

That was because her father was the man who may have (but maybe not!) killed the real estate tycoon in that Burbank parking garage.

Deep down she knew he couldn't have done it. Her father was a dork. A piano player — jazz mostly, but she also dug up old tapes of his rebellious rock/punk years in high school. His very first solo album was called *Jack Queen, the "Ace King," Live at Chris's.* I mean, seriously! How could you be afraid of anyone with that ridiculous moniker?

The man did not deserve the nickname the press gave him two years ago. The father she knew was no "killer." He was the kind of man who grew teary-eyed whenever they would drive past a road-flattened squirrel. The idea that he would actively choose to take someone else's life was absurd.

But knowing was one thing; proving was another.

And here was the really messed-up thing — the Girl Detective *needed* to prove it. Not for the courts, not for posterity. Not even for herself at this point. She needed to do it for her father. Jack Queen was freed on a technicality, and that kind of thing would haunt him forever. No, to give them both the best chance of a normal life AL (after leukemia), she had to definitively prove that he didn't do it. But she didn't want her father to know until she knew she'd solved it.

The Girl Detective's drug-fueled inspiration had been to hide the murder files among the files that were already in the room — at the base of her hospital bed, beneath the piles of paperbacks on the mini-desk in the room, inside the narrow cubby of her bedside table. Spread it all over and no one would notice it. Genius, right?

No. The opposite of genius. One bored father picking up the wrong piece of paper at the wrong time, and it was game over.

So now she turned her mind back to the problem, praying for a solution. No, not praying; she didn't believe in that. There was no Flying Spaghetti Space God floating over the hospital, just waiting to help all the good little sick boys and girls with the answers to their problems.

When the Girl Detective squeezed her brain hard enough, some kind of solution usually manifested itself. It was just a matter of time.

The drugs, however, seemed to be interfering with the solution-producing part of her brain. Maybe that part of her brain was already screaming, *Do you know we have a fucking narcotics freeway running into our heart muscle!?*

Through the venetian slats of the window overlooking the hallway, the Girl Detective could see her father's shape moving back down the hallway.

Funny how she would never forget his particular shape, even though she hadn't seen it in such a long time. It was like those parts of her mother that were burned into her very being: the way she moved, the way she smiled, the way she talked, the way she gave a hug.

Okay. Time was just about up. And when you're out of time, there's only one thing to do.

Stall for more time.

"KILLER"

"She's a piece of work, your sister-in-law," Hightower said when Jack met up with him in CHLA's bustling hospital lobby later that afternoon. "I had to get out of there to avoid her murder eyes."

"She's not wrong," Jack said, mostly to himself.

"About what?"

"Never mind."

"I know your late wife was her twin. Was she like that too?"

"Like what?"

"Like I said . . . a piece of work?"

Jack shook his head. "They couldn't be more different. We used to joke that all the bitchy genes floated over to Reese's side of the womb. But my wife adored her sister, no matter what. And she's taken good care of Matilda for the past two years."

"Not *that* good, apparently . . ."

"Hey," Jack said. "Don't do that."

"Geez, just trying to lighten the heavy mood," Hightower said. "How much do they look alike, your wife and your sis-in-law?"

"A lot more alike than I used to think."

"That's gotta be a head trip for you."

"Not really," Jack said softly. And that was the truth. They might have been tough to tell apart for most people, but not Jack. No one else on earth *felt* like his wife or captured the way she smiled when something amused her or laughed without restraint when something really amused her. Nothing like her touch or the sound of her voice. God he missed her. So much he was afraid to think about it for more than a few moments; otherwise he might lose his mind.

"Cool," Hightower said. "Hey, it's almost dinnertime. Let's go get a steak."

There was no way Jack would have left Matilda's side if she didn't have to undergo another series of pre-chemo tests—none of which he could be present for anyway. The Daughter insisted: go freshen up, maybe take a shower ("no offense, Father"), and come back later tonight. Jack promised he would.

Concerned parents pushed sick kids around in wheelchairs. There was a line growing for the elevator that led back down to the parking levels of the damned. The wall behind Jack and Hightower listed hundreds of names of donors to the hospital. A lot of them were names you would have heard of.

But Reese was right. *Someone* had to pay for all this. The hospital was great about taking care of kids in need, but they couldn't cover everything. And right now, Hightower's crazy scheme might be the only viable option.

"Where did you spend the afternoon?" Jack asked. He had horrible visions of Hightower making a menace of himself in the hospital cafeteria, stealing sick kids' juice boxes. They didn't serve booze in children's hospitals, did they? Please let the answer be no.

"I found a quiet little place just a block away," Hightower said. "Figured you'd need some quality time with the little one."

Somewhere quiet that wasn't the hospital sounded good. Jack needed to decompress; otherwise he might have an aneurysm. "What's the name of this quiet little place?"

"Teaser's," Hightower said. "Right over there on Hollywood Boulevard."

"Teaser's? Sounds like a strip club."

"It is a strip club."

"There's a strip club a block from Children's Hospital?"

"Of course. Parents need a little escape every now and again, right?"

"Sure. While little Timmy is having his back surgery, I'm headed over for a lap dance!"

"Exactly! You'll love this place."

"I am *not* going to a strip club."

"You know, I didn't take you for a prude. Knock it all you want, but the taco and burrito bar are pretty spectacular."

They ended up at a place not too far from the hospital, just across the LA River: Sizzler, which smelled like a grandparents' den. Jack had had no idea this chain still existed. Maybe it didn't. Maybe only in hell.

"The salad bar is my favorite," Hightower said. "You almost don't even need the steak."

Jack went through the motions as he put salad-type things on his plate. He couldn't have identified the things if you'd put a gun to his head. After drowning the whole mess with a pale pink salad dressing he couldn't place either, Jack took his cold plate and sat down. A waitress brought Hightower his steak — a sad, desiccated strip of sirloin. He looked up and added, by way of explanation:

"I need the iron."

It took all Jack's concentration to raise a fork to his face. He shouldn't be eating a fucking salad. He should be getting his shit together. One thing was clear. He might be guilty, but he'd been released from prison for a reason: to save his daughter's life. Fate worked in mysterious ways.

Hightower sawed into his sirloin with more effort than it should require. He stabbed the bleeding chunk with the tines of his thin fork, as if delivering the coup de grâce.

"Look, I didn't tell you because I wanted to give you a chance to breathe. A few days more wouldn't have mattered."

"Give me a chance to breathe? Fuck you, Hightower. I think you just wanted to go on a bender."

"Possibly. Can't change things now."

Hightower popped the chunk of steak into his mouth and chewed, waiting for Jack to respond. But Jack was too busy thinking about his options. This didn't take long, because he had zero options.

"I need a job," Jack said. "A real job, lots of money as fast as possible."

"No," Hightower said through a mouthful of food, "you don't. You've got a fat check coming your way, remember? And until then, I've got you covered. Help yourself to another trip to the salad bar, by the way."

Jack pushed the salad toward the center of the table. "Whenever you're done, I'd like to go back to my room, get my things, and start looking for work."

"Cool your jets. Let's think this through."

"Preferably somewhere near the hospital, so I can see Matilda as often as possible."

"I said hang on a minute! Jesus. At least let me finish my steak."

"I'll be out by the car."

"Come on, Jack. Don't be like that."

But Jack was already up and leaving. He didn't want to be rude. He just didn't want Hightower to see him weeping.

When the shock had worn off, the hard reality had set in. Jack was left with only one truth: unless he started making some incredibly smart decisions right about fucking now, his daughter was going to die.

Jack prayed Hightower would take his time with his sad little strip of sirloin and head back to the salad bar and maybe even wander over to the ice cream bar for some soft serve and chopped nuts. He needed time to recover.

Leaning against Hightower's car, Jack pressed his fingers to his face. His entire head throbbed. Jack hadn't cried in what...two years? Jack knew he didn't cry when he was locked up. That would be like slitting your wrists and then doing the doggie paddle in a shark tank.

"Hey...are you okay?"

A female voice. Soft, but no-nonsense. Jack dropped his hands from his face and blinked away the tears. Wait a minute. He recognized her. Dark-red lipstick, hair pulled back, leather jacket despite the heat. The girl who had been eyeing him in front of Reese and Louis's place. Her eyes carried great concern.

"I'll be fine," Jack said. "Thanks."

She tilted her head. "Oh, that won't do." And then she punched Jack in the face.

The punch was shockingly solid — a tight, hard fist colliding with Jack's nose and mouth at top speed. He saw a bright flash. His head snapped back.

Jack fumbled for some kind of response, but his brains were too scrambled for that. Dumb animal instinct lifted his paws in front of his face in case the girl tried to punch him again. Which she did, but not in his face.

All Jack knew was that something sharp exploded in his ribs and he fell to his knees in the parking lot. He bit his tongue and squeezed his eyes shut.

"That's all you get for now," she said. "Every time it's going to be different. I just want you to know that you're going to be in pain for the rest of your life."

"Yeah," Jack mumbled; he didn't think she heard. It was quite possible he didn't actually say the word, only imagined he did. His ass finally rested on the asphalt, and he tried not to throw up. The next thing Jack knew, Hightower was helping him up and leaning him back against his car.

"What the fuck happened to you?"

"Pretty sure I was just mugged by a sorority sister."

"Very funny. I think you passed out and landed on your face. How about we go back inside? They brought you a cup, if you want some ice cream."

"I just want to go home."

"Well, you're technically homeless. But I know what you mean. Let me settle up the check and we'll get going back to the roadhouse."

"I was serious. Did you see her? The girl who mugged me?"

"Nobody mugged you, Jack. I looked out the window and saw you'd done a face-plant on the asphalt. Pretty sure it's the stress."

"Does stress wear a leather jacket? Who the fuck *was* that woman? I think she's been trailing me since we were at the apartment. Did you notice someone following us to the hospital?"

"I would have noticed someone trailing us, amigo. I used to be a cop, as you may recall."

"Then how the hell did she know we'd be at a friggin' Sizzler?"

Hightower eyed him with something like genuine concern. "Do you think you have a concussion?"

FRIDAY, JUNE 1, 2018

"KILLER"

Jack woke up at 3:30 a.m. ravenous and thirsty and disoriented.

Traffic had been horrendous all the way back to the roadhouse, and it was full dark by the time Jack collapsed into bed with the intention of taking a restorative nap before returning to CHLA. He felt awful when he realized what time it was. He would have sent Matilda a text, but he still didn't have a phone. He didn't know where to find a landline. He didn't even know if her room *had* a landline.

There was nothing in his half-size fridge, so he staggered over to see if Hightower was awake. He was and wearing a T-shirt that read HAR-VARD LAW (JUST KIDDING).

"Happy to see you up and about," he said. "You had me worried about that whole concussion thing. Still seeing phantom chicks in leather jackets?"

"You're not supposed to let a person with a concussion sleep."

"You woke up, didn't you?"

The biggest wall in the room was covered in photos and documents and Post-it notes. The Weird Sisters were positioned to the left, as if they were a trio of adjunct professors about to give a topless lecture. Against another wall leaned the three cheap framed prints that Hightower had removed to make room for his collage.

"What's all that?" Jack asked.

"The case against Christopher Albin Dixon. The California Bear."

"Christ, not this again."

"Hey, you seemed interested enough yesterday. You agreed to help me!"

"Yesterday was a lot. I wasn't thinking straight. But I am now. And no, for the record, I did not agree to help you."

"Just hear me out, one last time."

"I need to get to the hospital."

"Why—are you feeling weird? Are you seeing flashing lights?"

"No—Children's Hospital. My daughter with leukemia, who you kept from me for two days? Remember?"

Hightower nodded in a way that made it seem like he was waving the suggestion away. Clearly, this whole daughter-sick-with-leukemia thing was an unforeseen complication of his master plan.

"Let me walk you through the case and then we'll go grab breakfast downstairs."

Jack checked the wall clock. It was 4 a.m. *God, shoot me.* "They're not going to be serving for another three hours."

"Well, it's a complicated case," Hightower said, then proceeded to explain that he'd stumbled onto this whole thing by accident. "Truth be told, I'm not that brilliant an investigator."

"You don't say."

Jack received a sour look for that one.

Hightower explained that toward the end of his rather unspectacular law enforcement career he was working in the records room. Not much to do down there but pull the occasional file for the cold case squad ... and read. So Hightower read. A large majority of the cases were as boring as tax code, but there were quite a few stunners. After a while, he got tired of flipping folders shut whenever anyone walked into Records, so he started borrowing files. "Like from a library," he said. The files piled up at home and then he realized he'd put in his twenty and then ...

Hightower waved his arm around the room. All the bankers boxes in his crowded motel room, guarded by the Weird Sisters, were full of proof (he claimed) of the monsters who had gotten away with it.

Jack was stunned. All these files were cold cases he'd *stolen* from LAPD Records.

"Borrowed" was the word Hightower preferred. But that didn't mean it wasn't a serious crime.

"You're unbelievable," Jack said.

"Thank you."

"Didn't mean it as a compliment."

"I didn't take it as one."

Jack didn't know what to do with a man who clearly felt no shame. "So you're basically saying that in one of these files, Christopher Albin Dixon was named as the Bear, but no one ever did anything about it."

"Um...not exactly."

One day his wife, Jeanie, had been reading this cheap true crime paperback about a series of unsolved 1970s and '80s SoCal home invasions—*LA After Manson*—and she mentioned a creepy detail: one killer had left a taunting message on the family fridge using magnetic alphabet letters. This intrigued Hightower. This was someone who knew a frightening message would draw media attention. Just like "PIG" did for those idiot Manson freaks.

"And when I started asking around, more than a few of my colleagues thought the Bear was a cop. Something in the way he worked. How he knew how to avoid...well, other cops."

"And by 'colleagues,' you mean your dead, drunk, retiree pal."

"Will you stop saying that?"

"Doesn't mean it's not true."

"It's not true! I'm sure there were others who liked Dixon for it, but what were they going to do without hard evidence? The feeling was, he'd stopped, so just let it go. Los Angeles had other problems."

"Why am I not surprised? Still, that's a long way from proof."

"Cynic. Anyway, when I started gathering a list of people who got away with it, the California Bear was number one on my list. We've got plenty of work ahead of us," he said.

"I told you, I need to find a real job. If you can't help me with that, then I probably should be on my way."

"Hold on, now. I thought about that last night, while you were all concussed and shit. I've got all your problems solved!"

"You do."

"Yes, I do. The California Bear wasn't just a sadist. He stole things — cash, jewels, drugs, electronics. This wasn't his primary motivation, mind you. More of a practical matter, I'm guessing. If you're taking complete control of someone's life, why not help yourself to some of their things?"

"Yeah, he sounds like a serious asshole. But how does that help me?"

"We break into his place, rob him blind. I'm sure he has stacks of cash tucked away. Cops do that, even if they tell people to do the opposite."

"I thought your plan was to blackmail him," Jack said.

"I'm just keeping our options open."

"Wait a minute . . . did you do that when you were a cop?"

"Do what?"

"Steal from people?"

"Of course not!"

"But now you're okay with robbing an ex-cop."

"An ex-sadist-torturer-murderer who *happened* to be a cop."

"And then kill him."

"Hey now." Hightower smiled. "I thought you were against killing him."

"I *am* against killing him! Or anybody! I don't do that."

"You mean, you don't do that *anymore*."

Things had a way of sounding strange this early in the morning; Jack could admit as much. But this conversation would have been surreal at any time of the day.

"I still can't believe that you broke the law and freed me from prison just so you could kill *another* man. There's no way to justify it. Not for justice, or the social good, or any of the other bullshit you've been serving up."

"You're right. I don't want to kill him. Not really. Well, maybe a little. But mostly I want to fuck with him. Make him suffer the same way he meant his victims to suffer."

"That's what the courts are for!"

"Well, the system failed in this case."

"That doesn't make it our business."

Hightower smiled. "Arthur Conan Doyle once said it's every man's business to see justice done."

Jack realized they could go round and round like this forever. No more.

"Let me put it to you as plain as I can: I'm not blackmailing a serial killer. No way, no how, not *ever.* Do you understand me?"

"Yeah, yeah, I hear you. Relax, man. You shouldn't get all worked up, especially after getting the shit kicked out of you by a teenager."

Jack sighed. "I'm going for a walk."

"Good idea. Clear that banged-up head of yours. And hey, after breakfast, I'll take you back to CHLA."

"Thanks. I'd appreciate that."

The Pacific was agitated this morning. Jack watched it bitch-slap the wide shore as he once again pondered his Alternate Universe Theory.

Jack "Killer" Queen's Alternate Universe Theory: two years ago, he accidentally stepped into a darker, more sinister reality right next door to the one he used to inhabit. Every day inside, Jack wracked his brains trying to pinpoint exactly where he'd crossed over into this world. The idea being, of course, that if he could find that juncture point that led him in, he could step back through the time-space crack or tesseract or whatever and return to his rightful world. So he replayed key moments in his life, decisions made, sins committed. But nothing presented itself as the obvious juncture.

The one thing Jack knew was that following Cato Hightower on his mission of blackmail was the *opposite* of finding his way back. That would be doubling down on this mad universe.

THE BEAR

The California Bear woke up with a dry mouth and a fogged-over mind. He called out for his wife. There was no reply. Where the hell was that sadistic bitch? Probably hiding cookies somewhere. He eased his aching body up and off his bed, feeling the usual twinges in his lower back and the minor lightning bolts up and down his arms. For a minute he wondered why he was in his mother's old bedroom; then he remembered. *Oh yeah.* Much had happened since 1984. The Bear fumbled for his cell phone on his bedside table.

The Queen of Mars had texted: she left early this morning for a meeting in Culver City. Meetings were all she seemed to do these days. Not that he minded her being occupied elsewhere. For most of their marriage they had pretty much stuck to their own corners, bound together by economic necessity as well as mutually assured destruction. It was a relief when one or the other was out of the house.

The Bear's heart was racing for reasons he couldn't understand. Did something happen last night? Did he do something he shouldn't have?

There were also five missed calls. All from Cubby. He tapped the screen and waited.

"What's up, Cubby?"

"Hey, chief. I don't think anyone's home."

"Home? What do you mean? Home where?"

"You know. Up in Port Hueneme. I've been staking the place out."

"Yeah, Port Hueneme," the Bear said, stalling until his memory reloaded. Right; the crappy Honda Accord. The dipshits gawking at him. The two losers who could possibly ruin everything. "What are you seeing up there?"

"Like I said, I think they're gone. The woman left a few hours ago and hasn't returned home. I left a few markers around, just like you taught me. You know, with the tape and doorways. But nothing was disturbed. Nobody's been here for quite a while."

"What about the guy I mentioned? Kind of fat, loud shirt, looks like a dipshit?"

"No sign of him. The place also doesn't have any kind of security. Like, nothing. It's a fucking joke. I was thinking about taking a look inside but wanted to check in with you first. I mean, if it's personal, maybe you'd want to do a little looking around yourself."

"I wish, Cubby. But no, the wife has me running around later today. How about you do it."

"You sure?"

"Yeah," the Bear said, even though he yearned to be out there again. He'd spent a few nights in Port Hueneme, back in 1982. He once almost abducted a young woman in some beachfront bar, intending to drown her in the ocean. No real reason; just an impulse. Fortunately, he'd resisted that urge. He wasn't the Oceanside Strangler. He was the California Bear, after all. His deal was breaking into people's homes and terrorizing them. If you were going to commit to this kind of life, you had to stay on brand.

"Well, I'll take plenty of pictures. I can grab you some souvenirs too."

"Nah, don't worry about that. I just want to know who these assholes are and what to expect."

"I can do that, no problem. Would it be okay to swing by later?"

The Bear thought about that and realized that would be a very bad idea. Cassandra had meetings this morning, but then she was bringing everybody back to their place, and the Bear would be expected to tidy up and prepare something for the grill. Everybody seemed to get a real charge out of that. The mighty California Bear! Flipping burgers and dogs! What a trip! He couldn't very well let Cubby, his protégé, see him reduced to such a pathetic role. Not when he was on the verge of finally claiming credit for his life's work. His *glories.*

"Better not, my friend," the Bear said. "I'm gonna be a little tied up. If you find anything, though, could you leave it for me in the usual spot? And if it's nothing, then just drop me a message on my burner."

"You got it. Okay, I'm going to give the place one more look, then slip inside."

"Enjoy yourself. In fact, you know what..."

"I know, I know. I've got plenty of gloves and those little baggies for my shoes. I've learned my lesson."

"That's not what I was going to say."

"Oh? What is it, chief?"

The Bear thought about it and realized, what harm could it do? In fact, it might help with brand building, come to think of it. He didn't want to run it by anyone or ask for permission. He wanted to make the choice and see what happened. Just like in the good old days.

"I want you to really *enjoy yourself,* Cubby," he said. "You follow me?"

Cubby was practically bursting with glee. "Oh, I do."

"That's a good little cub."

THE GIRL DETECTIVE

"What up, Padre?"

This was how the Girl Detective greeted her father upon his return to her room. She was wide awake and dressed in a fluffy robe and her pink knit hat, working on one of those stress-busting coloring books for adults.

However, this was just for show—to make the nurses (and Aunt Reese) believe she was keeping her mind active with positive things. For the past few hours, she'd been drawing up a list for Violet—Things to Say. Part of her investigation, she now realized, would involve a kind of ruse. Violet would be good as her personal Archie Goodwin. She already carried herself with the demeanor of someone much older—eighteen, possibly even nineteen, instead of her actual age of fifteen. Violet's sense of style "helped" too. Jackets over button-down shirts, and jeff caps whenever possible. Louis said her friend dressed like she was headed to Santa Anita to drink beer out of a paper cup and bet on the ponies all afternoon. This would also be useful.

Luckily, Violet had forgiven her for not sharing the news about her l-word diagnosis straightaway. She apologized and explained she had wanted to tell her in person, not over the phone, but alas. Violet still seemed hurt, but she understood. And she swore to keep it a secret. Which was a total lie, but the Girl Detective appreciated the gesture. Violet couldn't help herself; soon the entire freshman class would know. Fortunately school was practically over. Maybe even her

English teacher would forgive the Girl Detective for her hopelessly late paper.

Speaking of...

The Girl Detective had also made a shorthand list for herself—all the unknowns and all the possible paths (that she could think of, anyway) to provide answers.

Smoke House to Burbank Town Center; Distance? Cameras?

Receipts (and how to get copies)

Follow up the partial plate (possible sites to look them up?)

Insurance bros and their motives

But now all those notes were swiftly hidden within the pages of a goofy coloring book.

Her father looked like he'd slept in the same suit he'd worn yesterday. Which looked *a lot* like the same suit he wore when he was sentenced to prison. Not that she was keeping tabs or anything.

Aunt Reese was dead asleep on the pullout bed near the window. Sometimes she reminded the Girl Detective of her own mother so much that she wanted to cry. She took a mental snapshot of this moment, trying to fool her brain into thinking they were all together again, just like in the good old days.

"Padre?" her father whispered. "What happened to 'Father'?"

"Oh, you're still Father. I'm just changing it up. How did you get here? Is that old cop guy with you?"

"His name is Cato Hightower. And no, he's not here. He just dropped me off."

"Are you really staying with him?"

"I'm in a motel down in Santa Monica. But I'm going to find a room out here as soon as I can."

"Why don't you stay with Aunt Reese and Uncle Louis? You can have my room. You know, for when I'm here in the hospital."

"Pretty sure if I tried that," her father said, and then cast a furtive glance to the sleeping woman on the pullout bed, "Aunt Reese would probably try to smother me in my sleep."

"Well, you *did* beat up her husband."

"After he Maced me."

"*Still don't want to know about that,*" she replied in a singsongy voice.

"Anyway, I'm fine. When I'm not here with you, I can freshen up at the motel. Besides, I think I'm going to be doing some work for the old guy, so..."

The Girl Detective nodded. "Well, good, because you're going to need a cell phone if we're going to do this thing."

"Thing?"

"This father-and-daughter thing. I want to be able to text and call you."

"I'll work on that."

"You can probably just get a burner for now."

"A burner, huh. How do you know what that is?"

"Because I live in the world, and it is the year 2018? I'm surprised *you* know what a burner is. They don't allow them in prison, do they?"

"Are you kidding? That's one of the most heavily traded items on the black market. Some guards bring them in by the caseload."

"I'm shocked."

"You wouldn't believe half of the stuff that goes on in prison. It's nothing like you see in the movies."

"That's not what shocks me. I'm shocked that you didn't buy a burner and call your daughter every once in a while."

"I was trying to get time off for good behavior."

This was their way: the banter, the jokes—making light of the completely awful and deep-down hurtful. The Girl Detective knew it was her father's defense mechanism. She could see the wheels turning inside his skull right now, trying to pivot to something positive, anything to steer the talk away from the lack of communication over the past few months.

"Hey, you know what would be pretty boss, pretty dope?" Jack said. "You and I going somewhere for a few days once you're checked out of this place."

The Girl Detective stared at him. "Hey, you know what else would be pretty boss, pretty dope? You never using those words ever again."

Reese stirred lazily, then a switch flipped, and she sat up in a hurry. "Is everything okay, honey?"

"I'm fine, Aunt Reese. Dad's here."

Oh, the displeasure on her aunt's face at the sound of that word. *Dad.* Reese didn't even try to hide it. She stood up, straightened her pants, mumbled something about going to the cafeteria. She pushed past Jack, pumped a dispenser for hand sanitizer, then staggered out into the hallway. Their encounters would never be *not* weird. She would never forgive Jack for the loss of her sister (which was not his fault) or the upending of her life (fair enough). The only way to make things less weird was if Jack could get his life together again and make some money.

"The thing is, Father—I'm not getting out of here for a while. And when I do, I can't just go *anywhere.*"

"What do you mean?"

"Sit down and let me explain a few things to you. Oh, but first wash your hands. With soap and water. And then use the sanitizer. Unless you want to accidentally kill me."

The Girl Detective had absorbed a lot about her condition and tried to explain it in a way that would be crystal clear to her father. Leukemia is like a broken photocopier inside your bones, she said. The stuff inside your bones, the marrow, produces three different kinds of cells. The marrow acts as a photocopier making countless copies of these helpful cells. They fight off infections and keep you healthy.

But leukemia is like some asshole who decides to hijack the photocopier and print copies of their butt.

Sounds like fun, but it's not. Imagine a business. With a photocopier. And after a while, the photocopier prints nothing but copies of some guy's butt.

Eventually, said business would fail.

So the idea is to fix the photocopier, but in practice this means practically burning the company down to the ground and starting from scratch...all in the hope that when you open for business again, you've effectively rid yourself of the employee making all the butt photocopies. If it doesn't work, and you see even a few photocopies of someone's ass...you burn the company down to the ground and start over again.

"So you're not getting out of here for a while," her dad said.

"Probably not before three weeks, maybe a month."

"And then..."

"Well, as I understand it, then the real fun begins. Aren't you wishing you were back in the slammer?"

"The only place I want to be," her father said, "is here."

"That's sweet," she said, a sarcastic deflection to keep the tears at bay. "But when you're not here, you really need a phone."

"KILLER"

A few hours later, when Hightower picked Jack up from the lobby of CHLA, Jack immediately asked to be taken to a place where he could buy a cheap burner phone. Hightower said sure, right after they had lunch—he was starving *and* had big news to share. Jack had no choice but to agree (Hightower was the one with the car) but gently insisted on somewhere other than a Sizzler. Hightower beamed and said he had just the place, and best of all, it was two minutes away: Ye Rustic Inn, which turned out to be a corner bar in a strip mall on Hillhurst.

"Can't you go drinking later?" Jack pleaded. "I have a lot to get done this afternoon before heading back to CHLA."

"Au contraire, my friend. *We* have a lot to get done this afternoon."

"Which is maybe why you shouldn't go drinking?"

"Believe me, after I tell you my news, you might change your mind about your little sobriety thing. You're going to want to celebrate."

Jack did not, in fact, change his mind. He ordered a Diet Coke with a wedge of lemon. After considerable indecision—which inspired considerable eye rolling from the pretty, tattooed bartender—Hightower landed on a Fat Tire Ale. Because Jack was right, he explained. He shouldn't be drinking heavily when they had so much to do. Jack supposed that in Hightower's world, a beer didn't count as "drinking."

"So what's this good news?" Jack asked.

"Before we get to that," Hightower continued, "do you think names influence destiny?"

Jack blinked. "Come again?"

"You know, how accountants are always named Sheldon, or pilots are always Jim or John or Glenn. And then you've got the last names. Fire-fighters named McBurney or Hotz. Some asshole named Hamm working the deli counter."

Jack Queen frowned. "Is this leading up to some joke about me being a jack-off or a drag queen? Because, buddy, I've heard them all before."

"No!" Hightower exclaimed. "Christ, you're touchy. Let me start over. Take my wife, Jeanie. Perfectly normal name, right? Her maiden name is Poole. Jeanie Poole, no big whoop."

"Did you just say 'no big whoop'?"

"But consider her late-in-life career, and it's kind of absurd. She builds online family trees for people. You know, one of those genetic researchers. Anyway, online she's known as 'Gene Jeanie.'"

"Cool. Just like the Bowie song."

"What Bowie song?"

"Never mind."

"So my question is, did she fall into this line of work because of her name? What are the chances that a kid named Jeanie Poole would end up working in genetic research? My theory is that if you hear something enough, it burns into your brain. It influences everything."

Hightower sort of had a point there. But Jack was way too sober for this kind of barroom philosophy.

"Anyway, the reason I bring up my wife is because she needs a leg man. Someone to help her with research, errands, that sort of thing. And I could use a little help, too, with my own work. Before you say anything — don't worry, it's nothing to do with the Bear. It would all be legit work."

Jack was instantly suspicious. "What kind of work?"

"Background checks, skip tracing, that sort of thing. I kind of have a private eye thing going on the side. Lots of ex-cops do." For a moment, Jack thought Hightower was going to add *It's no big whoop.*

"This is a *real* job? Like, steady pay? You're not fucking with me?"

"Why would I do that? Did you think I sprung you from the pokey just to play an elaborate prank on you? Come on, man."

"Well, pardon my skepticism, but you're offering me a job on your wife's behalf, and she's never even met me."

"My wife is a huge fan of yours," Hightower said. "She'll never admit it to your face, because that's her way. But I caught her listening to your first album a few times."

This embarrassed Jack a little; he felt so removed from that album—in fact, from everything involving a keyboard. That performer was *not* him. Someone else had played those notes, improvised those riffs, joked with those audiences. Jack didn't like lingering too long on the old days, because back then his wife (then girlfriend) was looking up at him from the audience, smiling, and that would never, ever happen again.

"Did you like the album?"

"Jazz just ain't my thing."

"Fair enough. Solving cold cases isn't my thing either."

"You won't be working on any murders, I promise."

"Fine," Jack said, more or less on impulse. The least he could do was meet Hightower's wife and listen to what she had in mind. He had to save his daughter; maybe this was the way.

"There's got to be a cell phone place somewhere nearby."

"There's one in Port Hueneme."

"Exactly how far away is Port Hueneme?"

"You know LA. Everything is—"

"An hour away from each other. Right."

Port Hueneme was a lot farther than a fucking hour. Jack could only watch helplessly as Hightower steered his Honda down Franklin, then past the Hollywood Towers, and somehow levitated onto the 101. That he didn't clip anyone was a minor miracle. Once they were on the 101, Hightower impatiently weaved in and out of lanes, hoping to find the one that was moving the quickest. There is no such thing in Los Angeles. At any time, for any (or no) reason, freeway traffic will suddenly slow to a crawl or slam to a teeth-grinding stop. The best thing to do is go with the flow.

Jack had learned this long ago. Hightower must have missed this memo and attacked traffic like he had a personal vendetta. The San Fernando Valley eventually gave way to the hilly playgrounds of the rich — Agoura Hills, Calabasas, Malibu — before coasting down into Ventura County.

"I should warn you about something."

"Go ahead."

"The missus and I are not in a great place," Hightower said, as if he had been waiting for the right moment to deliver this devastating news. Until relatively recently, Jack had had no idea Hightower was even married.

"I'm sorry to hear," Jack said, biting his tongue before he could ask, *What does this mean for the potential job?*

"But it's not permanent. She's just going through some stuff. I don't know if it's the usual midlife-crisis bullshit or some kind of whackadoo menopause thing."

"One suggestion," Jack said. "When discussing this with your wife, I'd avoid phrasing it that way."

"Well, I would if we were on speaking terms."

"I thought you spoke to her this morning. About the potential job?"

"Well, that, sure. I meant we're not on personal speaking terms. It's a temporary thing, and the only reason I brought it up is in case she acts a little . . . weird."

"Maybe the Weird Sisters pushed her over the edge."

"What? No. Of course not," he said. "But they probably didn't help."

They were only sixty miles from Hollywood, but it felt like they had teleported light-years away. Lots of strawberry farms, a big military base, middle-class homes. Jack hated being so far away from Matilda. What if something happened back at CHLA? Right then he swore to himself that he'd never venture this far again.

Hightower insisted on stopping for some beers at a local deli because Jeanie probably didn't have any in the fridge. Jack followed him inside, hoping against hope he'd find a cheap cell phone. Shockingly, the deli had such a device in stock — a prepaid TeleFon brand, model 3000. The low,

low price of $39.95 meant a flip phone, which meant awkward thumb texting on a numeric keypad. But it was better than nothing. The very idea of being able to communicate with Matilda whenever he wanted was a miracle unto itself.

"Drug dealers love those," Hightower said, eyeing up Jack's purchase.

"And your brand of beer," Jack replied, "is a favorite for people on the brink of liver failure."

"Whoa-ho-ho! Easy there, Mr. Moral Conscience of Southern California."

Back in Hightower's car, Jack cracked open the plastic shell containing the phone and managed to power the damned thing up. He pulled out the pink Post-it note where Matilda had scrawled her number. Not that Jack could ever forget it. The 215-area-code number originally belonged to his wife and had been bequeathed to Matilda. He punched it in, then sent a short message, which took quite a bit of thumbing:

This is your Father speaking.

THE GIRL DETECTIVE

She thumbed in response:

Hello, Father. This is your Daughter speaking. What kind of number is this? I don't recognize the area code. Did you fly to a non-extradition country? Haha JK (maybe)

As her dad fumbled with an explanation, the Girl Detective did a little Google Fu and put it together on her own.

She thumbed:

Oh, I see this area code is used exclusively by the TeleFon corporation, which in turn is owned by a Chinese investment firm. You probably have the 3000 model which coincidentally is a favorite burner phone for many drug dealers

Her father abandoned his epic reply and typed:

Hightower said the same thing

Of course.

Where are you? She thumbed.

I'm in a place called Port Hueneme. Where the old guy lives. He might have a job for me

Some quick online mapping revealed that her father was currently... oof, pretty far away. Was this where her father might end up working? Horrors—if she survived her current ordeal, would she end up living in...Port Hueneme?

I'll explain more later. I love you

Urgent business in Port Hueneme. Five words the Girl Detective never thought she'd string together. Life was absurd.

Love you too, Old Guy #2

The Girl Detective might be trapped in her cell, but that didn't make her powerless. As long as she had Wi-Fi, she was Gouda (that is to say, good). With Wi-Fi, she could escape these four walls and ceiling and floor and IV machines and blood pressure cuff and everything else they put in here to torture her.

She wondered about her father, wondered what he was up to out in Port Hueneme.

She wondered about her family and how it had fallen apart so easily.

She wondered about how she'd ended up here so suddenly.

But no dwelling on that now; not when there was a case to solve. Multiple cases now, in fact. The Killing of Julian Church. The Port Hueneme Connection. And of course, the ticking-clock mystery of My Own Malfunctioning Body.

"KILLER"

Hightower's place was a modest two-story house in the middle of an absurdly long block lined with photocopied reproductions of the same house. His exterior needed paint. The lawn and shrubs needed taming. Hightower warned him that Jeanie's cat would probably try to shoot out the front door the moment he opened it so be on the lookout. Jack just nodded. He was exhausted and already tired of this. But what choice did he have?

The door opened. No cat.

The inside of the house, however, looked like a gang of burly Russians had tossed it looking for a secret dossier or something. No couches or paintings were slashed, which was about the only thing keeping their décor from being Early-Twenty-First-Century Home Invasion.

"Mind your step," Hightower said. "Jeanie's not much of a homemaker."

"Hey, this is your place too."

"Not these days," he muttered in reply. "Jeanie! Hey! You here?"

If Jeanie Hightower (née Poole) was home, she didn't acknowledge their presence. Jack wasn't sure what that meant in terms of their possible job discussion. He'd come all this way for that one reason, not expecting his (maybe) employer to be missing in action. Considering the state of the house, Jack couldn't help but wonder if maybe Jeanie didn't really exist—that she was a figment of Hightower's imagination. But such an accusation might be considered rude at this point.

Hightower loaded his beers into the middle of three refrigerators stacked side by side in an open space that appeared to be a dining room. Hightower noted Jack's puzzled expression.

"Jeanie never likes to throw anything away."

This ethos seemed to inform the rest of the house, because it appeared to be where all material goods came to die. Mess aside, the place seemed like the perfect starter home for a small family. Maybe that was the dream at one point. Jack couldn't help but wonder what it would be like to find a place like this, an hour away from LA and all its dark memories, and start over with Matilda. He wondered how the schools were.

"Let's go out back," Hightower said. "I'll put a steak on."

Which sounded good to Jack, because he hadn't eaten all day. But anticipation quickly turned to dread. The cut of the meat wasn't the problem. Sure, it was a New York sirloin style bought in bulk from one of those club-type stores. That wasn't necessarily a bad thing. But Jack watched in horror as Hightower coated the meat with a thick barbecue sauce best meant for drowning chicken nuggets shaped like dinosaurs.

"What are you doing?"

"Getting it ready for the grill," Hightower said.

"You're not supposed to smother a steak in barbecue sauce. If you grill it right, all you need is just a little salt and pepper. Maybe a touch of garlic powder."

"This is how I always do it, and I've never heard any complaints."

"That's because everybody was probably choking to death."

"Didn't realize you were so fancy, Jack. Why don't you head back inside and get yourself a beer."

"No, I'm okay."

"You sure you don't want something to wash down this horrible steak I'm going through the trouble of making for you?"

Okay, so Hightower was offended. Fair enough. But Jack considered covering a piece of steak in barbecue sauce a war crime, so the offense was on both sides.

The result wasn't exactly disgusting, but it was in that ballpark. The

BBQ-crusted piece of cow flesh reminded Jack of how the Scots loved to deep-fry everything. Hightower had done the Scots one better and removed all hints of savory steak flavor from the cut. There were no steak knives—Hightower couldn't find them. So Jack was forced to pry strips of the well (well)–done meat from the bone with a dull butter knife and attempt to finish the job with his teeth. This was not always successful. He half regretted turning down the offer of the beer, which might have helped. But no, better to keep his mind clear.

Hightower had a grand ole time with his meat-based abomination and sucked down a six-pack before shuffling out back to turn off the grill and smoke a joint and look at the stars. Jack stayed at the table and tried to stay awake, but exhaustion must have overtaken him, because he didn't realize he'd fallen asleep until he heard the racking of a shotgun directly behind his head.

GENE JEANIE

Amazing how stupid some people can be, thought Jeanie Hightower (née Poole, and leaning more toward the Poole with each passing day).

She had arrived home from a business trip to discover her house had been crudely tossed and burglarized. This was an unwelcome development. The absurd part: the perpetrator was seated and passed out at the dining room table among about a half dozen empty beer bottles like a drunk Goldilocks. His suit was dirty and wrinkled. He wasn't wearing shoes. One of his socks had a hole in it.

The sloppy home invader had also cooked himself two steaks and dirtied two different dishes, then felt at ease enough to just drift off to sleep mid-ransack. What happened to the smart criminals? Jeanie had enough time to recover the double-barreled shotgun from the front closet and give this asshole a pump-action wake-up call. There's no more terrifying sound in the world, Cato had always insisted. He was wrong about most things, but Jeanie knew he'd nailed that one.

The sharp *CUH-CHACK* had its intended effect: the would-be home invader sat up straight in his chair, clearly too terrified to turn around.

"If you picked this house at random," Jeanie said calmly, "you have the worst luck in the world."

"I'm inclined to agree with you," came a quiet, soft voice that took her by surprise.

"You know this is a cop's house, right?"

"Ex-cop."

"And you broke in here anyway."

"I didn't break in. I was invited in. By the ex-cop."

Jeanie should have known this had the greasy fingerprints of her husband. Only Cato would smother a piece of good steak in cheap barbecue sauce and grill it beyond recognition. But that didn't explain everything, and this asshole wasn't off the hook yet.

"I didn't see his car outside," she said.

"He parked down the street. He wanted to surprise you."

"Bullshit. He was hoping to avoid me."

The man at her kitchen table shrugged as if it were none of his affair. And Jeanie supposed he was right.

"Can you tell me why this place looks like a hurricane touched down in my living room?"

"Ma'am, I'm not trying to start anything, but is that shotgun loaded?"

"No. You don't get to ask questions. Whoever the fuck you are."

"My name is Jack Queen, ma'am. You must be Jeanie."

And with that, this whole surreal scene started to make a little more sense. Her soon-to-be ex had brought home his stray ex-con after all. Unbelievable.

"I am Mrs. Hightower," she said, "and you can turn around. You still haven't told me why you two geniuses trashed my home."

Jack Queen the ex-con turned around. "You mean it wasn't like this before?"

And that is when her husband entered the living room, unsteady on his feet, as if he'd been roused from a bender followed by a nap followed by another beer to kick-start his circulatory system. Which is how Cato usually looked, to be fair.

"Honey!" he said cheerily. "I see you've met Jack."

There was some confusing back-and-forth before Jeanie could convince her soon-to-be ex that their home had, in fact, been burglarized. Cato refused to believe it. But Jeanie knew this was his pride talking. Especially in front of his new best friend — this "Jack" guy. How could a former police officer completely miss the fact that his own home had been knocked over?

Never mind that it had to have happened in a relatively short window of time. Jeanie had left just a few hours ago to deliver a package to a client up in Santa Barbara. The perp had clearly been waiting for Jeanie to leave. Which meant someone had been watching her. Which creeped her right the fuck out.

No, she had a hard time convincing Cato because nothing of value had been stolen, he argued. Why would someone break in just to dirty up their place? Jeanie did a fine enough job of that on her own.

Which was the absolute wrong thing to say at this moment.

"My workspace may be a mess," Jeanie said, "but your entire fucking life is a mess."

"I am in complete control of all things," Hightower said. "Which is a lot more than I can say for you."

"You're not even in complete control of your bowels."

Jack "Ex-Con" Queen looked uncomfortable. "I'm going to step outside and let you two discuss things in private."

"KILLER"

"Hello, Father," Matilda said over the phone.

"Is this an okay time to talk? I didn't want to bother you while you were in the middle of something."

"All is quiet on the western front."

Jack laughed. "How do you know about that movie?"

"Because before it was a movie, it was a book, and we read it earlier this year in English class. Are you still in Port Hueneme?"

"Yes, and I'm listening to a couple of grown-ass adults argue."

"Your cop friend and...?"

"And his wife. They're having...troubles."

"Remind me to never get married," Matilda said.

This gave Jack pause for reasons he couldn't quite articulate. He changed the subject.

"I thought I'd be back in LA tonight, but that isn't looking likely," Jack said. "I'm sorry. Hightower's a little tipsy, and I don't have a car. I can try asking his wife, but I don't think she likes me very much."

"What makes you say that?"

"Well, my first clue was that she pointed a shotgun at the back of my head."

"Oh, Father."

She spoke the words all *ho-hum*, like such a thing happened every day. Maybe Matilda thought he was joking. Boy, Jack wished he was.

"Tell me what's going on with you," he said.

"So when will you be back here?" she asked.

"First thing tomorrow morning, even if I have to hitchhike."

"Okay."

The disappointment in her voice crushed him. "I'm really sorry . . ."

"Well, if you don't have to thumb your way back to civilization," Matilda said, "can I ask a favor?"

"Anything."

"Would you bring me doughnuts? I don't really care which kind. No, scratch that. I do care. I don't want any chain doughnuts. I want good old-fashioned LA doughnuts in a pink box. You know the kind I mean."

"I do," Jack said, smiling. "I will bring you a dozen."

"Mmm," his daughter said. "I can taste them already. But you should make it two dozen. We have to treat the nurses right, and I figure a sugary bribe will come in handy later."

"Smart thinking."

This was the first time in days—his entire new life as a free man—that Jack Queen felt like he could do something good for his child. Work prospects might be grim, and he might be hooked up with a pot-smoking drunk with a ludicrous scam bouncing around his fevered brain. But at the very least, Jack had enough money to buy doughnuts for his daughter.

As he enjoyed this fleeting warm feeling, Jack sensed eyes on him. He turned around to see Jeanie Hightower staring at him from the doorway. She had a drink in her hand. Something clear and carbonated with a wedge of lime floating among the ice cubes.

"Uh, sweetheart, listen," Jack said. "I'd better go. But I'll see you bright and early tomorrow morning."

"Don't forget to get a new pass at the front desk," Matilda said. "I made Aunt Reese and Uncle Louis share one, so you'll have one all to yourself. You are, after all, the Father."

"Yes, I am," Jack said, dangerously close to choking up. "I love you."

"I love you too."

After Jack pressed the END key, Jeanie stepped into the backyard.

In addition to her drink, she held a small pile of clothes under her arm. "That your girlfriend or something?"

Jack didn't care to explain, not right now, so he gave a quick shake of his head.

"I made up the couch for you," Jeanie said. "My living room looks like a FEMA site, but there's nowhere else to put you, unless you want to pull a sleeping bag out here."

"The couch will be fine, ma'am."

"Don't 'ma'am' me. Christ. It's Jeanie. Not Jean, not Jay, not Mrs. Hightower."

"Got it. Jeanie."

She stared at him for a long moment, as if scanning his soul. "My husband's crazy, you know," she finally said.

"I'm beginning to catch on."

"I'm not exaggerating or being funny," Jeanie said. "I'm too tired for humor right now. The man is a fucking lunatic. For example, those half dozen dead soldiers on my kitchen table. How many were yours?"

"None," Jack said.

"There you go. I made Cato promise no more hard stuff. I told him, you want to leave your head for a while, fine, but stick to a few beers, maybe an edible or a few hits from the vape pen. Reasonable, right? Well, all Cato hears is *no hard stuff*, so he goes and compensates for that by sucking down ten beers and chasing *that* with a hundred-milligram THC gummy and an entire pre-rolled joint. He's a master of the technicality."

No hard stuff, Jack thought. Good thing Jeanie didn't join them for her husband's mini-bender two days ago. He also wondered about the drink in Jeanie's hand, which looked suspiciously like a gin and tonic.

"All I'm saying is, proceed with caution," Jeanie continued. "I know you must feel like you owe him. But you should know what you're getting into."

"I hear you, m——" Jack said, then corrected himself: "Jeanie."

"Now, come on, out with your story. Who was that on the phone?"

"I don't want to burden you."

Jeanie's expression softened. The word "burden" had piqued her curiosity. She didn't respond verbally, instead making a *gimme gimme* gesture with her fingers.

Jack Queen realized he hadn't talked out loud about this stuff with anyone. Well, aside from Hightower. This would be his maiden voyage. How do you tell someone completely awful news? He supposed he'd had some experience with that after losing Matilda's mother. But that part of him felt hazy and distant. He wasn't behaving like a proper human being then — which, come to think of it, got him into this current mess.

"My daughter, Matilda, was diagnosed with leukemia," he said. "She was diagnosed two days ago, just a day after I was released from prison. I didn't find out until yesterday. Anyway, that was her on the phone. I was hoping to be with her at the hospital tonight, but then..."

"What type of leukemia?" Jeanie asked quietly. "ALL? AML?"

The immediate question surprised him. "AML," he said.

Jeanie took this in, nodding.

"I understand it's not the best kind, if there is such a thing," Jack said.

"No, it's not. How old is she?"

"Fifteen. Almost. Her birthday is next month."

Again, Jeanie took this in, nodding. Whatever was going through the woman's mind, she didn't feel the need to share. Instead she handed Jack the tidy stack of clothes. "These are some of Cato's things. Looks like your suit needs pressing, but I'm not equipped to do something like that. But if you leave your underthings in the downstairs bathroom, I'll have them washed and dried by morning."

"Thank you so much, Jeanie." She placed a hand on Jack's shoulder, squeezed, then gently guided him into the living room, where indeed she had prepared the couch with fresh sheets and a tasteful comforter.

"One last thing," Jack said.

"Yeah?"

"Did Cato talk to you about a possible job? For me, I mean?"

Jeanie sighed and shook her head. "He sure does like to promise things."

Jack nodded, not wanting to be rude, not wanting to scream *fuck* at the top of his lungs.

After Jeanie left the room, he peeled off his clothes and pulled on a pair of drawstring PJ bottoms that were somehow still too big, even after he drew the strings as tight as possible. The T-shirt was pale green and adorned with the words I KNOW HTML (HOW TO MEET LADIES).

Jack fell asleep a lot quicker than he thought he would.

GENE JEANIE

After putting the ex-con's clothes in the washer, Jeanie decided to throw a mattress sheet over her office futon. She didn't want to go anywhere near her drunk/high husband, who had decided to sprawl out on her bed in their former bedroom. She was pissed; they had discussed this. Cato shouldn't be here at all. But now was not the time for another knock-down, drag-out argument.

But when she realized what had been stolen from her office, Jeanie began to think maybe another argument was just the thing.

They had both taken a quick inventory of the house and determined that nothing had been stolen. There was no Hightower family jewelry to speak of. The flat-screen in their living room was six years old and featured a couple of dozen dead pixels, which gave a delightful snowfall quality to any show. The kitchenware was from Walmart or Target, usually bought on an emergency, as-needed basis. Cash? Please. No, the only item of real value was the two-year-old laptop in Jeanie's office, the one she used for work (and paid for with the proceeds of her fledgling business). She'd taken a quick peek inside her office during the post-burglary inventory, fearing the worst...but the laptop was still there.

Now, though, as Jeanie was placing scattered books back on her shelves and righting lamps and putting pillows back on the futon, there was an ice block in her guts. *Something was missing.* She could feel it. But what?

Not until she popped the opaque lid off one of her Sterilite storage boxes—temporary, until she could find a filing cabinet she liked—did she realize what it was.

Her files.

Not just some files. All of them were gone.

Whatever Cato was mixed up in had something to do with her DNA research. Which didn't make any sense. Their businesses—and she was using that term loosely when it came to Cato Hightower's schemes—were church and state, oil and water, dog and cat.

Then she remembered: "Cousin Christopher."

A month ago, Cato had come to her, looking sheepish, asking for help with something. He was trying to track down a lost cousin, someone he only remembered from a family reunion. He showed her the clumsy Ancestry.com page he was building, and it was clear he was trying to establish a family without linking it to his own tree. Jeanie was puzzled because she thought all of Cato's relatives were back in East Texas, not here in LA. But Cato insisted, and to be honest, she just wanted him out of her hair for a while. Within twenty minutes, she was able to pinpoint this wayward cousin.

"Who the fuck is Christopher Albin Dixon?" she said now, kicking her husband's upper thigh to wake him up.

"Hunh?" Cato said, rousing himself like a bear after months of hibernation.

"You heard me. 'Cousin Christopher.' He's not family, is he?"

"Uh…no?"

"So who is he?"

"Look, don't get upset. He's part of a case I'm working on. And we're close to nailing this motherfucker. You have no idea, Jeanie."

"Don't 'Jeanie' me. Who is he?"

Cato said nothing.

Jeanie pressed the issue. *"Who."*

After some throat clearing, her husband said: "Pretty sure he's a serial killer responsible for attacking twenty-six people from 1978 through 1984. But he only killed eight of them."

As if that made it better.

But Jeanie only half heard his response, because the moment he spoke the words "serial killer," her vision fuzzed over in a hazy red rage. A shrill whistle in her ears canceled out all possibility of comprehension. She wanted to kill her husband, serially, resurrecting his body so that she could kill him again and again and again.

Cato had invited a fucking serial killer into her home, and now he had the confidential and detailed family histories of every single one of her clients.

Of all the boneheaded things he'd done in their twenty years of marriage, this one might be the worst. And, boy, there was stiff competition.

"Your serial killer suspect stole my files," she said after a while.

"I know," he replied, realizing the gravity of their situation.

"You will make this right."

"I will."

"You've said that before, Cato."

"I mean it this time."

"You'd better."

"First thing in the morning. Believe me. I've got a plan."

"Don't," she said, "you dare tell me about your belief, or your fucking plans. I don't care about plans. I need you to fix this."

"Tomorrow it will be resolved."

Jeanie had heard this before. This time, she really wanted to believe her husband. Not just for her own sake, but for that clueless ex-con on their living room couch. He had no idea what a mess he had gotten himself into. Jeanie had no excuse. This devil, she knew.

THE BEAR

Would these fucking people ever leave? The Queen of Mars told him how important this meeting was—and he knew it was. But he didn't know why *he* had to be involved. He really shouldn't be involved, come to think of it. He was the talent, not some below-the-line worker bee. But try telling *them* that.

The socializing would be tolerable (maybe) if she'd put out a decent spread of snacks. Whatever happened to crackers, cheese, and pepperoni? A tray of Italian cookies, maybe? Instead she put on airs and served these tasteless crudités (a "veggie tray" for the non-fancy people) and a truly abhorrent dipping sauce she found online. Hell, he'd rather put up with the indignities of flipping burgers for these pretentious fuckwads. But the Queen of Mars had dismissed the idea, saying: *This is not* that *meeting.*

Worst of all, the dynamics were all off. The California Bear preferred to invade other people's homes, not the other way around.

"How's the scouting going?" the Producer asked.

"It's going okay," the Bear said. "I'm learning the houses all over again. The neighborhoods have changed a lot."

"Maybe," the Actor said, "the next time I could tag along with you? Get a feel for your process as early as possible?"

"That's not what we agreed on," the Queen of Mars said. "My husband made it clear that he works alone. Plus, you're a potential distraction. You being...well, you."

"At some point he's going to have to let us in," the Director said.

Let us in, the Bear thought. *Oh, I'll let you in.*

If it were up to him, the Bear would invite each guest—the haughty producer, the pretty-boy actor—and let them into his backyard shack to show them his "process." But halfway across the lawn, they'd feel a little sharp poke along their spine. The Bear would inform them that if they tried to pull away, or run, or resist in any way, the steel spike would be inserted between two vertebrae *just so,* paralyzing them from the waist down. And then the real fun and games would begin.

It's amazing how you can control people like puppets if you can make them believe their life is teetering on the edge of a permanent transformation.

By the way—the Bear had no special medical knowledge. The whole paralysis thing was a bluff. But the commanding tone of his voice sold it. His body size sold it. The tiny poke in the back sold it.

In the Bear's experience, most people were just *waiting* to be treated like puppets.

Once you had them in your control, you could basically make them do anything. Such as slip a noose around their own necks. Some, in the spirit of total submission and obedience, would even help the Bear secure their wrists behind their backs. That was the thing he liked the most—making his victims collaborators in their own predicament.

How much fun would it be to take each of his guests out to the garage this way? One by one, led to their own doom, knowing that the more they struggled to free themselves from their binds, the closer they were to death.

You want to know what it's like to be hunted by the Bear? Here, let me show you . . .

That would be so much more entertaining than a veggie tray.

"We don't have forever with preproduction," the producer said. "And I've got to start rolling soon. Can you give us a timeline?"

"When I'm ready, I'll let you know," the Bear said.

"Let's put something on the calendar," the producer said. He was smiling, but only from the nose down.

The actor, however, smiled with his entire face and body, just as he had been trained to do. "How about we book a lunch next week...say, Tuesday? You name the place, Mr. Dixon."

"I don't think I'll be ready by then."

"Just initial impressions," the actor said. "I don't need your entire process, but it would be such a huge help to start thinking like you do. The more time we spend together, the better. All I want to do is listen."

And all I want to do is cut you into little pieces, the Bear thought.

When the meeting was finally over, the Bear excused himself and ambled out to his shack, where he'd stashed some Nutter Butters earlier in the day. The Queen of Mars had been so busy lately, she didn't even notice him smuggle them in. She was losing her iron grip on the household.

Fortunately, the Bear now had an excuse to be spending so much time in the garage. He was the kind of predator who loved the tactile reminders of his prey; how objects felt, smelled, and even tasted opened the floodgates of memory. That was the only good thing that had come of this whole ridiculous arrangement: his glorious rebirth.

And yes, he needed these pathetic people to make that dream come true. Finally, his life's work would be recognized, even *celebrated* among a certain audience. If that meant he had to put up with absurd questions or studio genuflections, fine. But the power remained his.

Now that the Bear had returned, there was no stuffing him back in his cage.

SATURDAY, JUNE 2, 2018

"KILLER"

Jack snapped awake on a lumpy couch, not understanding where he was or even which reality this might be. Then he remembered: *Oh yeah... this one.* He was the houseguest of an alcoholic ex-cop and his surly wife. The ex-cop had freed him from prison, but he turned out to be a lunatic. The wife seemed sane by comparison, but also not thrilled with Jack's presence in her house. The current situation was not sustainable.

The horror of someone else's house was almost worse than prison. *Almost.*

Jack searched for a clock somewhere. Anywhere. Then he remembered his cheap burner phone. He'd plugged it into a wall socket before turning in. Jack twisted his body, reached out, and found it. The display read 5:45 a.m. Probably too early to wake his hosts. But why did that matter?

Maybe he could find a train back to LA. Or a taxi... though he didn't have the money to cover such a thing. And there were the doughnuts to consider.

The smart thing would be to wait until Hightower woke up and convince him to give Jack a ride down to CHLA. Whatever was going on in this household, it didn't matter to Jack. He just needed to be with his daughter.

The Hightowers' place looked even messier in dawn's early light. Neither Cato nor Jeanie was much for housekeeping. The way the sun hit certain surfaces, it was clear those surfaces hadn't been dusted since the early days of the Obama administration. Used drinking glasses of unknown vintage appeared in random places: a bookshelf here, an end table there. Overall, the home gave the impression of a wild party that had gone on too long and trapped two of its guests here forever.

And to think, not too long ago Jack had fantasized about staying here — *it's just a three-bedroom, but it's a very short walk to the beach,* Hightower had written in one of his earliest letters. Those words gave him something to focus on, transporting Jack out of his cell. The plan had been for Jack to crash here until the settlement money came in, and then he'd be able to rent a place for himself and Matilda in a good school district, wherever that might be.

Jack wandered into the kitchen, said hello to the half dozen dead soldiers still lined up on the table, and prayed for a can of Diet Coke to magically appear in the fridge. No such luck. The closest thing was a janky brand of lemon seltzer water that was probably intended as a mixer. The first sip tasted like floor cleaner.

Back in the living room, Jack was too keyed up to browse through one of the many historical novels lining the shelves (he guessed those belonged to Jeanie). But he also couldn't sit still. He found the remote for the flat-screen. Maybe a little subtle noise would rouse Hightower from his slumber.

There was some gangster movie on. Something Italian from the 1970s involving torture in a basement. That might wake up Hightower, but it also wasn't something Jack wanted in his brain right now. Maybe another day he'd feel in the mood for subterranean torment.

Mindlessly flipping through channels, Jack Queen realized that none of this world made sense anymore. He recognized none of the shows, nor the people populating them. Perhaps this was an alternate universe, after all.

Jack was so lost in his own thoughts he barely noticed Hightower shuffling past, headed straight for the kitchen. He killed the flat-screen and followed the ex-cop. When Jack opened his mouth to speak, Hightower somehow sensed the disturbance in the atmosphere and raised a hand — in warning. *Do not speak just now.*

Hightower pulled three ingredients from the fridge: a chilled bottle of bottom-rail vodka, an off-brand Bloody Mary mix that looked like it was sold in bulk, and a stalk of celery that was more brown than green. A splash of the mix in a pint glass full of vodka and ice cubes, a swirl with the diseased celery stalk, and Hightower's breakfast was ready. He gulped it down, exhaled, burped.

"That's going to be your only one, right?" Jack asked. "Because we have a long drive back to LA, and you're the only one with a license."

"We're going to Studio City, and then to LA," Hightower said, studying the bottom of his empty glass as if it might reveal a message from the gods.

"Why exactly are we going to Studio City?"

"To confront the Bear. He wants to play hardball and ransack my house, fine. We can fight dirty too."

"No," Jack said. "A thousand times no. There is no 'we.' This is your crazy scheme."

"What are you talking about? We've had this conversation already."

"Yes, and it ended with me saying no fucking way. And then you lied to me about a job."

"Damn, the mouth on you at eight in the morning," Hightower chided. "Besides, I didn't lie. This is part of your job, working for me."

"You said the work had nothing to do with the Bear."

"Oh, now you're going to tell me how to run my business?"

Jack inhaled deeply. Maybe some oxygen would help him fight the urge to punch Hightower in the belly.

"If you really think the California Bear is the one who ransacked your house," Jack said, "why don't you call the police? They can do all that forensic stuff in here. Maybe he got sloppy in his old age and left behind a fingerprint or some skin cells or whatever."

"And have the Ventura County Sheriff's Department take credit for my detective work? You're out of your fucking mind."

"Listen to the mouth on *you*," Jack replied.

"Oh, shut the fuck up. Can't you see this is good news? The only way the Bear could have found my address is by looking up the license plate on the Honda. That means he still has friends on the force. That also means he saw us as a threat. He's scared. We need to take advantage of that fear."

"Again with the 'we.' This is your scam. Leave me out of it."

Hightower again peered into his glass as if he could make a few more ounces of his Bloody Mary magically appear.

"Guess you're going to have to find some other way of supporting your daughter," he said quietly.

Jack felt his chest muscles twitch involuntarily, as if the ex-cop had landed a punch.

"Hightower, I'll always be grateful for your help getting me out," he said carefully. "But if you say anything like that ever again, I have no problem knocking you on your ass and going back to prison."

Hightower raised his hands like, *fine, fine, mea culpa.* "You'll regret this, but okay. It's your life, man."

"You can just drop me off at the closest Metro station."

"Whatever. Nice shirt, by the way."

Hightower's feelings were clearly hurt, but Jack didn't really care. The ex-cop put his glass on the kitchen counter, then ambled upstairs to get dressed. Jack used the downstairs bathroom to put on his wrinkled suit once again. At least Jeanie had kindly washed his undergarments, just as she'd promised. He found toothpaste in a drawer and used an index finger to clean his teeth the best he could, hoping a swig of nuclear-green mouthwash would take it the rest of the way home. He also used his fingers to erase some of the bedhead. Jack Queen needed to buy everything all over again.

Back in the living room, he called Matilda.

"Hey, Daughter."

"Hello, Father."

"I'm going to be on my way soon, but it might take a little longer than I thought. I have to take the train part of the way."

"It's all Gouda," she said. "I'm feeling a little tired this morning anyway, so maybe I'll wake up and see you here."

"That would be nice."

"But," she warned, "do not forget the doughnuts."

"I could never." Jack had, in fact, completely forgotten about the doughnuts and appreciated the reminder. He looked around for a pen to write himself a note on his hand. "A dozen, coming right up."

"Two dozen! There are a lot of nurses on the floor."

"I'm on it."

Hightower was coming down the steps, yelling ahead of him. "Okay, Jack. Gather up your things and strap on your balls. It's time to go Bear hunting!"

"Is that the cop?" Matilda asked. "What does he mean by 'bear hunting'?"

Thank goodness his daughter ignored the "strap on your balls" part of that command and focused on the mention of the Bear. Not that Jack was terribly eager to discuss the Bear with her either. The less she knew, the better. He'd have a couple of hours to come up with some kind of explanation.

"It's a long story. But I'll tell you about it this afternoon."

"Weird, but okay," she said.

"Any particular kind of doughnuts you'd like?"

"Come on, Jack, let's go! I want to surprise this fucker while he's still slurping his first Metamucil of the morning."

"Not Metamucil flavored," Matilda said. "Otherwise, surprise me."

They told each other "I love you" and hung up.

THE GIRL DETECTIVE

"Bear hunting." *Such a curious phrase,* thought the Girl Detective.

Put that with the other thing her father had mentioned — that Hightower the ex-cop wanted help catching criminals who had gotten away with it — made her wonder if this "bear" was a criminal. Well, of course he was. But was "bear" a nickname, or an actual name — like Baer, or Bayer? Was he just a big, furry dude? (Or a big, furry woman?)

The Girl Detective was very sleepy, especially after receiving her latest round of platelets. But the "bear" kept nagging at her brain. She needed to know what her father might be getting into.

Whoever it was had to be local. That probably meant the city of Los Angeles because Hightower had been LAPD.

She did a little Google Fu with "Los Angeles" and "bear," which yielded a whole bunch of stories (and videos!) about actual bears breaking into people's homes. Which was an amusing detour, but somewhat off topic.

So she narrowed the search with the term "crime." And, *Ah, there we go.* The California Bear. Apparently, he was a serial killer who hunted from 1978 to 1984 before suddenly disappearing. This was way before the Girl Detective's time — it was practically the Victorian era to her. But that's what made it interesting. She loved stuff from Ye Olde Tymes.

Did the goofy cop guy want her dad to help with a cold case? If so...cool...but why her father?

Not that she wasn't proud of her father. The piano-playing jazz version of her father, that is. Not the ex-con. Nobody ever believed he was a jazz musician, which always cracked her up. She supposed she could see their point. He never looked the part. He was six foot two and had the build of a thug for hire you'd see in lame action movies. No one could ever quite pinpoint his ethnicity either, which was also amusing.

She checked the message boards for anything she could find on the California Bear. For such an ancient case, there was a surprising amount of activity. Not with anyone her age, but millennial web sleuths were all about this dude. Probably because they were all trying to figure out if maybe, just maybe, their asshole fathers were secretly the California Bear.

Some posters like BearlyAshley99 had the idea that the California Bear wasn't a single attacker at all, but a group of them, trading off home invasions and murders so none of them could be traced back to an individual perpetrator. Basically, *Strangers on a Train on Steroids.* BearlyAshley99 had a series of posts about each victim, painting their social circles the best she could, then looking for connections between those people and the other attacks. Sure, there were coincidences here and there that weren't easy to explain, but it seemed like a lot of heavy lifting with little payoff. Still, the Girl Detective flagged her posts because at least she gave an exhaustive rundown of each victim and their friends. That could be useful.

Another sleuth, Mr_Claude (yep, *clawed,* she got it), was obsessively focused on the California Bear mask, posting links to every possible style of furry balaclava sold from the 1950s through the early 1980s, as well as a detailed breakdown of how the Bear's clawed glove might have been constructed, and how the materials might have been sourced. If you could track down where these items were sold, Mr_Claude maintained, you could eventually narrow it down to stores in a particular neighborhood. This dude hinted that he had a source in the LAPD that was going to let him look through the case files for tangible evidence. But this sounded like a lot of bragging to the Girl Detective.

Speaking of bragging: Carnivora83 was a frequent poster with a massive man crush on the Bear. His very handle was a reference to the bear's scientific classification, specifically the order—and it sounded more bad ass than the family name (Ursidae) or infraorder (Arctoidea). Carnivora83 was all about debunking online theories about the California Bear's identity. If someone linked to a piece with a new theory, Carnivora83 was there to maul it to death. The dude was great at swatting aside possible candidates, yet, strangely, never seemed to offer one of his own. Ol' Carnie loved to drop hints that huge revelations were coming. But they were always off in the distance, with nothing in the way of real facts. The Girl Detective was both annoyed by him and fascinated by his shamelessness.

Still another sleuth, ThinkPink, argued that the lyrics of a certain Pink Floyd album were the guiding influence for the California Bear's nighttime attacks. The Girl Detective was impressed by the line-by-line breakdowns of every lyric and how they tied into every attack—most notably, the Bear's fridge-magnet message: *One of these days I'm going to cut you into little pieces.* That was sort of interesting . . .

The Girl Detective was so absorbed in her message-board scrolling that her aunt Reese almost caught her. She quickly closed the window a second before her aunt looked at the screen—the woman was super nosy like that.

"How are you feeling, sweetie?" she asked.

"Just tired. You know, rocking the chemo and all."

The pained expression on Aunt Reese's face made the Girl Detective regret being so flip. She had to remember to be gentle with this one. Reese had a tough exterior, but that was just a front. Even on a good day, she and Uncle Louis barely seemed to be holding it together.

"How are you doing?" asked the Girl Detective.

"I'm okay," she said, before immediately reversing her position. "No, I'm not okay. But I don't want to dump on you."

"Can't you tell I'd appreciate the change of topic?"

Reese smiled for a moment, then resumed her scowl. "If you were ever considering a career in real estate, forget about it. The business is full of backstabbing pricks who would gleefully throw you in front of a speeding truck if it meant they'd make their commission."

"Ugh, I'm sorry," the Girl Detective said. "Who do you need me to hurt?"

Again, a glimmer of a pained, fake smile. "That's sweet, honey. But it'll all work out in the end, don't worry."

"You don't have to spend all your free time here. I know you're taking a lot of time away from work."

"There's no place I'd rather be," Reese said, and the Girl Detective could tell she meant it. Which made her feel all kinds of ways. Loved, but also more than a little guilty. Just because her own life had been upended didn't mean everyone else's had to be too.

"Hey, I heard from my dad," she said, now eager to change the topic again. "He's bringing doughnuts later."

"Oh," Reese said, then realized that the Girl Detective had noticed her disappointed tone. She tried to pivot. "Are you sure you should be having that much sugar? I mean, considering . . . ?"

"They're bribes for the nursing staff. I figure we're going to need them on our side."

"Smart thinking. What were you working on?"

"Just one last paper for English class."

"What's it about?"

The Girl Detective was caught off guard; Reese had never shown specific interest in her work before.

"*Strangers on a Train*," she blurted.

GENE JEANIE

After Cato and his ex-con left the house, Jeanie poured herself another Tanqueray and tonic over ice. Her head already hurt. The morning cocktail would not ease the pain, but it would fuzz it over for a while. The booze helped her focus. She was grateful for the ex-con not bringing up the hypocrisy of her drinking last night. If he had, she would have explained that living with an alcoholic was easier if you were on their level once in a while. At the very least, booze helped you resist the urge to strangle them in their sleep.

Jeanie then reconsidered, dumped the contents of the drink down the kitchen drain. She always worked better sober, and she had serious work to do. She opened her laptop, once again grateful the home invader hadn't swiped it.

What kind of monster had her husband unleashed? Jeanie fell back on the thing she knew best, and what had always saved her: research.

She was vaguely aware that there had been a serial killer called the California Bear lurking around Hollywood back when she was a teenager. But she grew up in Woodland Hills and paid no more mind to the Bear than she did the Zodiac, or the Hillside Strangler, or the I-5 Killer. They were not important unless they were breaking down *your* door.

The vital thing with research was to toss aside the useless. This meant 95 percent of the material out there. Social media, cheap paperbacks, tabloid stories, cheapie streaming documentaries. None of that mattered. She needed the good stuff. The primary stuff. People with stories to tell, and firsthand knowledge.

Jeanie cracked her knuckles, fingers poised over the keys, fully prepared to dive down the rabbit hole...

Wait.

Hold on, hold on.

She was forgetting something big. How could she have been so stupid? Jeanie rolled her chair backward across the plastic rug protector and stared at her laptop. Her entire desk too.

If this California Bear had broken into her lair...then he'd possibly left traces of himself behind.

She'd been the spouse of a cop long enough to know it might be a long shot—but always one worth taking. Now, where did Cato keep his old gear—specifically his latent-fingerprint kit? Not that he ever used any of it. *I just like the toys,* he'd once told her.

First, she checked his "office," which was not so much a functioning workspace as a room Cato treated as a plus-size storage closet. There were, for instance, stacks of signed hardcover mysteries from back when he was still on the force and fancied himself a future cop novelist along the lines of Joseph Wambaugh, Robin Burcell, James O. Born, Kim Wozencraft, and Dennis Meechum. He'd attended all the signings at places like the Mystery Bookstore in Westwood and Mysteries to Die For in Thousand Oaks. He bought the books, did the glad-handing, purchased the post-signing drinks. Cato, however, did not read the novels or spend any time trying to learn how to actually write. He thought he could just *manifest* himself onto the bestsellers' list.

Then there was Cato's movie phase—and that meant lunches with action movie producers and TV writers who worked on police procedurals, as well downloading scripts from the Internet and buying countless VHS tapes (later DVDs) so he could learn how to crack the code and speak the language. His big idea here was to become a big-shot consultant, raking in fat fees and soaking up the glory. This, too, went nowhere, and the remains of this effort were all over the place.

But no fingerprint kit.

She tried their bedroom again, searching through all his drawers.

Jeanie couldn't tell if their home invader had scrambled everything or that was just Cato being Cato. Still, no fingerprint kit. She was about to give up when she tried her own drawers, just in case her husband had tucked the kit underneath her garments. He'd been known to do that—his filing system was more or less "tuck it out of sight in the nearest available space."

There was nothing in the drawer with her yoga pants, nor in the drawers with T-shirts or bras and underwear.

But wait.

There was something weird about her underwear drawer. Her panties were folded in a way that was unfamiliar. God knows Cato didn't wash and fold her laundry while she was away.

Jeanie reached out and touched a pair of her dark-pink Hanes briefs . . . and realized her fingertips were sticky. And it wasn't gin and tonic residue.

Oh God.

Upon closer inspection, her fears turned out to be accurate. Not only had someone broken into her house and tossed the place. They'd *had their way* with her undergarments. *Goddamn you, Cato.* She fought the twin feelings of fury and revulsion. How dare someone do this. What the fuck was wrong with people?

She was going to have to burn the contents of this entire drawer and then run to Target to replace them all.

Jeanie took a moment to feel what she was feeling (trying not to throw up, which would only make matters worse). Then she turned to go find a pair of rubber gloves or something to clean up yet another mess.

Then she stopped as she realized: she didn't need rubber gloves. She needed a plastic baggie.

This monster had left a genetic sample. And that was the absolute wrong present to leave behind for a genealogist.

THE BEAR

Cubby dropped off the files late last night, as instructed. Good little Cubby. The Bear only had the chance to dig in this morning, while the wife was at Ralphs picking up something for dinner. Probably another vegetarian dish. The Bear had stopped asking for steaks long ago. You'd think he was asking her for meth and a stack of porn rags, the way she reacted.

The files confused him at first. A lot of it was nonsense — birth certificates, printouts of census reports, family trees, that sort of thing. All people he didn't know, and nothing to do with him. What was this shit? Why did Cubby grab *this* box?

The Bear didn't know about Cubby sometimes. He was a decent cop who fumbled his way to detective grade. Kid had a good heart. People generally liked him, which came in handy. And, of course, he was a sick fucker, much like the Bear.

The Bear would give Cubby a call now, but he was on the job. He continued flipping through the useless files. Maybe this was all nothing. Just because the asshole in the Honda Civic stopped directly in front of his house didn't mean he knew anything. Maybe he was a real estate speculator. Maybe he liked to jack off in front of roses. Who the fuck knew, who the fuck cared. The Bear had to admit he was running on high paranoia these days. With years of hard work and patience looking like it was about to pay off...

One more flip, however, and the Bear muttered, "Fuck me."

There was a file with a familiar surname on it. Not his surname, but one in the extended family. Couldn't be, could it?

A quick flip through the folder and the Bear knew the truth. Fuck, they'd found him through his fucking family tree. These were people he didn't even speak to anymore! Hadn't since the 1980s, but technology had linked them anyway.

The day he'd long feared had finally come, all because some dipshit cousin had paid $179.95 to spit in a plastic tube.

The Bear would readily admit he wasn't the world's greatest detective. Never claimed to be. But he could do some remedial digging into the assholes invading his privacy. And Cubby had done one smart thing. He'd thrown a business card into the box. Jeanie Hightower, professional genealogist.

Well, Miss Thing, let's see what kind of secrets *you're* hiding.

"KILLER"

"Pull in over there. Right by that doughnut shop. The pink one."

"Nah, you don't want to go there," Hightower said. "Let's get your sugar fix after we visit the Bear. There's this great place over on Olive Avenue in Burbank. Donut Prince. Their motto is, 'Don't get a divorce, get a doughnut.' Which cracks me up, even if it's shitty advice."

"I don't want to wait until Burbank."

"Fried dough is no solution to two decades of miserable cohabitation."

"Hightower. Listen to me. I need to buy the doughnuts now."

"So they can sit in the car for an hour and melt? That's stupid. Let's go take care of our business, then we'll head over to Donut Prince. I'll even spring for a few bear claws. You know, in honor of the occasion."

"What do you mean *our* business? This is your deal, not mine. I told you that."

"Fine, whatever. Damn, you're touchy this morning."

"Stop the car! Now!"

Jack was so insistent, Hightower did pull over to the side of Ventura Boulevard. "Christ, what's your problem?"

"I'm going to buy my daughter two dozen doughnuts. You can wait here for me, or you can go off on your own. I truly do not give a shit. But I am buying doughnuts."

"All right, all right!" Hightower complained. "All you had to do was ask."

As Jack waited inside the shop for his two dozen assorted doughnuts, he began to wonder if he should have just strangled Hightower in his sleep when he had the chance, then stolen his car. Jeanie probably wouldn't have objected. Jack already was a killer, if in his own heart and not the eyes of the law.

Back in the car a few minutes later, Jack tossed a paper sack into Hightower's lap. "Bought you a bear claw. You know, for good luck."

"Oh man," Hightower complained. "You just sealed my fate. You don't buy the ironic food item *before* the meeting. You always do it after! This is a serious jinx." Jack thought he was kidding but the ex-cop didn't break character. He was upset for real.

"You're welcome. Let's go."

"I'm not going to eat this now. I never eat before a business meeting. My stomach can't handle the stress, and then I'm off to find a bathroom. You know, with a book."

"I really didn't need to know that."

They continued down Ventura Boulevard. Jack looked for any sign of a light rail line, or even a bus stop. Now that he had the doughnuts, he didn't need to be tagging along with Hightower. But the chaos of the boulevard hid any obvious signs of public transportation, and before long they were in the Bear's territory. Hightower parked in the exact same place he had the other day.

"Now, here's all you have to do," he told Jack.

"I'm not doing anything but sitting here until you return," Jack said. "I may not even be here that long."

"What you're going to do is," Hightower continued, "lean against the car, you know, arms folded and shit. Do you have sunglasses? You don't want him to see your eyes."

"No."

"What, you don't have sunglasses? Fine, you can use mine. I'll be inside anyway."

"I mean no, there's no fucking way I'm doing that."

Hightower sighed. "Way to show your gratitude, Jack. I mean, I go through hell and back to spring you from prison, and all I'm asking you to do is stand next to a fucking car and look tough for a few minutes."

"I'll look tough from inside the car. Best I can do."

THE BEAR

The knock at his front door came a lot sooner than expected.

The Bear put his iPad on the end table, eased himself out of his lounge chair, and shuffled across the living room. He thought Mr. and Mrs. Hightower would take a little longer getting around to the actual blackmail part of their plot, but he supposed they were impatient. Maybe they really needed the money. Which was fine with the Bear. Desperate people were the easiest to manipulate.

Might as well get this over with.

"Mr. Dixon? My name is Cato Hightower. Former LAPD, just like you. Might I have a minute of your time?"

The Bear stood his ground, silently appraising the man standing before him. It was difficult to imagine this turd of a human being in uniform. His bulky torso was barely contained by the tropical button-down shirt he had draped over it. The man's hair was both thinning and unruly. He was clearly nervous, but even worse — this guy thought he was covering it up completely with a veneer of casual banter. *Hey, man, I just want to rap with you for a second.* Pathetic.

All morning the Bear had been idly wondering how to play this. Strategy depended upon your opponent. One look at this guy and the Bear realized his strategy was simple: *Fuck it. Let's watch this idiot hang himself.*

"Come on in," the Bear said, pushing open the door to allow his visitor to pass. Cato Hightower hesitated for a moment. Maybe he was nervous about being too close. Or having his back to the Bear, even for a single second. This was actually sensible. The Bear had considered hiding a tire iron by the door so that he could brain the stupid asshole from behind and dispose of his body quickly.

The Bear glanced at the street and saw the shitty Honda Accord with someone in the passenger seat. Not the wife. Some burly guy — same as the other day. Hightower's mysterious accomplice. This meant he had to employ a different strategy.

"Wow, is it hot in here," Hightower said. "Don't feel like turning on the AC?"

"Can I get you something to drink?" the Bear asked. "An iced tea, maybe, to help you cool off?"

"No, I'm okay," the fat ex-cop said. "I'd like to just get down to it, if that's okay with you."

"This is your show."

The Bear guided him to the kitchen table. Good a place as any.

"I don't want to insult your intelligence," Hightower said, "so I figure we should get down to brass tacks."

The Bear had to truly stifle a laugh there. First was the reference to intelligence. That was rich. And then followed up by the "brass tacks" cliché. Whatever tacks this guy had in mind, they wouldn't be brass, or all that sharp.

"I don't know what you mean," the Bear replied. "I don't know who you are, or why you're here."

Hightower smiled and shook his head. "Let's not play that game. A few days ago I rolled up in front of your house. Not long after, my own house was ransacked. Doesn't take Sherlock Holmes to put that one together."

"Your house was burglarized? Have you reported it?"

"Cut the shit, man. I know you're the California Bear."

"Now, this is interesting. Not only do you think I'm a serial killer, but you think I'd come out of hiding after all these years just to rob your house."

The fat man sighed. "So you're going to play that game. Fine with me. Let me lay it all out for you. I have California Bear DNA from the case files. I ran it…through certain proprietary databases. A family tree popped up. Your family tree. A little more detective work, and…well, there you go. You're the Bear. It's no use denying it."

"DNA databases?"

Hightower laughed and slapped the surface of the table. "I really didn't think you'd go the denial route. I mean, c'mon. You were a cop. How many times have you heard this bullshit? You know who you are, and what you are, and I'm here to tell you I know who you are and what you are."

Christ on a whole wheat cracker, this guy was too much! It was going to be *so much fun* to fuck with him. And then kill him.

The Bear didn't want to allow himself to get *too* excited. It had been decades since he took a life, and it had never happened quite this way before. The Bear always went on the offense, at a time and place of his choosing. This was defense, in his own house.

Still, it was kind of exciting. The Bear had to work hard not to lose his stony cop exterior and break into a wide, gap-toothed grin.

"So you know who and what I am," the Bear said. "Congratulations. What are you going to do about it?"

"Hopefully nothing," Hightower said with a broad smile. "I mean, I see no reason to fuck up your shit. Looks like you've got a nice life here."

"That's mighty kind of you."

"Not to mention the streaming TV deal."

The Bear sighed. "Streaming TV deal. You read about that, huh?"

"Yeah, I read *all* about it. Congratulations! I'm impressed by that chick director you have on board. Any word on casting? I mean, they'd need someone big and brawny to play you in your prime. Unless you'll be portraying yourself in the reenactments?"

"No, they'll be using someone else."

"That's what I thought. I mean, they have that computer stuff that de-ages you, but I imagine that costs quite a bit and you wouldn't want a computer-effects budget eating into your profits."

This asshole did his research. The Bear gave him that much. He almost wished his wife were here so he could press her nose into this stinking mess. The Bear had told her: don't make a fucking announcement, it's too risky. She countered by saying no one knew his identity except for the director, producer, and actor, and they had all signed iron-clad NDAs. Well, if this dipshit figured it out, surely others were on the verge of doing the same. *Somebody* was talking! Could it have been Cubby—the only other human being alive who knew about the deal? No. The kid would know better. If Cubby turned traitor, he knew the Bear wouldn't hesitate to chop off his head and use the hollowed-out skull as a urinal for the rest of his days.

"What do you want, Mr. Hightower?"

"I want to be compensated for my silence."

"What kind of compensation did you have in mind?"

"I thought I'd allow you the courtesy," Hightower said, "of making the first offer."

"That is awfully courteous."

Oh, this guy was way too much.

"Well," the Bear said, sitting upright in his chair, "here's the real deal. I don't have the kind of offer that will turn your head. Whatever you imagine I'm making, I assure you, I'm not. There are a lot of complicating factors, and I know you don't give a damn about any of that. But I wanted to be sure to calibrate your expectations."

"So, calibrate," Hightower said. "What are we talking?"

"I don't have much in the bank, and whatever I do have, my wife keeps a close eye on. I can't just take money out without having to do a lot of explaining."

Hightower grinned. "You don't have to tell me. I'm married too."

"That's right, you are. Jeanie, her name is, right?"

"Right. And by the way, I'm going to need my wife's files back. She's a little freaked-out that you took them. I mean, I understand and maybe even admire the bold move, breaking into my house like you did."

"Thank you," the Bear said. "That means a lot, coming from you.

Anyway, the files are out in my shack, along with my life savings in a coffee can. All cash. Money my wife doesn't know about. You're welcome to it."

"Uh, how much of a life savings we talking about?"

"Oh, I don't know," the Bear said. "If I had to ballpark it, I'd say it was around twenty grand. Maybe a little more."

Hightower frowned, then shook his head. His fingers tapped the surface of the kitchen table as if he were punching numbers into a calculator.

"You're right. That's not exactly an offer to make me turn my head."

"But is it enough for your . . . silence? Is that how you put it?"

"I don't know. But it's definitely the start of some silence."

"The start?"

"I mean, twenty grand is not a lot. Even you have to admit that. And I've got a partner to think about."

"Is he the tough-looking guy outside? The one in your Honda Accord?"

"Yeah. He deserves his cut, which means even less on my end."

The Bear made a point of frowning, as if he did sympathize with this poor blackmailer's dilemma. Yep, the money they were trying to extort from him wouldn't last very long. Not in LA. Not in this economy. Boy, was that a shame.

"I don't know what to tell you," the Bear said finally. "You can either take what I have, or you can go tell the police everything you think you know."

The Bear knew there was zero chance this buffoon would leave empty-handed. Con artists never accepted a loss. There had to be *something* to show for their efforts. Most likely, this Hightower didn't believe him about the twenty grand and assumed the Bear had more tucked away somewhere. That was the other thing about con artists — they assumed other people thought just like they did.

The best part of this whole thing was the Bear didn't have twenty grand in a coffee can. He had maybe a couple of thousand out there — money for sweets and other distractions — that the Queen of Mars didn't know about. Or maybe she did and didn't care.

"Let's see this money," Hightower said.

"It's out in the garage," the Bear replied.

He was fairly certain how all this would play out. While the Bear was fetching his can of money, this ex-cop would be eyeballing the interior of the garage, looking for other hidey-holes. Which was perfect, because the ex-cop would be distracted and wouldn't see what was coming next.

"You want to text your partner and invite him inside?" the Bear asked.

"Nah, he's fine where he is. Take me to that coffee can."

"Let me get my keys."

The Bear reached for his keys, which happened to have a four-inch metal spike attached to the main ring. Oh, this was going to be fun.

"KILLER"

Jack wondered why the hell he was still sitting in this oven of a Honda Accord while Hightower was inside doing something incredibly stupid. If Jack had any brains, he'd drive the car straight down to CHLA, deliver the doughnuts to Matilda, and forget any of this ever happened. It was not too late. If Hightower decided to blackmail him, that was fine. What the ex-cop was doing right now was far worse. It was mutually assured destruction.

Did Jack have any brains? Jury was still out on that. But he also didn't have any car keys. Hightower had taken them with him inside the serial killer's house.

Public transportation was always an option, but without a real cell phone, he couldn't plot a course. A cab was a luxury he couldn't afford. There wasn't much he *could* afford at this moment. A box of fucking doughnuts. That's all he had to offer his daughter.

This is why you're still sitting here, Jack. It isn't the car keys or the lack of a handy bus map or anything else. You're sitting in this increasingly sweltering car because you're hanging on to the desperate hope that Hightower's plan just might work.

And it might make all the difference.

After climbing out of the passenger seat, Jack removed his suit jacket, folded it neatly in half over his arm, then draped it over the two dozen doughnuts in the back seat. He stretched in the hot sun and wondered how long this was going to take.

Jack looked down the quiet block of single family homes. The people who lived here probably thought they had it all figured out. Attended the right schools. Shook the right hands. Somehow managed to not get ground up by the massive gears of life. And yet—if Hightower was to be believed—they ended up living on the same block as a sadistic serial killer.

While he was lost in these hot reveries, Jack's pocket vibrated. His cheapo cell phone—probably Matilda, wondering where he was. Not to mention the doughnuts.

But it wasn't Matilda.

Come inside. We're all set.

No name popped up, but it had to be Hightower. He was the only other person with this number.

Jack looked at the serial killer's neat little house, which was bathed in gentle morning sunlight. Just another Saturday morning in the San Fernando Valley. How many other crimes were playing out in similar homes all over Southern California? How many ex-cons were in the same position as Jack right at this very second—standing outside a home, contemplating yet another crime?

Instead of delivering a box of doughnuts to his daughter. His daughter who was fighting for her life. Whose survival might very well come down to her father committing yet another crime.

At least blackmail wasn't the same as manslaughter. Unless things turned ugly in there . . .

Jack stared at the text message again. Just five words, but what did "we're all set" mean? That was annoyingly vague. If they were all set, then why did Hightower need him to "come inside"? Why couldn't Hightower just be direct for once?

I'm good out here, Jack thumbed.

And that should do it, right? Hightower wanted to see his crazy scheme through, then let him. Jack would find another way to pay the hospital bills. None of them involving a crime. There had to be financial aid of some sort, especially for families in their situation. Yeah, ol' Dad was a jailbird, but they couldn't hold that against Matilda.

Jack's phone buzzed again. Before he even looked, Jack imagined Hightower's reply, which would be something along the lines of Don't be a pussy.

Instead the text read: If you don't come inside, say goodbye to your cut.

Which was uncharacteristically straightforward of Hightower. This also made it easier to give a straightforward reply.

Like I said, I'm good.

THE BEAR

"What the hell is wrong with your partner?" the Bear asked. "He doesn't want his part of the cut? Are you two even partners?"

Not that Hightower was in much of a position to answer. The man was almost choking to death and flailing around like an insect inside a mason jar.

The old spike-to-the-spinal-column trick had worked beautifully. The Bear thought the fat man might wet himself, he was so surprised. Hightower tried some panicky charm, claiming he was just kidding about the whole Bear thing, it was kind of a prank, really. But he wasn't saying much now, with a noose around his neck, which was tightly secured to the binds around his wrists. To avoid strangulation, the fat man had to twist his own arms up behind his back, a predicament that left the dipshit desperately wriggling around at the bottom of the empty pool.

"Or is he just hired muscle?" the Bear asked, mostly thinking out loud. "Yeah, I'm guessing your lovely wife, Jeanie, is the brains behind the operation. After I'm done with you two, I think I'll pay her a visit up in Port Hueneme."

The choking sounds coming from Hightower's throat took on greater urgency, which was also amusing.

"Save your breath, there, partner," the Bear said. "I don't want you passing out on me."

But right now Hightower wasn't the issue. It was the tough guy out on the street. The reluctant blackmailer. When the Bear choked out the ex-cop and took his phone, he realized he was taking a bit of a risk. He didn't know Tough Guy's name. There was no guarantee his number would be on Hightower's device.

But the Bear suspected he would be—and he was right. Apparently, this fool only called or texted two people. One of them was his wife, Jeanie the Genealogist, with the 805 area code. The other was a number that looked suspiciously like a number for a burner phone, which would make sense. The Bear was pretty sure that if he sent a text to that number, Tough Guy would respond.

Come inside. We're all set.

And Tough Guy responded right away. Just not in the way the Bear thought he might.

I'm good out here.

What? Was this guy his partner in crime or just a menacing-looking Uber driver? The Bear decided to cut to the chase:

If you don't come inside, say goodbye to your cut.

A few seconds later:

Like I said, I'm good.

What the hell did that mean? What kind of blackmailers *were* these guys?

The problem was, the Bear needed Tough Guy to come inside as soon as possible. The sooner Tough Guy stepped inside, the sooner the Bear could brain him, then dump him into the empty pool too.

The pool—the best feature of this house, if you happened to be a serial killer coming out of retirement. Such a setup was perfect for a quicklime body pit. The very idea just filled him with delight.

Imagine: resuming his work after all these years and having the most convenient place to hide the bodies. With no telltale smell of decaying flesh! That was the joy of quicklime. People assumed it dissolved bodies like magic. Au contraire, mon frère. For centuries, quicklime was used to hide the odor of decomposition mainly so animals wouldn't go digging up shallow graves and spreading disease. The lime, weirdly enough, preserved the bodies. Which would be perfect, especially if the Bear installed a see-through cover. He could come out here, roll up the rug, and gaze upon his handiwork. As a bonus, he could even throw in some extra quicklime, causing the chemical reaction to heat the garage any-time he wanted.

Now to lure Mr. Tough Guy back here. *Okay, so how do we do that?*

The Bear removed a garden tool from a pair of nails he'd driven into the garage wall. It was a long-handled rake, three prongs, meant to pull weeds and till the soil. But now he used it to reach down eight feet to ease the noose around Hightower's neck a little. The man flinched when he caught sight of the metal claw approaching.

"Calm down, you idiot. You're only making it worse for yourself."

But it wasn't until the Bear finally loosened the rope that his prisoner began to stop struggling enough to be able to breathe. A low moan came out of Hightower's mouth.

"Hey, asshole," the Bear said.

The ex-cop groaned again.

"What's your friend's name?"

"Fuh-fuck you."

"I'm only going to ask one more time. Then I'm going to use this gar-den tool to pluck out one of your eyes. I might even force-feed it to you. Bet you won't be feeling too sassy then."

"Jack."

"Is that what you call him? Jack? Not John or Jay or anything else? You're not trying to fool me, now, are you?"

"No...it's Jack."

The Bear thumbed his next text.

Jack, I need you right away!

Floating dots meant that "Jack" the Tough Guy was considering his response. The dots seemed to float like they didn't have a care in the world. Wheee. Maybe Tough Guy was drafting a few options, erasing them, then trying another few, just to make sure he had the perfect reply.

When it finally came, after all that buildup, the Bear couldn't help but be a little disappointed:

Fine.

Disappointed, but only at first. Because now he had someone else to fuck with. Oh, this was turning out to be such a wonderful day!

THE GIRL DETECTIVE

She felt horrible, of course, but it wasn't just the aftereffects of the chemo treatment — her first. And to think . . . there were nine more rounds of this to go. *RIP my life,* she thought.

No, it was something else. Something she couldn't quite place. An unsettling feeling, beyond her illness and exhaustion and the IV tubes and monitors and constant interruptions.

Oddly, it was the unexpected quiet of this moment — with Aunt Reese out for a quick lunch with Uncle Louis — that sent her spiraling. The Girl Detective was usually very good at staying in the moment. There were plenty of facts on hand to ponder and analyze; there was always more research to be done. All of this was great at keeping the larger terrors at bay . . .

. . . right until they didn't.

And the Girl Detective realized she was alone in a room, with something in her blood that was actively trying to kill her, and her mother was gone, and her father was somewhere in the city on some weird mission with an ex-cop, and it all hit her hard: What was going to become of her family?

She wished her father would hurry up and walk through that door.

In the meantime, she decided to lose herself in other people's miseries with more California Bear research on the message boards, culling little factoids from BearlyAshley99 and Mr_Claude and Carnivora83 and ThinkPink and dozens of others.

One interesting thing: The Bear was in full costume (the furry mask, the claws, the gauntlets) for only the final three killings. In the popular imagination, he was wearing the mask and claws all along, just as they assumed Jason Voorhees wore a hockey mask in every Friday the 13th installment. This was simply not true; in fact, it could be argued that Jason wore it for only a film and a half. (The Girl Detective had watched all the movies; Uncle Louis had a DVD box set.) Jason killed a victim for the hockey mask halfway through part 3 and was wearing it when he was killed by Corey Feldman during the finale of part 4. Jason wasn't in part 5 (some other killer wore the mask pretending to be Jason), and from part 6 on, Jason was more zombie than serial killer, and the mask served to cover up all of that ick. So the big question was...why did he start wearing the mask toward the end of his run? Was he worried about people recognizing him? Or was it the nickname that made the Bear decide to dress the part?

Another thing the local press made a big deal about were the colorful plastic letter magnets on the fridge. In the popular imagination, that was the Bear's primary method of communication—much like the Zodiac had his letters and the Unabomber had his manifestos. Apparently, the California Bear had...Fisher-Price.

Truth was, the Bear did it only twice. The first time was a spontaneous act. He was raiding someone's fridge in 1980, post–fun and games, saw the plastic letters on the fridge, and thought, why not? He arranged them to read:

C-U-T
Y-O-U
I-N-T-O
L-I-T-T-L-E
P-I-E-C-E-S

He'd been forced to use numbers by the end there because he ran out of *E*'s and *I*'s. Maybe the set came that way, or a kid lost them at some point?

But wow, did that get a reaction in the press! The Girl Detective knew that predators were usually ignored by the media until they did something colorful or weird. But leaving a message? Oh, that was guaranteed to land you on the front page. She had to grudgingly admire his craft.

During his next hunting expedition, the Bear must have brought along his own set of plastic magnetic letters to spell out a new message.

N-O-N-E
O-F
Y-O-U
A-R-E
S-A-F-E

She had to give Mr. California Bear that one. He kind of nailed it.

"KILLER"

Jack "Killer" Queen followed the narrow cement walkway leading to the front door of the (alleged) house of the California Bear. This gave him a strange out-of-body feeling, as if he were remembering something awful right before it happened.

The door had been left ajar a few inches. Which was weird. He remembered Hightower stepping inside, then the door slowly closing behind him and clicking shut. Had it popped open by itself? Did Hightower open it to let him in?

"Hightower? Hey, man — are you in there?"

He reached for the door handle but stopped just before touching it. What if this was a ruse? Maybe the elderly serial killer had gotten the drop on Hightower, knocked him out, then stolen his phone? And then just used it to lure Jack inside to kill him? Okay, no. That was crazy paranoia talking. For one thing, the text used his name. No way the California Bear (if that's who it was) would know that. And Hightower wouldn't be stupid enough to tell him.

Jack pushed open the door, then stepped inside. "Hey, it's me. Hightower, where are you?" Maybe he should just pull out his burner phone and call him? That way, the ringing would give him some kind of clue.

The décor inside the house itself was Basic White Americana, remodeled sometime in the late eighties or early nineties, with furniture to match. A ceiling fan and two standing fans tried to push the hot air out of the room, but they weren't doing a very good job. Either there was no AC or this Dixon guy was too cheap to turn it on, even in June.

Jack wasn't expecting this place to look like the lair out of *Silence of the Lambs* or anything. But it was all so ordinary that he couldn't help but think that maybe Hightower had screwed this one up.

The living room blended right into the kitchen, with a dining room table marking the dividing line between the two. No one was in sight. Okay, fuck this. Jack dialed Hightower's number.

There was a ringtone directly behind him. When Jack started to turn, he felt a sharp poke in his back, like someone was trying to skewer him.

"Don't move," a gruff voice spoke, hot breath on Jack's neck. "I push this spike into your back, you're paralyzed for life."

Before being sent to prison, Jack took a quick one-session self-defense course meant for convicts. It was a gift from a drummer friend who'd served a little time for DUI and possession. *Hope you never need it,* Howard had said, *but in case you do...*

Jack had never needed it in prison, but it sure came in handy now.

Because he used the element of surprise—and the back of his skull—to slam the old fucker in the face.

Tried to, anyway. The old man had reflexes and largely sidestepped the blow. Jack rushed forward and tripped over his own feet, sending him to the hardwood floor. His cheap burner phone slid across the floor. Not his most graceful moment, but at least he wasn't paralyzed.

"Hightower!" he yelled. "Answer me, man!"

Christopher Albin Dixon still had the weapon in his hand—a metal spike. "You want to see your friend? I'll take you to him."

"I don't want any part of this," Jack said. "Let me just take him and go."

"It's much too late for that."

"Yeah, I had a feeling you'd say that," Jack said as he climbed to his feet. "I know you've got that scary little nail there, but if you don't drop it, I'm going to beat the living fuck out of you."

The old fucker smirked and then charged at him with the spike—

faster than Jack had anticipated. Jack used more of that self-defense class to block the hand with the spike and then went for the man's throat. If this was the California Bear, he was a shadow of himself, but there was a surprising amount of strength left in him. They wrestled a little, with the old man wiggling around as if better footing might help him prevail. It would not. Jack twisted the man's wrist. The spike, along with a set of keys, dropped out of his hand, then Jack pushed him backward into the kitchen cabinets. The old man, winded, slid down onto his ass.

Jack scooped up the keys and the metal spike. "Where is he." Not a question. A demand.

The old man slammed a fist into one of the cabinets. At first, Jack thought he was throwing a temper tantrum. A spring-loaded drawer popped open. Dixon reached in and lifted out an automatic pistol.

"Thanks for picking up my keys," Dixon said, aiming the pistol at Jack's belly.

THE BEAR

This was no professional muscle; this man, despite his size, was an amateur. Maybe he took a shopping mall Krav Maga course at some point. But nothing more than that. He was big on bold moves with no follow-up plan.

The Bear, meanwhile, was all about contingency plans. He had weapons and bindings everywhere in this fucking place. It was the one thing he refused to compromise on. Surprisingly, the Queen of Mars hadn't given him too much grief about it. If she only knew how close he'd come to using those things on *her* over the years.

"I'm sure you know that I could cut you in half with this thing," the Bear said, "and nobody would even blink. You're an intruder, just like your pal Hightower. God bless the Castle Doctrine and the state of California."

"Don't do this," Jack the Intruder said. "This is all a big misunderstanding."

"Yeah, I had a feeling you'd say that," the Bear replied, thoroughly enjoying himself. "Turn around and get down on your knees."

Jack the Intruder was trying so hard to project toughness but was trembling hard. Another indication that this was no professional. Whatever was between him and Hightower was personal. Maybe they weren't friends after all. Or maybe he was a family friend, roped into a favor that took a gruesome turn. The Bear would find out everything soon enough.

"You can't do this," Jack said. "People know we're here."

"Who? Jeanie? Don't worry about that. I'll explain everything when I see her later. Is there anybody you want me to notify? A sweetheart? A wife somewhere?"

"Please," the man pleaded. "Don't."

Oh, this was delicious. The Bear had forgotten how powerful this made him feel! The decades were gone, along with the bland suburban trappings of his life. This truly was a resurrection. He'd lost nothing. *Nothing.*

"Turn around," he repeated. "And down on your knees."

Jack the Intruder drew it out as long as he could, which was fine with the Bear. He needed time to catch his breath, pull himself up off the floor, and find the heavy-duty zip ties he'd stashed somewhere in here. Unless the Queen of Mars had moved them.

"Please listen to me..."

Nope. Here they were, in the junk drawer.

"Put your hands behind your back and lock your fingers together like you're praying," the California Bear said. "And feel free, if you're so inclined."

"KILLER"

The hard plastic cut into his wrists. Jack was quick enough to try to hold his wrists as far apart as he could without Dixon noticing, potentially giving himself a little wiggle room to escape. But the latter was wise to that and pulled tighter on the plastic ties.

"What's your name, son?" Christopher Albin Dixon asked.

"I'm nobody," Jack replied.

"I already know your name is Jack. That's your Christian name, though I wouldn't pretend to guess at your faith. What's your last name?"

"Fuck you."

"You and your friend down there seemed to have a limited vocabulary. I think I'm gonna call you the Fuck You Brothers."

"Where is Hightower?"

"Lounging in the pool. And don't change the subject. I asked for your full name."

As he spoke, the Bear started patting Jack down, as if arresting him. Jack realized the Bear was looking for his wallet and identification. Fortunately, he didn't have them on him — they were out in the car.

"Where's your fucking wallet?"

"I don't have one."

"Right. Because you're nobody."

The man's voice was a little weak on some of the syllables, and cracking in places. But that did not do a thing to disguise the menace beneath. Jack knew this kind of voice well. It was the voice of authority, someone used to being obeyed, no questions asked. Any levity was about power and control. This was Christopher Albin Dixon's show; Jack had merely wandered onto the set. His only chance was to try to reason with him—somehow convince him that hurting him would only blow up *his* life too.

"Please put the gun down," Jack said, "and let's talk like sensible adults."

"You want me to put my weapon down," Dixon repeated. "You sure about that?"

Jack realized his mistake. Oh, this man was going to put his gun down—right in the middle of Jack's skull. He sensed the movement a second before it was too late. Jack lunged forward. The butt of the pistol didn't connect with bone. But Jack couldn't control his sudden momentum and his face collided with the edge of a wooden coffee table.

The blunt edge of the table caught Jack just under his nose and along his cheekbone. Jack's face went numb for a merciful second...until the pain roared in.

Jack didn't resist as the old man pulled him up onto his knees and then finally to a standing position. He felt the gun on the back of his neck. There was no self-defense trick that would help him now. As he was forced across the lawn to the freestanding garage, Jack couldn't help but feel like he was in a waking nightmare. Bright sun, palm trees, bamboo shoots along the fence. Ordinary civilians to the left and right. He could cry out for help. He could also feel a bullet severing his spine at the base of his skull, and there would be no more Jack.

Dixon pushed him through the garage door and then grabbed the back of his shirt before he could take another step. Jack's eyes adjusted to the darkness, then he looked down. What he saw confused him. Hightower was indeed inside an empty pool. But there was no water, and there was a complicated noose around the man's thick neck, the ropes wrapped around his arms and wrists.

"I can't believe you two knuckleheads," the Bear said. "I mean, you could have just made an anonymous phone call. Provided you have proof of any of these wild allegations."

"Are you denying you're the Bear?" Hightower asked.

"Oh no," the Bear replied. "I am the California Bear, and I am going to cut you both into tiny little pieces."

And then he pushed Jack into the empty pool.

THE BEAR

The thing is, the Bear would have desperately loved to fuck around with these two for a while. Maybe even force one of them to hurt the other, and vice versa, in some kind of sick competition. Winner gets to leave the pool. Spoiler Alert (as the Hollywood fucks liked to say): the Bear would be the only winner.

But you had to give them hope.

Sadly, time was an issue. The Queen of Mars was due back home at *some* point, depending on the checkout lines at Ralphs. Or maybe she went somewhere else after grocery shopping? The Bear didn't want to get into this with her, because then it would become a whole *thing,* with conversations and brainstorming sessions and meetings and all that. For once, the Bear just wanted to make a decision without someone second-guessing him or rolling their eyes or telling him how he'd screwed it up.

The Bear needed to know how these two knuckleheads found him, then kill them and cover them in quicklime and seal the pool and let science do its thing and...oh shit, he needed to take their car and dump it somewhere too. That would be tricky. It had been so long since he'd had to dispose of a compromised vehicle that all his former contacts were useless. That would require some brainpower.

For the moment, he supposed, he could drive it over to the Fashion Square, where it could sit for a day or two. But then the Bear would have to rideshare or hoof it back...and that was a pain in the ass. Was dumping the car somewhere on Ventura Boulevard too risky? No, maybe that was the way. Who would notice one more shitty Honda Accord? Cubby could take care of it later tonight...

Well, wait just a goddamned minute, the Bear thought. The car. Could these idiots be foolish enough to leave some of their "research" materials in the car? Chances were good, because they were stupid. But also because he'd imagine they'd have some kind of "evidence" to wave under the Bear's nose, make him realize they meant *business.* Yeah, he needed to go look inside that car.

"Throw me your keys, Hightower," the Bear said.

"You think I'm going to help you erase all traces of our existence?" Hightower said. Ah, he was regaining some of his sass. "No way. Come down here and get them yourself."

"Give him the keys," muttered his partner, Jack.

"What? Why?"

"Just give them to him!"

The Bear could guess what Jack was thinking. Jack was clearly the Mensa member of the two. He thought that having the Bear distracted and out of this garage was their one shot at freedom. Not a bad idea, but hopelessly flawed. For reasons these two assholes would soon discover.

"No fucking way," Hightower said. "The car is paid for, free and clear, and I'm not just going to hand it over to a psychopath."

"Fine," Jack said, and began tugging at Hightower's cargo shorts. "I'll take them myself."

This initiated a sloppy and pathetic wrestling match at the bottom of the pool. These two had no idea how ridiculous they looked. As much fun as this would have been, the clock was ticking. The Bear needed to get a move on.

"I could just go and smash a window," the Bear said, genuinely trying to be helpful.

"*No!*" Hightower yelled, then elbowed his partner in the stomach. Jack curled up like a pill bug. The keys slid out of his hand. Hightower snatched them up, then grunted as he clumsily threw them up to the Bear's outstretched hand. The keys missed by a good two feet.

Luckily, they landed outside the pool so they wouldn't have to do this all morning long.

"Be right back," the Bear said. "Don't go anywhere."

GENE JEANIE

Jeanie stared at her violated panties, which were resting inside a plastic bag on her kitchen table, phone in hand.

God, this fucking day. She thought about a gin and tonic but reminded herself to stay on task. There'd be time for drinking later. After this particular errand.

She needed someone to run the genetic sample. There were plenty of private companies who ran DNA analyses, but none of them would be able to match the semen to a human being with a name. That was the purview of law enforcement. The only person who came to mind—aside from her husband—was her ex-husband, also a retired cop. Yes, Jeanie Hightower (née Poole) was a serial cop wife. Maybe after she and Hightower called it quits, she'd wise up and marry a dentist or a professional wrestler or a stage magician, just to change it up a little.

Yes, her ex was the best bet, but she wasn't prepared to make that call yet.

So strange to think that this new career started as an escape from her *second* failing marriage. Jeanie had bought a discounted subscription to a commercial genealogy site, spit into a tube, and spent the next few weeks obsessively filling in the gaps of her family tree. She told herself that looking into her past might explain where she was headed in the future. Even then, she knew that was bullshit. This was nothing more than a glorified *New York Times* crossword, or a thousand-piece jigsaw of a field of fucking strawberries. Genealogy was a puzzle, and Jeanie was extraordinarily good at puzzles.

And the most reassuring thing of all: people can try to reinvent themselves, but deoxyribonucleic acid doesn't lie. DNA is fate, and it's destiny. Jeanie had come to believe that and embrace it. This was why she'd rededicated her life to it.

What other choice did she have? Accept the choices that led her to this point? Choices that were largely out of her control? No. DNA explained it all. We all enter this world programmed a certain way, to follow a certain pattern. It took a superhuman effort to deviate from that pattern.

So why be so hard on herself now that her second marriage wasn't working out? Maybe she wasn't genetically disposed to be happy or raise a family. None of that mattered now. What mattered was her clients. If she could focus on them, everything else would sort itself out. That's what made it a business — and a calling.

Give me access to your *family tree,* she promised her clients, *and I'll obsessively fill in all those missing pieces that you don't have time to fill in.* Gathering clients was tough at first; there was a lot of amateur competition. But soon word of Jeanie's prowess began to spread. In two years she had gone from a single (flaky) client to an extremely robust client list, so robust that she was paying all the bills and was even considering *turning down* work. This would have been unthinkable a year ago. She should be proud of herself!

Should be.

For now, the best thing she could do was research this California Bear with a real-life source who knew a thing or two about him. But who would that be? Reaching out to someone in the cold-case squad of the LAPD didn't feel like the right move — not until she understood more. Jeanie's questions would raise other questions, and she could be mired in someone else's obsession. No, thanks.

As she mixed another drink, she ran through her mental Rolodex of recent clients. Were any of them true crime buffs? Criminal lawyers? Journalists? Not that she could remember.

There had to be someone . . .

And then it came to her: a husband-and-wife team who ran tours of Los Angeles. But not grisly, sensational tours that reveled in pain and misery. They were more interested in history and literature and civic life...with tastes, of course, than ran to the macabre. Jeanie had taken a few of their bus tours with a friend a few years ago and appreciated how they never celebrated the monsters and always found a way to humanize the victims. The Black Dahlia tour, for instance, focused on Beth Short as a young woman trying to make it in a sometimes hostile city. She was painted not as a born victim but as a woman who'd made one small yet tragic mistake—trusting someone a little too much.

Yes! Kim and Richard would be a perfect resource. It was almost 11 a.m.; they would probably be leaving for one of their Saturday afternoon tours soon. Maybe she could reach them in time...

"KILLER"

They remained in a messy tangle at the bottom of the pool, and neither of them was very happy with the other. It would be funny, were they not at the mercy of a vicious torturer-murderer who had dozens of ways to make them hurt.

"You ripped my fucking pants," Jack said.

"You gave away my car," Hightower replied.

"It's a piece of shit. Nobody will miss it."

"Says the guy who currently relies on said piece of shit to get around."

"Never mind your car. Let's get the fuck out of this pit."

"It's a pool, not a pit. And that sick fuck has greased up the sides with something. It's impossible to climb out of here."

"Have you tried?"

"Of course I've tried!"

"Yeah, I'm sure you tried real hard.'

Jack extended a foot out to the nearest pool wall. Hightower was right. It was coated with some kind of slippery substance. Like furniture polish, only slimier. Matilda's mother once made the mistake of polishing his upright piano, keys included. ("The thing is made of wood, isn't it?" was her defense.) This was the earliest argument of their marriage; Jack eventually forgave her. But Jack also forbade any type of polish in the same room as his musical gear.

"Okay," Jack said. "Let's focus. We need to come up with a plan before the old bastard gets back."

"Call him an old bastard all you want, but somehow that wily prick managed to trap us both. I told you he was a pretty big deal."

"Did you hear what I said about focusing?"

"I'm just saying, I feel less foolish about him getting the drop on me. Because he got the drop on you awfully quick too."

"That's because you basically gave him your phone. And told him my name! Why would you do that?"

"Because I might want to see a 3D movie again someday."

"What?"

"Never mind," Hightower said. "Okay, let's do it your way. Let's focus. Looks like he has your wrists bound up with zip ties. This is good news."

"I'm not quite seeing it that way," Jack replied. "I tried to leave a little wiggle room, but he was wise to that trick. He cinched me pretty tight. My fingers have gone numb."

"Well, make them un-numb, because you're going to need them. The secret to zip ties is the little locking mechanisms in the little buckle doo-hickey. If you can break that, you'll be out of them in no time."

"What *doohickey*?"

"You know, the little plastic buckle thing where the band slides through."

"The locking mechanism is inside that buckle?"

"That's what I'm saying!"

"The hard plastic buckle that would be unbreakable on a good day, let alone with numb fingers? Yeah, sure, I'm on it. How about you try to untangle the knots around your wrists? You're tied up with fucking rope."

"Rope that's been cleverly tied around my neck so that the harder I struggle, the more I choke. Is that what you want? For me to choke myself out?"

"Yes, if it makes you shut the fuck up."

THE BEAR

Oh, sweet and gentle Jesus, would you look at that.

The Bear tossed aside Mr. Nobody's jacket and looked at what at first seemed like a mirage. He reached out and touched the pink box. They were real. He gingerly ran his finger under the Scotch tape and lifted the lid. The doughnuts inside were also real. They looked and smelled incredible. Before he even knew what he was doing, the Bear shoved a Boston cream into his mouth and devoured the whole thing in roughly three bites. The sugar hit his system like crack cocaine and his brain was overwhelmed with bliss.

Never mind the weird fact that two dozen doughnuts were sitting in the front seat. Who does that — stops at a fucking doughnut shop on their way to blackmail a suspected serial killer? Were these supposed to be for the big celebration once the Bear handed over fat stacks of cash?

The Bear lifted the boxes like they were the Ark of the Covenant and kicked the car door shut. Then he remembered the jacket, which might have a wallet inside. And possible files! *Let's stay on mission,* he told himself.

The Bear placed the boxes on the hood. But he also couldn't resist cramming a devil's food doughnut into his face as he searched the car. He chewed slowly, savoring the rush. Tried to, anyway. It was impossible to eat a doughnut like a Zen monk.

There were no files, but the jacket did contain a wallet, along with a state-issued (CAL-ID) card. JACK BENNETT QUEEN, the name read.

Well, okay. Finally he had a middle and a surname. Both would be useful. He finished the devil's food doughnut as he searched the glove box for registration. No surprise there: the car belonged to CATO DIPSHIT HIGHTOWER. That wasn't the man's given middle name, of course. But it should be.

Before the Bear ambled back inside, he couldn't resist a third treat — a chocolate-covered Long John, which had been his favorite when he was on the job. A Long John was like two doughnuts for the price of one. Who could complain about that?

The Bear took his treasures, locked the car, and headed back inside. His brain was more awake and alive than it had been in years. This felt *so good*. Why had he let that fucking cunt deprive him of this feeling for so long? No more. From now on, he was going to run the show his way, no exceptions.

Starting with these two. If the Queen of Mars didn't like it, she could leave. She'd failed to realize the naked truth: she no longer had anything to hold over him.

"KILLER"

Despite his skepticism, Jack tried like hell to find that hard plastic buckle (doohickey) with his increasingly numb fingers. He thought he'd found it, only to realize he was frantically trying to pull apart an edge of his own belt.

And then the garage door opened, heralding the return of the Bear. Was that grunting he was hearing? Or was it more like masticating?

"Oh fuck," Hightower said.

Jack twisted his body around to see what had Hightower so freaked-out and understood immediately. The Bear was chewing, and smiling, and holding a long-handled Black & Decker string trimmer—commonly known as a weed whacker.

"You ever see what these things can do to human flesh?" the Bear asked. "Buddy of mine on the force once decided to trim the edges of his lawn while barefoot. He'd had one too many Dos Equis and lost three of his toes. Not his best day."

"Come on, man," Hightower said. "Let's talk about this!"

The Bear responded by pressing the plastic trigger on the handle of the trimmer, which erupted into a fierce *WHRRRR* that, in the confines of this garage, sounded like the engine of a Harley-Davidson. The hard string whipped the edges of the pool, a chilling sound that sent electric shocks down Jack's limbs.

"Oh, we'll talk. This won't kill you. But you're not going to enjoy the rest of your lives after I start in on you two. Maybe I'll have a contest. First one to spill everything is given the easy way out."

"Your neighbors will hear the screams," Jack said.

"Yeah, that's a good thought. And I appreciate it. But they're used to me playing loud music back here while I do lawn work. You guys feeling like a little Pink Floyd? Nah, that's too mellow. Maybe some James Gang."

The Bear pulled the trigger again. WHRRRR *WHRRRR*. And then another WHRRRR *WHRRRR,* in the same exact cadence.

Jack understood what he was doing. He was approximating Joe Walsh's opening guitar riff to "Walk Away."

"Don't do this!"

The Bear just smiled. He rested the trimmer against the garage wall, then reached down for something on the ground. Jack couldn't see from this angle. Was this another Black & Decker torture device? Was this how this sick old fuck got his thrills?

No. It was a doughnut.

A bear claw, to be precise, from the boxes he'd left on the front seat of Hightower's car.

"Tell me, Jack Bennett Queen," the Bear said. "Who's Matilda? She's the only other number on your shitty little phone. Is Matilda your sweetheart? You into older women?"

He took an obscene bite of the doughnut. Crumbs and flakes of dried glaze tumbled down his chin. He chewed and made yummy sounds.

The temperature of Jack's blood plummeted below freezing while his brain began to vibrate wildly inside his skull. *No. This can't be happening.*

"You motherfucker." Jack pulled against his zip-tie binds with all his strength, not really caring if he cut off his own hands in the process.

"Something for you to think about, Jack Queen. Because I'm going to find her next. And then I'm really going to have some fun with her."

He took another jaw-unhinged bite, which made the Bear look like a python trying to snarf down an antelope. Through a mouthful of fried dough he kept talking.

"Thing is, I'm not really into men. I mean, I'll take a certain amount of pleasure with you two. But ladies . . . ah, now, that's what really gets me going. Young, old, don't matter. I'm an admirer of the female form in all their lovely shapes and sizes."

Jack *snapped*. He didn't care about the physics of his situation, that there was no way to free himself, let alone gain some kind of foothold that would launch him out of this pit of hell. His rage was almost enough to make him levitate, and a primal roar blasted from his mouth as powerful as a shock wave.

The California Bear flinched, then took an uncertain step backward, frozen mid-chew, eyes wide open. It was as if some great truth had been revealed to him, and he was wrestling with its implications . . .

"KILLER"

At first, Jack thought the Bear was putting him on — puffing out his cheeks, eyes rolling back in his head. Like a pantomime of death. Mocking Jack and Hightower for the hell they were about to endure.

But then the man's flesh turned pale white, almost translucent, and broke out in a slick sweat. He dropped to the ground, completely disappearing from view. There was a gurgling sound coming from his unseen throat. And then nothing.

"What the fuck just happened?" Hightower asked.

"I think he just had a heart attack," Jack replied.

"Had a heart attack, or is having?"

"Why? Do you want to climb up there and give him mouth-to-mouth?"

Jack started to pull on his binds only to discover that they were no longer around his wrists. Somewhere between going nuclear with red-hot rage and watching the Bear drop dead from a coronary, he must have snapped them loose. His hands were still numb, and his wrists were raw and bloodied, but he could move his fingers. Slowly the feeling came back.

"You snapped the locking mechanism!" Hightower exclaimed. "See, I told you. Works like a charm, every time."

"Shut the fuck up and roll over."

Untangling Hightower was a lot more difficult than Jack had imagined. The Bear had applied some Eagle Scout–level knots to this bizarre rigging. Working with partially numb and trembling fingers didn't seem to help much either. Every time he'd tug on a knot, just about to work it loose, Hightower would start coughing and choking and cursing, not always in that order.

And then there were the slicked-up sides of the pool to deal with. They tried scrambling up and out on their own, but that was like trying to run down a city block in the freezing rain. They slipped. They slammed into each other. Whatever they tried, they could not maintain a foothold long enough to reach the edge of the pool.

"I'll push you up," Jack finally said, figuring out that he could prop one foot against one of the jet nozzles and give Hightower something to push against. This, too, took more effort than it appeared. As a bonus, Jack spent an unusually long time confronted with Hightower's ample ass, which was a memory he wanted scrubbed from his mind immediately.

Hightower finally made it over the edge of the pool and froze in place, his legs dangling in midair like Winnie-the-Pooh.

"Oh Christ."

"What is it?" Jack asked in a sudden panic, wondering if the Bear had faked everything and was lying in wait, ready to torture them all over again.

"He's . . . really dead."

"Good."

"It's horrible, Jack. Oh, fuck me, it's horrible."

"Help me up out of here. You can cry about it later."

But when Jack finally made it up and over, he saw what Hightower was talking about. Christopher Albin Dixon, the California Bear, was not just dead. He was gruesomely, absurdly dead—jaw open, partially-masticated dough hanging off to one side of his mouth. Surrounding his corpse were the remnants of two dozen doughnuts in their pink boxes, lids open. Doughnuts meant for his daughter, now part of the strangest crime scene Studio City had seen in quite some time. Possibly ever.

Or was it even a crime scene? The crimes (forcible detention, assault) had been the Bear's, not Jack's, unless you count aiding and abetting a would-be blackmailer. Somehow, though, Jack "Killer" Queen felt that—karma-wise, anyway—he was now responsible for two deaths. After all, he'd insisted on purchasing the doughnuts that did the Bear in. Did that make Jack a serial killer too? Or did you have to do three before earning that distinction?

"Let's get the fuck out of here," he told Hightower, pulling the big man to his shaky feet. Hightower couldn't stop looking at the Bear's dead body, fascinated and repulsed. Jack tugged on the man's arm. "Come on!" As if in a trance, Hightower finally allowed himself to be dragged out of the garage.

Jack knew better than to cut through the house. He opted for a route along a narrow garden path that would lead them to the front lawn. As they were about to clear the front of the house, he heard a noise. Jack threw out an arm to stop Hightower, as if the man were a child in the front seat of a car and they'd braked suddenly.

"Wait a minute," Jack said.

The sound was a key turning a lock in the front door—or trying to, anyway. Then the voice of an older woman: "Christopher? Did you know you left the door unlocked?"

Hightower looked stunned. "That must be Mama Bear."

"Fuck!"

The moment she stepped inside the house, Jack dragged Hightower over the lawn, across the street, and to their car . . .

The car that would work only if you had the keys.

Keys the Bear took.

Fuck fuck *fuck* . . .

If this was an alternate universe, it was the cruelest one imaginable.

Jack led Hightower to the other side of the car, then gently eased the man down into a sitting position on the curb. He wasn't exactly catatonic, but he was experiencing some form of mild shock. In short: he was useless.

"Listen to me," Jack said. "You stay here, out of sight."

This snapped Hightower out of his trance. "Where are you going?"

"To get the fucking keys to the car!"

"No."

"What do you mean, no? If I don't go back for the keys, we're walking out of here. Sooner or later, someone's going to notice your car and check the registration. And then we're as good as fucked."

"No."

"Will you stop saying that?"

"Check the right rear tire well."

"Why?"

"Hide-a-key box. I got tired of losing my keys in bars, so I stashed an extra in a little box there. It's attached to the frame with magnets."

For perhaps the second time in his life, Jack wanted to kiss Hightower on his dumb lips. The first time was when the man managed to free him from prison. And now, when Hightower had enough foresight to give them an escape route from this nightmare.

The key was there. Jack insisted on driving, despite not having a license. He tucked Hightower in the passenger seat, pulled the shoulder belt over his frame, locked it in place. Jack slid behind the wheel and gave himself a moment to just . . . exhale. Somehow, against all odds, they were getting out of this.

Jack reached into his pocket to pull out his burner phone and tell Matilda that he was finally on his way.

The phone wasn't in his pocket.

Fuck fuck *fuck* . . .

This *was* an alternate universe. The cruelest one imaginable. No doubt about it.

The phone was in the garage with the rapidly cooling corpse of the Bear. Or it was somewhere in the house. The cheap burner phone wouldn't matter . . . except that Matilda's number was stored in its memory. He couldn't leave it behind and risk involving her in any way.

"I have to go back inside," Jack said.

"What? Why?"

"My phone is inside."

"No. Drive away. Now. I'll buy you a new crappy burner phone."

"I'll be right back. Wait for me!"

This was crazy, this was crazy...

Jack traced his steps back the way he'd just come with Hightower. Across the lawn (praying Mrs. Bear wasn't looking out her front window at this exact moment) and then moving along the side of the house toward the backyard. He paused at the edge of the yard and scanned the area the best he could without revealing himself. Would she stay in the house? Or would she venture out into the garage, knowing her creepy husband usually hung out there? He had no idea about their domestic life or habits. Maybe she wouldn't notice he was gone for hours.

"Christopher! Where are you?"

It was her voice, from somewhere in the house. Okay, she was going to notice pretty soon. Shit!

Jack darted across the lawn, opened the garage door, slipped inside, and closed the door behind him.

At his feet was the still, very-much-dead corpse of the Bear. The man-beast looked like he was the centerpiece of an avant-garde tableau: *Still Life with Sugar Jelly.*

Jack crouched down, heard his knees pop. He hesitated, then told himself to stop being a coward. He felt around the Bear's body, patting him down, feeling for anything close to a burner phone. But there was nothing. Nothing but doughnuts. This was not good.

He scanned the interior of the garage. The trimmer was still propped up against the wall, and there were assorted boxes and a big black trunk with a padlock on it. If the phone wasn't here, then it must be . . .

The garage door opened. Sunlight blasted its way inside.

"Who the fuck are you?"

Mrs. Bear was staring at Jack. Once Jack's vision adjusted, he saw she had piercing green eyes and an angry, downturned mouth. For a horrible, eternal moment, both were locked into a death stare, neither of them quite knowing the protocol in a situation like this. Who was supposed to flinch first? She was about to look down at her dead husband, so Jack acted on sheer impulse.

He punched her hard in the face and ran.

As he ran, he looked over his shoulder and saw her sprawled out on the grass. But there was no time to linger. He pulled open the back door and launched himself through the living room / kitchen before skidding to an awkward halt. There it was, on the table. His burner phone.

Jack scooped it up. Had Mrs. Bear seen it? Opened it? Possibly written down or memorized the number attached to the mysterious name "Matilda"?

There was no time to ask; he had to hope for the best.

Mrs. Bear had locked the front door. Jack fumbled with the locks for what felt like a dangerously long time. He didn't even understand how he finally opened the door; it just happened, and he hurled himself through the doorway.

Halfway across the Bear's front lawn, Jack received another shock.

Hightower, and his car, were gone.

THE GIRL DETECTIVE

She tried not to dwell on the fact that her father (and the doughnuts) was hopelessly late. She tried not to think about her dark premonitions and overall bad feelings.

The Girl Detective, instead, focused on research. Maybe if she was working on her father's case, it would be enough of a jinx that he would come right through that door and catch her in the act. That would be worth it — him catching her. Just so long as he was here in the room with her.

But even as she kept herself busy, the Girl Detective couldn't avoid glancing at the door every few minutes. Who was she kidding? Felt like every few seconds.

The only interruption from her vigil was a routine visit from Meghan to take her vitals. The nurse noticed there was something off with her new bestie.

"Everything okay?" she asked.

"Just waiting for my dad to show up," the Girl Detective replied.

"I'm sure he'll be here soon, sweetie."

"He'd better. I dispatched him on a very important mission."

Meghan smiled. "Oh, did you? Is this a secret mission?"

"For now. But once he arrives, you'll know all about it, don't you worry."

Meghan smiled, then booped her on the nose. "Don't *you* worry."

The Girl Detective couldn't help but smile. But the smile faded once Meghan left the room.

Her view from the room provided her with a semi-clear view down the length of the hall, all the way to the double security doors where the nursing staff could buzz in visitors. Which meant she not only checked the door obsessively but also peered down the corridor, praying for those double doors to open and a Padre-shaped being to come walking through.

Hopefully carrying two giant pink boxes.

"KILLER"

This was not good.

This was, in fact, a disaster.

Even if he started running toward Ventura Boulevard right this second, how long would it take for Mrs. Bear to wake up, call the police, and give them a description of Jack? He might be able to have some fun and games with them for a while, but he would not escape an LAPD dragnet. He would most likely be spending tonight back in jail, a second murder charge hanging around his neck...

An earsplitting screech of rubber on asphalt pulled Jack out of his mental spiral. He whipped his body around, which was a good thing, because Hightower's Accord was weaving all over the road and nearly hit Jack as it braked to a messy halt beside him.

"Get in!" Hightower exclaimed.

"Slide over — I'm driving, you asshole!"

"You don't have a driver's license."

"And you don't have a fucking brain," Jack replied. "Slide over!"

To his credit, and Jack's surprise, Hightower complied without a word, crawling over the center console and into the passenger seat. Jack climbed in, not bothering with a seat belt. He put the Accord into drive and peeled down the street.

For most of the trip Jack tried to concentrate on the streets and directions. His mental map of Los Angeles was still blurry. He asked Hightower for advice now and again, but the man would just grunt a word or two while staring out the windshield. Jack wished he had the luxury of being able to shut down mentally.

After about fifteen minutes of weaving around the streets, he remembered the doughnuts.

"Where was that place you mentioned? The doughnut shop?"

"Donut Prince."

"Yeah—where is it? I can't see Matilda empty-handed."

Never mind that both came close to not having hands at all—if the Bear's lawn-trimmer threats were to be believed.

"Olive."

Meaning Olive Avenue in Burbank. Meaning he needed to take Barham over the hill, past Universal, then whip past Warner Bros. Okay, it was coming back to him now. Jack even remembered the shop Hightower was talking about. It was close to a comic book shop where he'd taken a much younger Matilda every so often.

Jack pulled his sleeves down over his raw, bloodied wrists and hoped the bruise on his face wouldn't freak out the doughnut-shop proprietor. Thankfully the Bear had left Jack's wallet (and the small amount of cash he had tucked inside) in the car. When he asked for two dozen assorted, no one gave him a second glance. This time, however, he made sure not to ask for a bear claw. It was too soon.

Olive took them to Victory, which led to Griffith Park and an entrance to the 5. Then it was off at Los Feliz Boulevard, and a climb up the hill to Vermont, a left, and then downhill pretty much all the way to Sunset. Another left and they arrived at CHLA.

Hightower hadn't said anything for this final portion of the trip.

"Uh, are you okay to drive home?"

"Yeah. I'm great."

"You say that but you're squinting. Can you even see?"

Jack imagined they looked like a pair of lunatics. The Honda Accord was sloppily parked, blinkers on, in front of the main entrance to the children's hospital. Jack stood there with two pink boxes of doughnuts in his arms, trying to break through to Hightower, who was behind the wheel but looking as if he'd fail even the most rudimentary of sobriety tests.

"I'm fine," he mumbled. "Get in there and go be with your daughter."

Hightower spoke as if under heavy sedation, possibly not even understanding what he was saying. Jack could empathize. After the events of this morning, he felt like his soul had been separated from his physical body.

"You sure?"

Hightower waved at him as if he were a pesky fly at a picnic.

"Should we talk about things for a minute? I mean, at the very least to get our stories straight?"

"No story," Hightower responded. "Nothing happened."

"Uh, something *very much* happened."

Finally the ex-cop locked eyes with him, and Jack was able to see the man's actual eyeballs. They were bloodshot. His pupils were dilated. But he could see.

"Nothing. Happened. You understand me?"

"Okay, okay . . ."

Hightower pulled the driver's-side door shut and peeled away from the curb, blinkers still on, then disappeared down Sunset Boulevard to points unknown.

Not his problem. In fact, the way Jack saw it, he'd just saved Hightower's life. (Sort of?) If he had peeled away from the California Bear's house, he probably would have never seen Hightower ever again. And the ex-cop would have been dissolved in that stupid pool, erased from existence forever. Which . . . okay, that was awful, and Jack knew he couldn't live with himself. But still, the scales had to be balanced. There was no way Hightower could hold anything over him any longer. Right?

Jack checked in at the front desk and carried the doughnuts to the elevator and made it to the oncology floor. At least he'd accomplished this much: bringing the sweet treats to his daughter. She'd never have to know the original two dozen ended up partially digested in the belly of a monster.

On the elevator, the shiny metal doors allowed Jack to take stock of his current physical condition. The verdict: not good. He was more or less covered in slime. His pants were ripped. His wrists were a mess. A sizable bruise was visible on his face, even in the warped reflection in steel. A few splashes of water on his face weren't going to cover any of this up. Matilda was going to notice. Jack was going to have to...explain. In detail.

He had no idea where to begin.

GENE JEANIE

The seagulls were all over them. Jeanie knew it was a mistake to order French fries along with their beer-battered cod strips.

"So your genealogy work led you to a serial killer," the producer said with a brilliant smile. "I thought this kind of thing only happened in the pages of *The New Yorker*."

"I didn't say that," Jeanie replied. "I was helping another client who later turned out to be looking into this specific case. I'm not even sure if it's real, which is why I reached out to my friends Kim and Richard. Who reached out to you."

"Interesting," the producer said. His name was David Peterson, and he lived in a wildly expensive condo in Burbank above a Whole Foods (she looked it up) practically across the street from the Warner Bros. back lot. That Mr. Peterson the producer was willing to drive more than an hour to Port Hueneme on a Saturday afternoon spoke volumes. Either he was keenly interested in this case — or he was keenly interested in Jeanie. Maybe both? Her photo was on her website; she was sure he'd checked her out. Nobody did anything in LA unless the optics were right.

"I just want to know if this is something I should take seriously," Jeanie said. "You know. Seriously enough to bring to the police."

"Yes, your friends mentioned that, which is why they reached out to me. As I told you on the phone, I'm kind of obsessed with this case. To a professional degree."

"You said you were working on a movie about it?"

"Well...not exactly. It'll be a short documentary series. But very high-end. All the streamers are going crazy for them right now. And this is a case that's largely been forgotten by the general public."

Jeanie had chosen this outdoor fish-and-chips restaurant near the harbor because of the general public. Not that she couldn't handle herself; she carried a canister of heavy-duty pepper spray (5.3 million Scoville Heat Units) in her bag at all times and knew enough self-defense to take out an eye or badly damage a pair of testicles. This is what happens when you marry two cops in a row.

But Peterson didn't look like the pushy, grabby type. He was more professorial, about her age, maybe a shade younger, slender, dressed in casual slacks and a button-down shirt beneath a form-fitting cashmere sweater. Probably his jaunty weekend look, or something he pulled on when slumming in Ventura County. Either way Jeanie felt underdressed. Though she did choose a blouse that showed off ample cleavage and open-toed shoes to showcase her pedicure. Jeanie was glad she'd done a little self-care earlier in the week.

"So," Peterson said, waving away another seagull that was trying to sneak in for a French fry. "What would you like to know?"

"Okay, first tell me what a producer does. On this kind of project, specifically."

"I'm flattered to be asked! Nobody ever notices the producer. Writers complain that they're the unsung heroes of Hollywood, but really...almost no one considers the people who scrape together the money, twist the arms, package the talent...I mean, a lot of people slap their names on movies and call themselves producers, but very few know how to get the job done."

"I can imagine. Was it difficult getting the studios interested in the California Bear?"

Again, Peterson smiled. The *exact same smile*, in fact, that told Jeanie it was well-practiced and delivered almost unconsciously, no matter what statement was to follow.

"You have no idea!" he exclaimed. "It's been my next project for about twenty years now. Okay, I kid. But it has been on my slate for quite a while. I have a partner, an actor you've definitely heard of, who's also been obsessed with this case since he was a kid. He grew up here, collected all the newspaper clippings, and so on. And for years, we've tried to make it happen, but we always heard the same notes. Why the Bear? Why *now?*"

"What changed?"

"Well...that's the interesting part. Let me ask *you* something first."

"Okay..."

"Is there such a thing as a confidentiality agreement between you and your genealogical clients?"

"Well, there's a code of ethics, but it doesn't quite cover something like this. Are you wondering who my client is?"

"A little." Again: the smile.

"I do keep their identities confidential. But I am wondering if...well, if they've somehow used a family tree to discover the identity of the California Bear."

"And you were wondering if I'd tell you about my best guess for the suspect."

"Something like that."

"Of course," Peterson said, "I can't reveal that. For so many reasons. I mean, the spoilers alone."

Jeanie tried her own version of the smile, which for all she knew looked menacing. "Just between us?"

"Well, now we're back to the interesting thing, Jeanie," he said. "Because I finally have an answer when some studio asks me why the Bear, why now."

"You know his identity."

"I believe we do. No, in fact, I'm certain we know. My actor partner and I have teamed up with a web sleuth who's been researching the case for years. You know, like that book that just came out about the Golden State Killer?"

"*I'll Be Gone in the Dark.* Michelle McNamara."

The smile again. "You are a true crime fan, after all."

"I read all kinds of things. But yeah...who am I kidding. I'm a woman of a certain age so of course I'm all about murders."

"So as a fellow true crime fan and obsessive, I will share this much...just between you and me. We not only have his identity, *but the California Bear himself* is cooperating with the project."

"You're kidding," Jeanie said, even though this was not exactly a shocking exclusive. The Deadline piece she'd dug up this morning broke the same news.

But Peterson hammed it up anyway, pulling a pretend zipper across his mouth and raising his eyes to heaven as if playfully asking God's forgiveness.

"Is the Bear going to take you around on a tour of his crimes?"

The producer's eyes almost popped out of his head with excitement. "*Even better.* We're taking the idea of a true crime reenactment to the next level. It's something nobody has ever done before."

"You're going to have him kill more people."

Oh, did that make Peterson howl in delight. "No...because that would be wrong. But it's something along those lines. Most documentaries can only hint at the mind of a psychopath. We've found a way — and a visionary director — who can offer more than a hint."

"Sounds pretty exciting."

"Oh, it is. I hope you'll watch."

"But...let me ask you something. Isn't your project guilty of withholding evidence of a crime? I mean, that technically makes you and your actor friend accessories."

"Quite the contrary. We're helping bring a killer to justice."

"While also making a tidy profit," Jeanie said.

Peterson took that arrow with grace. She was sure he had grown used to fielding that question throughout his career. Hollywood types loved to talk about the social issues, the artistic intent. But often it came down to a simple question: *Will this project buy me a second Lamborghini?*

"Art isn't free," he said by rote. "There's a reason it's called the entertainment *business.*"

"I suppose."

"Besides, we're going to be telling the victims' stories. That's going to be very important to the survivors and the families of those we lost. They'll finally have something like closure."

Once you lock down the life rights, Jeanie thought.

"So this Bear of yours is going to confess?"

"Well...you'll have to watch the series." Again, with the cherubic innocent look.

Jeanie struggled to play it cool, but inside she was screaming. Of course Cato would try to blackmail a man for a crime that he was perfectly willing to confess to...for the right price, naturally. She was sure the California Bear, whoever he was, wasn't doing it out of the goodness of his heart. Maybe he was terminally ill and saw this deal as a way to provide for his family. Maybe he was terminally ill and wanted a taste of infamy before he croaked. Maybe he was terminally ill and still mentally ill and figured, *Fuck it. Let me just tell my story.*

But she *had* to know if Cato had stumbled on the real thing or just another suspect.

"What if," Jeanie said, "I just run a first name and middle initial by you."

"One nod for yes, two for no? Is that it?"

"Something like that."

Peterson thought it over. Or at least pretended to. This, of course, was Jeanie opening her kimono first. What did he have to lose?

"Go ahead."

"Christopher A.," she said softly.

Peterson smiled, shook his head, and then shooed away a seagull. "Ah, see, I had prepared myself to be impressed. Gobsmacked by the wonders of forensic genealogy, even! But no."

"Are you sure? What about an initial for the last name...which is *D?*"

Peterson shook his head, which Jeanie supposed was two for *no.* "Let's put it this way. Your client is poking around in the wrong den."

THE GIRL DETECTIVE

She emerged from a restless, painkiller-induced sleep, but the first thing she saw was the giant pink box on her overbed table. And that filled her with delight. The pink box meant doughnuts were here, but more importantly, so was her father.

Where was the old man, anyway?

Ah—there he was, on the guest couch / pullout bed by the window. He was sprawled out and asleep. Tough day at the office, she supposed. She'd have to ask him about that when he woke up.

There was only one box, which meant her padre had the good sense to drop the other box off at the nurses' station. Those dozen doughy treats would buy an awful lot of goodwill. The Girl Detective used an index finger to gently lift the lid and reveled in the sugary glory within...

But her joy was short-lived, because her hospital room door opened and in walked a small gaggle of health care professionals, including her oncologist. All wore stern expressions. Which was never a good thing, especially on a Saturday night.

"Dad," she said.

The appearance of bodies stirred her father from his slumber. He didn't wake up so much as jolt back into this reality, as if a half dozen armed gunmen had stormed into the room.

"What's going on? Matilda—are you okay?"

"It's okay, Dad. It's just the doctor."

"What's wrong?"

After the startled hospital staff managed to calm him down, they asked to speak with him in private. The Girl Detective prepared to object, but her father, God bless 'im, saved her the trouble.

"Whatever you tell me," he said, "my daughter can hear directly."

The staff exchanged glances, as if wondering if this was okay, and if so, who would give final approval. After they shared the news, the Girl Detective realized that yeah, maybe her father should have heard it first, so he could retell it to her in a kinder way. Doctors could be so blunt with matters of life and death.

And this was such a matter. Further genetic testing had revealed that the Girl Detective was fighting an even more formidable opponent. If leukemia was an archvillain, then she was currently wrestling over the Reichenbach Falls with the cancer version of Dr. Moriarty.

Her leukemia was not just AML, but a variant called monosomy 7. That meant she wouldn't survive without a bone marrow transplant.

SUNDAY, JUNE 3, 2018

GENE JEANIE

Come on, Cato, pick up your damn phone. This is lousy, even for you.

No word from him in twenty-four hours. This was not a record by any stretch. The man enjoyed his benders and occasionally had the good sense to sleep it off in a Motel 6 somewhere. But this stretch of silence was disturbing, considering that the last time she heard her husband's voice, he was headed off with an ex-con to blackmail a possible (but unlikely, if David the producer was telling the truth) serial killer. If something had happened . . . okay, fine, let's say it went completely wrong. What was the worst-case scenario here?

The worst-case scenario would be that Dixon *was* the Bear, and he didn't respond well to the blackmail threat. The result would be Cato and the ex-con dead, their bodies hidden, with no resolution, no answers, forever.

Stop it, Jeanie. Let's not go there just yet.

Even if Christopher Albin Dixon wasn't the California Bear, he could be just an annoyed former cop who didn't take kindly to crazy accusations on a Saturday morning. Threats could have been issued. Punches thrown. Arrests made. But if Cato was in jail, wouldn't he call her? If only to arrange bail, if nothing else?

What the fuck was going on?

After her disappointing meeting with David, Jeanie had decided enough was enough. She called her ex-husband, Bob, and said she had an important favor to ask. He laughed as if it were the most absurd thing ever. *Really now.* Which pissed her off, but now was not the time for a fight. She tried to convince him that this was serious. That some maniac had broken into her house and left cum all over her underwear drawer and...

"What did you say?"

"You heard me. And I think it's someone you guys have been hunting for a long time."

"Who would that be?"

"The California Bear."

Her ex sighed. "You think the California Bear, a serial killer who hasn't been seen in close to forty years, jacked off onto your panties? What have you been reading lately?"

She ignored the crack. "Does the name Christopher Albin Dixon mean anything to you?"

"Former LAPD, but I don't know him. Why? Wait...do you think he's the Bear? Is that what you're asking me?"

"Never mind. Forget that I asked."

"I'm sorry," he said. "I just don't know what you want from me."

"Can you run the sample for me or not?"

There was a long silence before Bob cleared his throat and said, "Okay, if it's important to you, I'm sure there's something I can do."

"Thank you."

"What if it comes back with a match to your husband?"

Now, that was a clever trap. There was no way to respond to that question without it being a dig at Cato — the two hated each other with the passion of a centuries-old blood feud.

"Then that's a conversation I'll have at some point."

Bob laughed. "'Pardon me, dear, the next time, could you just use a Kleenex?'"

Jeanie ignored that completely. "How do I get it to you?"

"Drop it same-day delivery and I'll get it to the lab this evening. But I'm sorry. That was funny, right?"

"Thank you, Bob. I appreciate it."

"Yeah, well . . . what are exes for?"

The conversation had devolved from there. They ended the conversation like they always did during the twilight of their relationship: awkwardly.

There had been no word from Cato all night long.

Now it was six in the morning and Jeanie was wondering if she should pour herself a mimosa to keep her anxiety in check. That was a socially acceptable brunch selection, right? And this was Sunday, after all. For all she knew, her husband was sleeping off a hangover right now.

But what if he wasn't?

Jeanie realized she didn't know how to contact the ex-con or his family. His daughter, Matilda, was a patient at Children's Hospital Los Angeles, but she didn't want to bother a poor girl in middle of a chemo regimen. Things weren't that desperate . . . yet. But even more reason to acknowledge that Cato was being a serious asshole right now. He had to know she'd be worried sick, despite all the awfulness of late.

She resisted the urge to drown her worry in an orange juice and semi-cheap bottle of champagne and thought about her options. Until the semen sample came back (pardon the awful pun), there really wasn't much she could do.

Around eleven her cell phone sounded. It was her ex-husband, Bob, again.

"Hey, Jeanie. Are you watching the news by chance?"

"No, I'm at my computer. Why? What's going on?"

"You remember you were asking me about the California Bear yesterday? Like, completely out of the blue?"

Of course she remembered. Please God, no. Not the worst-case scenario.

"Well, check out KTLA."

"KILLER"

Hospital shift change at seven meant that Jack's brain roused him from his semiconscious state at precisely 6:50 a.m. He told his brain to do this; it was a skill he'd picked up in prison to avoid surprises. This morning, he wanted to make sure he was fully conscious when the nurses entered the room, because they usually brought with them the battle plan for the day.

Matilda appeared to be asleep, which was a good thing. It had been a long night of restlessness for both of them.

Jack shuffled down to the visitors' bathroom on the oncology floor and washed his face, hands, and forearms with water as hot and soapy as he could stand. Then he remembered he didn't brush his teeth. He did so with toiletries found in the gift shop, then repeated the washing process and looked at himself in the mirror. The bruise across his face was now quite prominent and would probably encourage questions. He'd already come up with the lie that he'd bumped into something in the unfamiliar hospital room. Matilda knew better, of course, and probably wouldn't let it go until he told her the truth. *Oh, it's nothing, I just smacked my face on a serial killer's coffee table.*

He managed to return to the room before the nurses appeared. Matilda was still out. He borrowed her iPad and found a web browser that led him to the online version of the *LA Times.* Jack found nothing there, but a quick search revealed a link to a KTLA news report labeled BREAKING—and detailing the puzzling death of one Christopher Albin Dixon, former detective with the Los Angeles Police Department.

Using his finger, Jack raised the volume so that he could hear the reporter without waking Matilda. Seemed the retired detective was found dead in his backyard shack. The official cause of death had not yet been released, but his widow was already claiming foul play. Only Jack and Hightower knew the truth: death by misadventure...and doughnuts.

Two men had been harassing my husband for days, a very stern Mrs. Cassandra Dixon told the reporter. In real life, she had looked wild and feral, but apparently she'd locked down her emotions for the camera. *And I have reason to believe they are the ones responsible for his death.*

Why do you believe that? asked the earnest reporter, who looked like he'd just graduated the year before.

Let's just say the scene of my husband's death made no sense, the Bear's widow said, *and the Homicide Department is actively investigating whoever did this.*

"That doesn't sound good," Matilda said, startling Jack, who quickly closed the window. He handed the iPad back to his daughter.

"I'm sorry," he said. "I didn't mean to wake you up."

"I wasn't really asleep," Matilda said. "I figure if I fake it long enough, my brain will think it's actually happening and will just go along with it."

"Yeah. Same here."

"So that was Mrs. California Bear on the news just now?"

"Hey. You're not supposed to know about that!"

"Dad. Please. You thought I wouldn't put it together? Tell your old pal Hightower he probably sucks at poker. That 'bear-hunting' crack was a little too on the nose."

"You figured out his plan from that one stupid joke?"

Matilda rolled her eyes as if that didn't even merit explanation. "And I'm guessing the people who were 'harassing' Mrs. Bear's husband were the two of you? Which would explain the bruise on your face and the state of your only suit."

"You're amazing." And Jack meant it. Nobody he knew had an intuitive brain like Matilda's. She'd been this way since birth, practically. For instance, she figured out the truth about the tooth fairy long before the blood had completely dried from the first lost incisor.

"I can keep a secret," Matilda said. "But tell me about this 'scene of my husband's death' making no sense. Did you accidentally leave clues behind?"

"Well, not exactly."

"That does . . . *not exactly* . . . put my mind at ease, Padre. Tell me what you two left behind and spare no details."

"Something we couldn't take with us, because at the time, it didn't seem to matter much. And we ultimately figured removing this . . . *something* . . . would only raise more questions."

"You can keep tap-dancing around this mysterious something, or you could save us both a lot of time by just straight up telling me."

Jack knew she was right. Why was he being so weird about this? Maybe it was his lingering desire to shield her from any part of this fiasco. The less she knew, the more it couldn't hurt her. But Matilda was not one to let things go, especially when they sparked her curiosity.

"The remnants of two boxes of doughnuts," Jack said.

"You left two boxes of doughnuts at the crime scene? Like, for the lolz?" For a second, Matilda's face twisted up in confusion. It only took her another second to put it together. "Oh my God. You carried my doughnuts into a serial killer's house?"

"This is why I didn't want to tell you," Jack said. "In fact, I didn't want to go to the house at all. I thought by picking up the doughnuts first, Hightower would drive me straight here, but as it turned out . . ."

"No, I understand your rationale. And I appreciate being at the top of your to-do list for the day, even if the second item on your list happened to be Extort a Notorious Rapist-Murderer from the 1980s. What I don't get is, why did you bring the doughnuts inside the house when you went to talk to him?"

"I didn't."

"So how did they end up at the crime scene?"

Jack sighed. "The Bear found them in the car and brought them to his garage. And then he started eating them."

"Interesting," Matilda said. "A picture is being painted. Go on."

"And to be honest... well, the stupid doughnuts saved our lives, because as it turns out the Bear was not doing too well, health-wise, and eating a bunch of them kind of gave him a massive heart attack."

"Well, I suppose dragging in a beehive would have been too cliche," Matilda said. "And now I see why the Widow Bear would be suspicious, seeing that her husband was not supposed to eat a single doughnut, let alone twenty-four."

"I think he had, like, *four* of them before he keeled over. I don't know. I didn't count the leftovers."

Matilda processed these new details quickly. "Okay, this could be serious trouble."

"What do you mean? I told you, he's dead. I felt him for a pulse. He's not coming back."

"Never mind that for now. Where did you buy the doughnuts? And does the Bear family have two cars, or only one?"

"One? Maybe? I have no idea. Why does this matter?"

"Because, Father," she said, "if they have one car, and the Widow Bear was using it at the time, then the sneaky Killer Bear would have had to walk for his two boxes of doughnuts. If you purchased them somewhere out of a plausible walking distance, considering the Bear himself was an older fella..."

"Then they'll know someone else was in the garage," Jack said, finally understanding.

"I'm guessing you bought them somewhere between Port Hueneme and Studio City?"

"Some random place near the 405. Technically he could have walked there..."

"But you know the LAPD will be all over that doughnut shop. And not for the obvious cliché reasons."

"Do you think they can link me to the shop?"

"You probably used cash instead of a credit card, since you're fresh out of the slammer. Which means it comes down to the server and if they remember you enough to make a positive ID."

Jack's mind was spinning. He hadn't considered any of this, but the way Matilda put it together with such ease...made him feel like the world's most incompetent would-be extortionist and killer.

"I think her name was Jenn McG," Jack said, almost muttering to himself. "With two *n*'s. I remember that on her name tag. The two *n*'s bothered me."

"If you remember her, there's a good chance *she* remembers *you*. But that's not what worries me the most right now. The Widow Bear mentioned two guys harassing her poor old serial killer husband. Now, you and I know there were two guys there..."

"But how could *she* possibly know that?" Jack said, getting it. "She only saw me. Shit!"

"You said that someone trashed the old cop's house in Port Hueneme. Maybe it was the Bear. Maybe he had help from his wife. Or maybe someone else entirely. In short: it's very likely the Bear had friends helping him out. At least one."

"Shit. Shit, shit, shit."

"Hush now, Father. The nurses could be walking in any second now, and excessive cursing is a sign of low character. Here's the funny part, though."

"There's a funny part?"

"Oh yes, there is a funny part. And you're going to love this. Because do you know what a group of bears is called?"

"Not...a group of bears?"

"No, I mean the collective name. Like a *colony* of ants. Or a *murder* of crows."

"Oh, right — like a flock of seagulls?"

"That's not the official term. I believe it's a *scavenging* of seagulls. But I'll let you have that one."

"Okay, okay, I give up. What's a group of bears called?"

Matilda smiled. "A *sleuth*."

THE GIRL DETECTIVE

My to-do list, thought the Girl Detective, *is wildly out of control.*

At the top of that list were her physical needs. These needs interested her the least, but she was forced to embrace the irrefutable truth: without a functional body, there could be no detecting. Which meant preparing for her third round of chemo later today. To do that, however, she needed more platelets. Fortunately, yet another donor had come through for her and the nurses had plugged her into yet another bag of chunky urine. The Girl Detective wished she'd called it something else when joking with her father a few days ago, because the very sight of it now makes her . . .

Ah yes, violently ill. The expected yet horrific side effect of chemotherapy. They pump her full of meds to take the edge off the nausea. Unfortunately, that also takes the edge off the Girl Detective, who succumbs to fits of childlike . . . well, goofiness.

Even her dad noticed. "Wow, I haven't seen you this silly since you were four years old."

"But when I was four," the Girl Detective said, "did I do this?"

At which point she gave her father the double middle-finger salute, pulse oximeter dangling from her left index finger.

"No," her father said. "No, you did not do that." But at least he finally smiled, which was nice to see.

Second item on her to-do list, and almost as important, was detailing the world of the California Bear, and if he indeed had a *sleuth* or not.

The Widow Bear was an interesting complication, begging the huge question: Did she know? Or was she completely oblivious to her husband's bloody past?

A quick search of "Cassandra Dixon" revealed practically nothing, which was suspicious. Or maybe not. The Girl Detective had an acquaintance back in school whose father was a patrolman with the Burbank Police Department. She had been forbidden to have any kind of social media profile, namely because her parents paid a lot of money to scrub their personal details from the Internet. This was standard practice with cops — the last thing you wanted was some criminal you'd arrested coming after your kids in school or your spouse when they were visiting their favorite restaurant. An ex-cop like the Bear — hell, especially the Bear! — would have likely scrubbed his personal deets from the interwebs too.

But the Girl Detective had more tricks up her sleeve than a quick Google search. She would have to explore that once the nausea had passed.

Third item on her to-do list, of course, was the continuing investigation into the (possible) crimes of her father. But this was practically impossible with him in the room. She'd have to send the old man on missions to the cafeteria, or . . . ooh! Better yet, out there in the big, bad city, just to give her some time to do more research.

Better to focus on the first two items for now. Because truth be told, if the whole California Bear situation blew up, the third item wouldn't matter at all.

THE BEAR

The serial killer who used to be the California Bear says nothing, does nothing, because the California Bear is dead.

Christopher Albin Dixon's body rests on a slab in the back of the Angeleno Valley Mortuary. The last set of clothes he wore is folded inside a plastic bag. No one will ever wear them again. His wife won't want them; they'll be thrown away by the end of the week.

This is not a slasher movie. Christopher Albin Dixon will not magically reanimate the moment a young blonde steps into the room and reach for his mask and glove. Dixon's body would be physically incapable, even if his spirit was still lingering on this plane of existence and willing to do so.

Dixon's corpse will soon be wheeled out into another room for a final viewing before cremation. Nobody knows about this except his wife, and she won't be visiting. Cassandra Dixon doesn't believe in the afterlife, only this one. Visiting the meat puppet that was once animated by her husband's brain activity would make as much sense as visiting a dustbin full of his hair, or a pile of his nail clippings. He's gone; there is nothing that can change that now. The rest is just a series of formalities, required by the laws of the state of California.

Except that's not entirely true.

In truth, people die three times.

Once, when their bodies stop functioning — when the heart gives up its ceaseless pumping, the blood no longer circulates through arteries and veins, and the last neurons flicker and fade.

Then they die again when their bodies are buried or cremated.

And finally: they die the last time someone speaks their name.

MONDAY-WEDNESDAY, JUNE 4-6, 2018

THE GIRL DETECTIVE

A sleuth of bears.

The collective name for the species known as Ursidae still greatly amused the Girl Detective.

She dove deep into the postings (and ramblings) of Bear lore on Reddit. But her fever was getting the best of her, making the words swim and the meanings elusive. Apparently, this was normal with chemo. Fevers spike, fevers drop, repeat endlessly, forever (or at least as long as chemo lasts). Nurses fuss; nurses relax. Nurses tell you to be careful; nurses tell you this is all completely normal. This phase of chemotherapy also happens to be the time when she's isolated the most. Aside from her dad and Aunt Reese (and okay, maybe Uncle Louis) no one else is allowed in her room as she's shot up with radioactive fluids in an attempt to kill the thing that's actively trying to kill her.

Oh, and also: destroy her hair.

The Girl Detective was no dummy; she knew this was a very strong possibility. But knowing it is not the same as hearing the doctor and nurses say it — *you are definitely going to lose your hair.* She could feel it thinning already.

Oh, and Tuesday (day five of chemo) brought another delightful complication: the need for matched platelets. This doesn't happen to every patient, but for some, the platelet donor must have the *exact same blood type* as the recipient. Otherwise, a painful and bright and itchy rash breaks out. Which makes resting super difficult, if not impossible. Why did her body hate her so much? Hadn't she been decent to it all of her fourteen years?

Finding the kind souls willing to donate platelets at all—a much more time-consuming process than an ordinary blood donation—was difficult. Now try to find the same kind souls who happened to have an O positive blood type and...well, those weren't odds that would thrill anyone.

Try solving a mystery when your skin is on fire, you're vomiting all the time, your internal battery feels like it's hovering at 5 percent, and your overheated brain decides to nuke itself every once in a while, giving you the sweats.

But strangely, her focus on solving the mystery was the only thing that kept her in this world.

On Wednesday they had a funeral service for the Bear. Or at least, the man they all assumed was the California Bear.

There wasn't much coverage online, to the Girl Detective's disappointment. If she were not stuck in this medical prison, she'd be out there in her thrift-store dress, blending in with the mourners, chatting people up, gathering clues. For a moment she thought about enlisting her best friend, Violet, to be there as her avatar. But that wasn't Violet's strong suit, the chatting up of strangers. (The Girl Detective wasn't even sure that was *her* strong suit, but she thought she could fake it.)

Sending her father would be a really bad idea—cops routinely checked out wakes and funerals for possible suspects.

But damn, this chapped her ass. (Even more than the platelet rash.) She knew that if the California Bear had a *sleuth,* they'd all be gathered graveside. Mourning him. But quite possibly also plotting some kind of retaliation. Maybe they wouldn't do that while standing around the urn. But the Girl Detective knew at some point, the Bear's sleuth would gather around a table somewhere, martinis in hand, and talk the business of revenge.

A real detective like Holmes or Poirot or Philo Vance would find a way to be at that post-service restaurant, perhaps disguised as a server, to eavesdrop. The Girl Detective even had a caper in mind, inspired by her parents taking her to the Smoke House in Burbank for their first holiday dinner in California. You see, there was a girl who went around taking photos of the guests, selling a modest package of prints for a reasonable price. This struck her as a brilliant opportunity. If the Girl Detective ever had a reason to investigate someone dining at the Smoke House, she'd pose as the photo girl to not only listen in but also take a handy series of surveillance shots.

Instead, she was chained to this stupid hospital bed.

"KILLER"

Jack wasn't a praying man, but now he prayed to God — begged whatever higher power might be out there — to allow him to trade places with his daughter. He had never felt quite *this* helpless, completely unable to make any of this better. He thought losing his wife, Matilda's mother, was the worst thing that could ever happen to him. Jack remembered taunting the higher power: *That's it? That's the worst you can do to me? Well, fuck you.*

Note to self: never taunt a higher power.

The next three days blurred into one another, punctuated not by dawn and dusk so much as by the twelve-hour shift changes at Children's Hospital. He spent as much time with Matilda as possible, only taking breaks to head back his sister-in-law's place to shower and change (in Matilda's room), avoiding Louis.

He managed to retrieve some of his own clothes from the storage locker he'd rented before heading off to prison. Everything felt big on him and was a bitter reminder of the past. Every shirt had an association with the life he used to live. *Oh yeah — wore that button-down when I had a gig at the Hotel Café down on Cahuenga. And here are the pants I used to wear to auditions — my lucky pants.* At least none of them had giant gashes in them. But it all felt like wearing someone else's skin. Was it bad luck to wear a dead man's clothing?

When Jack wasn't paying careful attention to the pediatricians and nurses and oncologists and infectious disease specialists who paraded in and out of Matilda's room, he obsessed over money. How could he possibly support them through this ordeal? Jack had pretty much liquidated his savings while retaining the services of his defense lawyer. All he had left was an assortment of musical gear (two keyboards, amplifiers, microphones, stands) in the storage locker. If—and that was a *big* if—he could sell it all, that would keep the wolves at bay for a couple of weeks at least. Staying at his sister-in-law's was a temporary solution at best. He needed a way to make rent, even for a one-bedroom (Jack would happily take the couch...once he bought one).

Somehow making this worse was the phantom payment from the state of California, hovering out in the distance, like the bunch of lush grapes and cool water Tantalus kept reaching for. If Jack had a check in his hand today, his worries would cease. But as the lawyer handling the case explained, it would be shocking if he saw any kind of settlement before the end of the year. Most likely, it would take a year or more before they had cash in hand. (Speaking of, Jack owed that lawyer payments too.)

Maybe a loan could help, but against what? Jack didn't have a job and had no idea what he might be qualified to do. Ever since high school he'd made his living with music—live gigs, session work, teaching. Somehow, he'd made it work. The idea of touching a piano keyboard again, however, made him tremble with anxiety. Even if he'd wanted to perform again, he wasn't even sure his fingers would remember what to do.

There were still some local club owners who were friendly to him. If he couldn't perform, maybe he could bartend. Or if his stint in prison made that a no-go, he'd even work as a barback or clean up after hours. That kind of salary, however, wouldn't do much to pay for rent, even in the most modest of LA dwellings.

Jack felt like he was falling down an elevator shaft, his limbs wriggling, useless, trying to reach out to anything to break his fall. The only object in sight was the elevator car, rushing up the shaft to splatter him on its roof.

"Hey, Padre."

"Yeah, sweetie?"

This was Wednesday morning, a few hours before shift change.

"Did you know the Bear only wore the mask and the clawed glove for his last three home invasions? I thought he wore them all the time, since the very first attack."

"I didn't know that. Have you been up all night reading that stuff?"

"It's sort of like Jason in those Friday the 13th movies," she said, ignoring his question. "He didn't put on the hockey mask until, like, halfway through the third movie, when he stole it from one of his murder victims. Yet, that's what everybody knows about him. The hockey mask, the machete, the *ki ki ki, ma ma ma.*"

"Have you watched those movies?" Jack asked, with no small amount of horror.

"Uncle Louis has them all. I spun through the best of them, which, for the record, includes part 2, part 4, as well as parts 6 and 7."

"Did they let you watch pretty much anything?"

"Why wouldn't they?"

"Some movies may have been a bit too much for someone your age. Or younger."

"As if I don't know how to gauge my own sensitivity and triggers to certain content? Please, Father."

"Fair enough."

Then later that afternoon:

"They're having a memorial service for him."

"For who?"

"The Bear," Matilda said.

"Oh."

"Now, I'm not saying you should go," she continued, "because that would be the most rookie mistake ever. But do you know anyone who might be able to attend? You know, scope it out a little?"

"Scope it out for what?"

"To see the Widow Bear and any possible accomplices? Better we know what's coming at us ahead of time."

"No one's coming for us."

"Not yet. I have a feeling this isn't over."

Jack was beyond frustrated that he didn't know how to put this toothpaste back in the tube. Once something caught Matilda's imagination, there was no distracting her from it. But this, of all things! This wasn't something she should even *know* about, let alone stay up all night reading about and obsessing over. Jack realized he was really stretching it with the higher power and all, but he wished he could go back in time and smack Hightower across the nose with a rolled-up newspaper the moment he first said the words "California Bear."

GENE JEANIE

At what point do you call the cops about your wayward ex-cop husband?

In addition to his benders, Cato had gone off on long marriage "sabbaticals" before. Usually they were mutually agreed-upon and meant that Jeanie had the house to herself while Cato went off to some cheap hotel near a beloved dive bar to get his head together. Jeanie actually looked forward to those breaks. A kind of peace would settle over Jeanie, and she'd start to think that maybe she'd be fine without a partner.

The most recent sabbatical, however, had been the longest in their marriage. It started when Cato insisted on bringing home a stray ex-con to live in their house for a while. A few days, at the very least. Possibly a few weeks, maybe a month. Jeanie had stated her opinion clearly: *No fucking way.*

But he's a good guy! A musician!
I don't care if he's the West Memphis Three, you're not bringing
    a stranger into our home without us having a serious
    conversation.
Who pays the rent around here, anyway?
I do! Or did you forget?
I mean until recently! Don't I get credit for floating your ass until
    you figured out what you wanted to do with your life?
You're such an asshole.
Oh, I'm the asshole? You're the one who wants to make a single father
    homeless on his first days out of prison.

Now that Jeanie had met the ex-con, she knew Cato had been right. Jack Queen *wasn't* a bad guy, as far as she could tell. In fact, Jeanie kind of liked him. But that didn't matter. What mattered was Cato's stubborn insistence on having it his way, and that her own safety (and boundaries) didn't seem to matter much. This time around, Jeanie started to think that maybe this was it — perhaps a terminal line had been crossed. Maybe their marriage had a twenty-year expiration date attached to it, and the relationship was coming to its natural conclusion. Just like it had with Bob (who, to his credit, was arranging for the analysis of a semen sample found in his ex-wife's underwear drawer). But still, this was another failed attempt at the life she'd always wanted.

Late Monday morning Jeanie thought about pouring herself a gin and tonic but instead walked onto her front porch for some fresh air. She needed a clear head.

Stepping outside was not as peaceful as Jeanie imagined. Across the street there was a parked car she didn't recognize. This kind of neighborhood, this kind of block? You got to know the cars pretty well — who belonged here and who didn't. This one didn't.

And the person behind the wheel was staring in Jeanie's direction.

The face was difficult to make out since the driver's-side window was fogged up. Jeanie couldn't really see the eyes of her observer so much as *feel* them. Once the observer realized he was being watched in return, he turned on the ignition and peeled out of the spot. All Jeanie caught was the make and model of the car (a black Audi) and a partial license plate (4HK something something something).

Could it be the same person who'd broken into their house a few days ago? Were they back for something else, or were they waiting for Cato to return?

Was this some unfinished business with the dearly departed California Bear?

Back inside, Jeanie did her usual round of checking and securing all doors and windows, just in case. She turned their alarm system to "at home" mode, which was something she probably should have on all the time anyway.

And then she poured herself that G and T. A double, with an extra wedge of lime.

Are you doing the same somewhere out there, my dear husband? Having a little prenoon drink (or five) to wash away the memories of whatever you did to that retired rapist-murderer?

When Jeanie watched the news on Sunday, she knew Cato was most likely okay... physically speaking. There had been some kind of confrontation, and Christopher Albin Dixon (aka the Bear) had died in the struggle. The official report was diabetic shock, and maybe that had been the case. Jeanie didn't think her husband was capable of murder, let alone a clever murder disguised as a blood sugar problem.

But Cassandra Dixon, the widow, was not shy about telling reporters she suspected foul play. And not at the hands of *one* killer, but two. Such as... Cato and his ex-con friend.

If this were true, her husband might have panicked and fled to Mexico. (Jeanie checked: his passport was still tucked in their fireproof box of important documents, as was their marriage certificate.) So, no Mexico.

Where, then? Jeanie knew Cato opted for beach towns whenever he could. The man liked to stick close to the ocean, which was the whole reason they lived in fucking Port Hueneme. (It was the only beach town they could sort of afford.) Was he down in Venice? Hermosa? Long Beach? Further south in Orange County? Was he not responding to her calls and texts because he believed they were being monitored?

She spent the remainder of her Monday drinking, sobering up enough to make dinner and do a little more research into the California Bear and his blushing bride, then leaving her husband an angry voicemail before passing out. Before all that, however, she mailed her soiled panties to her ex (boy, the look on his face when he opened that same-day delivery envelope) with a little note: "Please. It's important."

Tuesday morning the black Audi was back—parked just down the street in a different location, but still within viewing distance of the Hightowers' home through the windshield.

This time Jeanie was able to capture the entire license plate. She accomplished this by cutting through her own backyard, then through a series of neighbors' yards, before approaching the Audi from the rear and snapping a photo with her cell phone.

The driver spotted her, but too late to do anything about it. Her silent observer again peeled away, almost fishtailing down the street before hanging a violent right turn. *Yeah, go and run, asshole. I'll know who you are soon enough.*

Jeanie texted the photo of the license plate to her ex-husband, who responded within minutes. Apparently, license plates were easier than semen samples.

Instead of a text, however, Jeanie received an urgent phone call.

"Hey, it's me — that license plate you sent me? It's a cop."

"Local?"

"No. LA."

"Interesting," Jeanie replied. "Are you at liberty to tell me why a member of the LAPD might be parked in front of my house in Port Hueneme?"

"Jean, come on. You know I shouldn't even be telling you this much. I just wanted to put your mind at ease it wasn't splooging burglars again."

"Well, you've done a marvelous job of putting my mind at ease."

"Hey, don't take it out on me. Talk to your idiot husband. I'm sure it has something to do with him."

"I would if I could, but...never mind. Any luck with that...uh, sample?"

"I'm hoping to *come* back at you with an update soon."

"Okay."

"Did you see what I did there?"

"I did, Bob. Thank you."

Her ex-husband made a sad little chuckle on the other end of the call.

"Something wrong?" Jeanie asked.

"No...I guess I'll just never get used to hearing you use my actual name. Still feels weird after all this time."

Jeanie understood what he meant. When they were first married, all young and stupid, they used pet names with each other all the time. Using each other's actual name meant something was very wrong. By the end of their relatively brief marriage, they were using neither pet names nor actual names, instead opting for dismissive insults like *you selfish asshole* and *you castrating bitch*. As time went on and wounds healed, they found their way back to their own names, right where they started.

"Well, I appreciate it."

"Gotta run, Jean. Stay safe, okay?"

Jeanie's version of staying safe was locking herself back inside her home, turning on the security system, and drinking her dinner. At least this time she did not leave Cato a rambling angry voicemail.

Which may have done the trick, because early Wednesday morning he called her, slurring, from either exhaustion or booze. Most likely both.

"You fucking asshole," she said. "Where are you?"

Granted, this wasn't the most loving of greetings. But it had been four days with no word, and Jeanie realized she was very hungover.

"I'm fine," Cato said. "I'm only calling because I was worried about you."

"Worried about *me*? Why?"

"Well, when I didn't hear from you yesterday, I was worried something was up."

Jeanie imagined metal bolts sealing her mouth shut; otherwise she'd blurt out something incredibly mean. With a man like Cato Hightower, it wasn't worth picking apart the contradictions of any of his (frequently asinine) statements. You simply had to accept them for what they were: products of an emotionally stunted and profoundly broken mind.

"I was busy," Jeanie said. "And you?"

Cato exhaled in relief, as if he had been longing for someone to ask him this very question. "I'll be okay, I promise. I just needed some time to heal and get my mind together."

"Heal? From what? Were you hurt?"

"Jack didn't tell you?"

"Why would Jack tell me anything? I've been waiting for you to call me since Saturday."

"Oh...oh, honey, I'm sorry. I thought Jack would have reached out to you and let you know what was going on. He knew I was in no condition to talk to anyone for a while."

"I think," Jeanie said, trying to keep her tongue in check without resorting to the metal mouth bolts, "that Mr. Queen has enough going on in his life without having to worry about you and me."

"Yeah, I guess that makes sense. Did you happen to hear the news?"

"I've been following it, yes."

"Well, then you know that things didn't quite turn out the way I'd planned. But I think the worst is over, so maybe I'll be back in a day or two—"

"No."

"No?"

"That would be a very bad idea."

"Why?"

"We shouldn't talk about it right now."

"Why not?"

Jesus, Cato, read between the lines. "I'd rather have this conversation in person."

"Oh. Okay, if that's what you want. Maybe then you can come to me. I'm down at the—"

Jeanie cut him off. "Nope. Don't tell me."

"If I don't tell you where I am, how will you know where to go?"

"Tell me without telling me."

"You're confusing the living shit out of me right now, honey." Cato's words were slurred slightly, which meant he either woke up and had a breakfast cocktail or this was the cumulative effect of drinking through the night.

"Considering everything in our lives," Jeanie said slowly, "it might not be a smart idea to discuss very personal topics over a cell phone, which have been known to be easily tapped by law enforcement agencies."

"Oh fuck. Oh . . . oh fuck!"

Praise the Lord, the light of reason finally penetrated the man's thick, bony skull.

"So if you can tell me without telling me," Jeanie said, "great. Otherwise, we'll figure out another way."

"Okay. I'm, uh . . . you know that place with all the weird animals?"

"You've just described half of Los Angeles County."

"No, I mean that specific place. The one with the huge-ass brunch with all the omelets? And the . . . you know, the stuff on the roof? And where everything is green? I don't know how else to say it."

Cato was horrible at charades, and Jeanie was sure that trying to paint a mental picture without resorting to specifics was breaking her husband's brain. Fortunately, she was an excellent detective. Putting together a full story out of the thinnest of clues is what she did for a living.

"I know where you mean," she said. And she did. Patrick's Roadhouse, on the PCH on the outer fringes of Santa Monica. They'd had brunch there a lifetime ago. But Cato couldn't stop talking about the portions and the price, which were a mark of quality in his book.

"When are you coming down?"

"When I do," Jeanie said, then ended the call. If Cato could leave her hanging for days on end, then he could deal with a little uncertainty too.

THURSDAY, JUNE 7, 2018

THE BEAR

The memorial service had been small but tasteful.

Remains had been rendered to ash, as requested. Dixon, in preparing his will, hadn't wanted any fanboys digging up his frail old body someday and using his skull as an ashtray or some such macabre goth nonsense. He knew about the sad tale of outlaw Elmer McCurdy. At one time Elmer had been a feared desperado—a successful bank and train robber who'd been cut down in a shootout with the police. And perhaps his legend would have died right there. Except an enterprising mortician tried an experimental embalming technique on ol' Elmer, which had the strange result of turning him into a twentieth-century mummy. Elmer's corpse toured America in carnivals and freak shows, changing hands a few times along the way before ending up, strange as it may sound, inside a spook house in Long Beach, California. Along the way, people forgot Elmer had been a flesh-and-blood person. It was only after a worker accidentally broke one of Elmer's arms, revealing a jagged human bone beneath the "plaster," that people realized what had happened.

So, no, the Bear did not want to share Elmer's fate. Cremation it would be.

After a few days, the Bear's widow would be able to pick up his ashes. To her mind, there was no rush. And that's where the mortal remains of the California Bear were this morning: on a shelf at the mortuary.

Two conditions of permanent death had been met.

However, not the third.

Plenty of human beings still had the California Bear on their minds. And in that sense, the Bear still lived.

But the Bear was alive in yet another way, a specific tangible way that almost no one else knew about. His flesh and blood was prowling the streets of Hollywood. In fact, right now he was watching a house — a single home on Rodney Drive in Los Feliz. He could see the woman inside.

Look at her. Pacing around her living room, cell phone to her ear, curtains wide open, not caring who was watching her. The front window had the perfect dimensions of a movie screen, and it was as if she were performing for him. Which, in a way, she was.

Only she didn't know it.

The gate was not locked, and it was absurdly easy to reach the front porch undetected. As he moved closer to the glass, he could pick out her end of the conversation.

"...have until the end of next week. Can you believe that? I was counting on this place all month long. Where the hell am I going to find a place that—"

She stopped and turned in the Bear's direction. The Bear dropped down below the window. The wooden porch must have creaked under his weight. Or his movement caught her eye. Didn't matter. This was a learning moment. The Bear wouldn't repeat his mistake.

"No, nothing. I thought I saw something outside. So anyway...can we sue these fuckers? I mean, we had an agreement. I know it wasn't exactly a contract, but...anyway, I gotta go. I'm meeting my manager up the street."

The Bear watched as she pulled on a denim jacket adorned with buttons that dripped attitude (GIRLS JUST WANNA BE LEFT ALONE and I AMBIEN THE BEST PERSON I CAN BE, among others), pushed her feet into a pair of boots, then left the house and headed north on Rodney before hanging a sharp right onto Russell. It was late for a meeting with her "manager" (whoever that was), but that didn't matter, because an empty house was exactly what the Bear was hoping for.

There was nothing easier than slipping inside — the lock on the back door was the original, strangely enough. The Bear made his way inside.

The Bear had been obsessing over it for the past few days, writing endless drafts in his head. I-M B-A-C-K wasn't specific enough. Hell, any number of killers could be claiming a comeback. People remembered the

Bear for his mask and glove, not always the colorful plastic fridge letters. That was a bit of a deep cut for hard-core Bear geeks only.

In the end, it was probably best to go with something tried-and-true. Maybe it was borderline plagiarism, but it would surely send shock waves in the right places. And that was the point.

The Bear took a knee, opened the camping satchel (with the rest of his housebreaking tools) he had strapped to his sizable waist, and pulled out the baggie of magnetic letters. It was a little hard to see in the dark, never mind the slightly obstructed view because of the mask, but fortunately the letters were large enough.

I-M
G-O-I-N-G
T-O
C-U-T-
Y-O-U
I-N-T-O
L-I-T

A light in the kitchen snapped on. Letters tumbled out of the Bear's paw and scattered on the hardwood floor.

"What the fuck!?"

It was the girl in the denim jacket, who'd apparently made her way back to the house without the Bear realizing. Another downside of the thick, furry mask: obstructed hearing.

"Holy fucking shit! You really scared me." She sighed, then leaned against her kitchen counter. "Jesus, man."

The Bear, in his furry mask and glove, *growled* at her, then stood up to full height.

"That's pretty good. I'll admit, you did freak me out a little bit. But wait...I thought the project was canceled. I mean, I'm getting ready to head down to Ye Rustic to read my manager the riot act. Are we still on? Was this one big fake out to make me lower my guard?"

Oh, how the Bear loved this. This dumb bitch had no idea what was about to happen to her. And it made it more delicious, especially when he reached out with his clawed glove and seized her by her scrawny little neck.

"HEY!"

She tried to yell again, but the Bear squeezed tighter. He maintained his iron grip as he slid her along the kitchen counter until she was prone against the wall. She pulled at his hand, trying desperately to rip away the glove as the razor-sharp tip cut into her flesh. *Go ahead, keep struggling. It will do no good. You're at my mercy. And I have none.*

And then the girl jabbed him in the chest with four fingers and instantly his arms went numb.

The Bear released his grip and staggered back a few steps, wondering what had gone wrong. Before he could find a satisfying answer, she whip-kicked him in the head — once, twice, a third time, each blow making it more difficult to think or even understand what was going on.

"Two years of Brooklyn Krav Maga, motherfucker," she said. "I hope the cameras are rolling, because *you really cut me,* you prick. Let's dance."

By that time the feeling had returned to his arms, so the Bear hammered his gloved fist directly into her face with all his body weight behind the blow. Her eyes fluttered and she went down.

And she stayed down, fortunately, because it took a full minute for the Bear to fully regain his senses. She was supposed to be terrified, not fight back. Looking down at her prone body, he wondered if he should finish her off. But no, that wasn't right. That was not the way of the California Bear. His victims had to be terrified out of their minds at the moment of their deaths, or it didn't really count.

The Bear decided to leave the rest of the magnets on the floor and exit as quickly as possible, leaving the door open in his wake. Message — or enough of it — had been sent. This was no time for further conversation or a confrontation. The Bear quickly skulked out the way he came in, consoling himself with the thought that, well, the original Bear didn't kill someone his first time out either. At least the message had been sent.

FRIDAY, JUNE 8, 2018

THE GIRL DETECTIVE

Current hemoglobin level: less than seven, which was not a great thing if you want to, say, move around the hospital room and visit, say, the bathroom without collapsing in a messy tangle of limbs.

Yes, embarrassingly, the Girl Detective almost took a spill right on the cold blue tile. Thankfully, she reached out for the wall-mounted handrail before she totally went *splat*. After steadying herself, she called out for her father to help. He was right on the case ... which was a huge relief, as well as a huge embarrassment. The Father didn't seem to mind at all, but she was completely mortified.

Note to self: use the wheelchair when your hemoglobin is stupid low. You don't do any detective work if you're laid up with broken bones *and* going through chemo.

After freshening up the best she could in this tile prison, the Girl Detective checked her phone for local news. A certain news item jumped out at her. Nothing too out of the ordinary, except for ...

Wait. A home invasion at a house in Los Feliz. These things happened, but ...

Hold the freaking phone. The home invader was wearing a furry mask and used some kind of claw-glove to gain access to the residence? And left a message in colored plastic magnetic letters on the fridge? He *growled* at the startled homeowner before running away?

Now, maybe her chemo-addled brain was playing tricks on her. But from what she understood, this was pretty much the exact MO of the California Bear . . . who had been buried just two days previous.

The Girl Detective's mind swirled with possibilities. Let's dismiss the idea that this was mere coincidence; she didn't believe in them. The real Bear died nearly a week ago, and now here was someone doing their best Bear imitation. Who was behind the mask? And more importantly, *why?*

"Padre."

Padre was currently searching through his address book, which he had recovered from storage. "Yes, Daughter," he mumbled.

"Did you hear about the home invasion in Los Feliz last night? Like, just a few minutes away from where we are right this very minute?"

"Uh, no. Mostly because I was paying close attention to my ailing daughter."

"Okay. I'm going to send you a link to a message board . . . oh wait. You have a janky burner phone. I can't send you a link. Hold on. Let me bring it up on the iPad."

A few taps later the message board was on the screen. She handed the iPad to her father, who put down his address book and scrolled. She waited patiently for him to finish processing the information. The man wasn't the quickest reader in the world.

"Huh," her father said. "That's sad."

"That's it? 'Huh'? Don't you see the connections?"

"That poor woman. Says she was an aspiring actress, with a background in musical theater—"

"No! Not that part. Check out the part about the perp wearing a ski mask and gloves."

"If he was a burglar, that's kind of the smart thing to wear, isn't it?"

"The glove had sharpened fingertips that cut her neck pretty bad. And I'm pretty sure Isotoner discontinued their Freddy Krueger line somewhere back in the nineties."

"So that makes him the California Bear? Honey, the Bear is dead."

"Keep going."

Her father lowered his voice now. "*And I'm one of the very few people who know he's dead.* So either Christopher Albin Dixon wasn't the California Bear, even though he admitted he was..."

"Go on, Padre. You're getting there."

"Or someone else *knew* he was the Bear, and they've decided to take his place."

"Bingo."

"Ah, but, Daughter, you're making a huge leap. The article says nothing about the burglar wearing a furry mask. Just an ordinary ski mask."

"Look at the address again."

Jack squinted as he read. "The 1700 block of Rodney Drive..."

"Do you know what else happened on the 1700 block of Rodney Drive? Back in 1980, that's where the original California Bear claimed his first victim."

GENE JEANIE

Cato was in the room, all right. Through the thin motel door Jeanie could hear him stumbling around, probably trying to find a shirt, possibly pants. She knocked again, wanting to call out to him, *Don't worry about decorum. It's only me.* But maybe their relationship could use a little more decorum. Maybe this was Cato making an effort.

When the door opened, Jeanie realized how very wrong she was.

"What happened in here?" she asked. "Did someone break into your shitty motel room too?"

"I haven't exactly had time for housekeeping."

The interior looked like a Category 5 hurricane had touched down in a stoner's dorm room, scattering take-out food containers, stray pieces of soiled clothing, and empty beer cans in its wake. The only things that were somewhat organized were the crime files on the bed, laid on top of one another like cards in the world's grimmest game of solitaire.

"So, what have you been doing, aside from drinking yourself to death?"

"I'm only drinking beer during work hours," Cato said. "Gotta keep my head straight."

Jeanie could have stepped through the loophole in that statement. "And at night, you're doing what?"

"Using whatever tools are at my disposal to achieve unconsciousness. Speaking of . . . can I get you something?"

"What's with the files?"

Cato glanced over at the bed as if he were also surprised to see them there. "Those? I'm just organizing my research files for our next case."

"Whose next case? What are you talking about?"

"The California Bear thing didn't work out. Probably for the best. I mean, one less psycho sucking air off the planet, the better."

"Cato..."

"But there are plenty of other people who think they got away with it. So we're going to turn our attention to them. Like, there's a downtown real estate douchebag who used to run a ring of housebreakers all over the Hollywood Hills. I know, because twenty years ago I was the guy who was trying to nail him. Okay, not just me, but I was definitely part of the task force—"

"Cato."

"And there's this couple who I know framed their handyman for a high-end jewelry robbery, only the handyman didn't do it, and those rich fucks just did it for the insurance money—"

"Cato!"

"What?"

"The California Bear thing isn't over."

"Honey, listen to me. I'm wrong about a lot of things, I'll grant you that. But not this. The Bear is dead. I watched him die."

"Sure. I believe you watched someone you *thought* was the California Bear keel over and die. But then how do you explain how someone very much like the California Bear broke into a house in Los Feliz last night? The same house, in fact, where the Bear claimed his first victim?"

"I'm sorry...say that again?"

"You heard me. And while you're at it, maybe you can explain why I'm being watched all the time."

Her husband grew angry. "Who's watching you?"

"If I knew the identity of the person watching me, I would have mentioned their name. That's why I said *someone*. But it must be related to your so-called case."

"Fuck me—"

"No. *Fuck you!* For doing this to me! Do you know somebody jacked off in my fucking underwear drawer last week?"

"Why . . . why would someone do that?"

"I don't know. Maybe because that someone is insane, and you provoked him? My question now is . . . what are you going to do about it?"

Cato looked around his pigsty of a room as if he'd find an answer to that. There would be none. If anything, her husband would just come up with another pathetic excuse or lie or twisted bullshit meant to make her stop asking questions. Jeanie was done with it. Done with it all.

She slammed the door behind her, which felt satisfying in the moment, but the feeling had dissipated by the time she was headed north on the PCH. All she felt now was defeated.

THE BEAR

The Reborn Bear slipped his headphones over his ears and cued up his music: Talking Heads' "Psycho Killer." And no, this song choice was *not* too on the nose, thank you very much. This was because this new Bear has chosen the acoustic version, a rare outtake featuring slashing strings and an extra verse. No one else would have thought of it.

Truth be told, he was not sure what kinds of music his predecessor listened to. Many victims reported seeing old-school foam headphones against his ears when he prowled and hearing the tinny sound of some kind of "modern rock music" blasting from them. But only the original Bear knew what was playing. And those secrets had apparently died with him. Unless he kept those original tapes stashed away somewhere in his house in Studio City.

The Reborn Bear desperately wished he could have had that conversation with the original. So many conversations, about so many things, starting with: *Why am I even alive?*

The Bear made the decision not to wear the furry mask until he was inside the house this time. Wearing it in public would only attract more attention. Especially in this neighborhood-watch-crazy town. Besides, he wanted to be able to hear everything—no more surprises. That meant the headphones had to go away too, even though the music really put him in the mood for tonight's adventure. He continued uphill.

Finally it came into view. The second official scene of the crime—a wedding-cake house on Micheltorena Street in Silver Lake. The place was a rental, which was a plus. This meant detailed views of the property were available on the rental website, which gave the Bear all the information he needed. Imagine this kind of resource during the glory years of the late seventies and early eighties! The Bear found a hiding place in the yard and waited until all the lights went out in the house, one by one. After giving them enough time to fall asleep, the Bear stretched his legs, pulled on his mask and glove, and ambled toward the back door.

There was no complex security system to deal with, so the Bear had the time to practice on the back door with his glove, repaired and sharpened this very afternoon. The razor-sharp claws ate through the wood around the lock with surprising ease. Someday this would become second nature, like using a fork. When enough wood had been chewed away, the Bear was able to use his human hand to pry the lock loose. He juggled it for a moment, enjoying the weight, before flinging it across the grass and down the slope.

Now he was inside and making his way to the fridge.

The Reborn Bear had decided on a different message this time. Something to set him apart (slightly) from his predecessor. Because the original Bear had stopped short of the truly terrifying thought. Cutting someone up into little pieces was all well and good, but what was one to do with those pieces?

G-O-I-N-G

T-O

E-A-T-

Y-O-U

A-L-L

U

Again: a light snapped on. This was absurd. Was his predecessor interrupted like this? Only now did the Bear realize that he must have left the message *after* he'd had his way with the occupants of the house.

He was doing it in reverse. The click-clacking of the magnets on the fridge must have tipped off the sleeping residents. Well, lesson learned.

The Bear put his letters away and positioned himself by the doorway. Seemed it was time for a confrontation. His blood trembled with excitement. This feeling was incredible and far more intense than he'd imagined.

"Whoever's in there, I'm warning you—leave now!"

Leave now, or what? You'll scold me to death? Please.

The footsteps approached the doorway. The Bear flexed his fingers inside the clawed glove. Which part should he slash first? The torso made the most sense; it was the broadest target. But that would not inspire fear in the quite the same way as . . . say, gashes across the forehead and eyes. Imagine: blood dripping down your face, your vision compromised . . .

Yes, that would be best. The Bear waited for the face to appear.

"Wait," a voice said. "Hold on. I'm confused."

"Who is it, honey?"

"It's the fucking California Bear. Only now he's not running away."

"After all this time? I thought the shoot was canceled."

The Bear stood up straight and faced the couple, who shuffled into the kitchen weary and not afraid in the least.

"Are we . . ." the male started to ask, then lowered his voice. "Are we being filmed? Or is this some kind of test run?"

"Hold on," the female said. She squeezed the male's hand. "Did we miss a text or something?"

"Maybe it was all part of the plan? To let our guard down?"

The Bear took a step toward them. Showed them his glove with the freshly sharpened claws.

"That's very realistic," the female said. "But can you, like, break character for a second and tell us how we're supposed to play this?"

The Bear took another step toward them.

"Shit, are we fucking this up? Are we filming now?"

The Bear slashed his claws across the male's robe-clad arm, slicing through the fabric as well as flesh. The male screamed. The Bear reached out, grabbed the man (thick glasses, young—a hipster type) by the throat with his human hand and pressed him against the doorway. The Bear growled, then dragged his claws down his terrified victim's face, scraping off his thick glasses in the process, which delighted him to no end. The male screamed even louder.

Something heavy and hard crashed into the back of the Bear's head. If not for the cushioning of the mask, it would have probably fractured his skull. Dazed, he turned to see the female with a nine-inch cast-iron skillet in her shaking hands. This was not how it would end. No way. The Bear slashed out at her, again and again, until the skillet fell out of her hands, and she screamed and screamed and screamed...

SATURDAY, JUNE 9, 2018

THE GIRL DETECTIVE

For a dead guy, the California Bear had been pretty busy.

First Los Feliz, now this big house in Silver Lake. There was an actual attack this time—leaving two people torn up and bleeding and absolutely terrified.

The Girl Detective could see the hills of Silver Lake bathed in the first glimmers of dawn from her hospital room window. Could one of those rooftops belong to the actual house? Well, to determine that she'd need the actual address, and that wasn't available (yet). The latest attack happened a little too late (2 a.m.) to make the news cycle. The Girl Detective was reading about it on the Reddit message boards, which were big on lurid detail but short on specifics—to protect the innocent, according to the Redditors. But if she had to guess, she already knew the address. It would be the same location where the Bear had mauled his second and third victims back in the fall of 1981.

"Father."

"*Nuh?*"

Father was still asleep on the makeshift couch/bed thing in her room, directly below the windows that offered her the view of the hills of Silver Lake. To the Girl Detective, it had the strange effect of making it look like her dad was sleeping under the foundation of Silver Lake itself, oblivious to the suffering of its residents above.

"Wake up, Father. It happened again."

"Whuh? What happened?"

"The Bear. Last night, he was right," she said, gesturing toward the windowpanes behind her father's head, "*over there.*"

"Is there a story in the news? Did they link it to the Bear?"

"No, nothing in the mainstream press yet. But I have my sources."

"Seriously, Matilda?" Ah, finally...the pushback. Now her father was completely awake.

"Fine. I have message boards. There's a whole subcommunity of California Bear freaks, and this morning there were a dozen posts about the break-in. Someone even posted photos of the broken door. Looks like he clawed at the wood until he just pulled out the lock."

"But this could just be fan fiction, right? People faking it for the...how do you kids say it? For the LOLs?"

"Don't *ever* use that phrase again," the Girl Detective replied. "But if it *is* fan fiction, then they should sweep the fan fiction awards later this year on the grounds of sheer realism."

"Why would someone be doing this? It makes no sense."

"Whoever this guy is, he's still figuring things out. Apparently, he was interrupted leaving another message."

"What was the message?"

"There was only a partial sentence on the fridge, and this is based on rumor, mind you...but people are speculating the complete message was, 'I am going to eat you all up.'"

"This is absolutely insane, right?"

"Maybe, but I think you and your old-man cop friend roused some other rough beast from its hibernation. Maybe it's multiple someones. Maybe it's an actual conspiracy. A sleuth of bears, as it were. People who had been watching and waiting for the OG Bear to die, and now that he has, it's...well, open season."

Now her father was sitting up straight, rubbing the sleep out of his eyes, trying to tame his hair with his fingers. It wasn't helping, but at least the old man was making the effort.

"I've gotta meet up with Hightower. Maybe there's something he's not telling me about this case. Which, by the way, would not surprise me."

"What was his evidence?" the Girl Detective asked. "How did he figure out the Bear's identity? Or was he just guessing?"

"Long story short, his wife does genetic research, and she used a DNA sample from one of the crime scenes to track down his family tree."

Now, this was an exciting turn! "A DNA sample…from the actual case files? Does Hightower have access to them?"

"Access to them?" Her father laughed. "He straight up stole them from the LAPD."

"Padre, serious talk now. When you find him, bring back those files. If I have even, like, an *hour* with them, I think I can help you figure this out."

"I have total faith in your abilities, honey. But I'm not sure I'll be able to convince Hightower to bring them here."

"Well, *I* have total faith that you'll bring them back," the Girl Detective replied. "Along with two dozen doughnuts."

"That's extortion," her father said, "in addition to handling stolen evidence."

"No," she replied, "that's my fee."

THE BEAR

The producer was not pleased. He pushed the laptop back across the table. "Fuck me. This isn't you, is it?"

The Bear just smiled at the producer. He had been waiting for this moment for years. Oh, how the worm had turned. The Bear and David Peterson went way back. Too far back. Years of false hope, broken promises, and free work had led them all here, to this moment. And it was delicious seeing the growing panic creep onto Peterson's perpetually smiling fucking face.

"I don't understand," the Bear protested. "I thought this is what you wanted. Making the Bear relevant again? *Why him, why now,* and all that? That's what you've been telling me for years."

"Seriously, are *you* fucking doing this? What the hell is wrong with you?"

"Relax, David. I'm just pointing out that someone seems to have stolen your thunder."

Years ago, it was always a respectful *Mr. Peterson.* No more, the Bear vowed.

"There's no more thunder, kid," Peterson said when he finally caught his breath again. "The project's on hold. Possibly forever. I mean, we might have been able to salvage some of our investment, but this thing is as dead as the Bear himself."

"What happened? Just bad luck, with the old guy's heart giving out?"

"First . . . assure me this isn't you."

Yes, it's me, and you're next, Davey boy . . . I'm going to cut you into little pieces . . .

. . . is what the Bear saw, spelled out in bright colorful magnet letters on the inside of his skull.

"David, come on. I'm not a psychopath."

"Okay, fine," he said. "Then this is probably one of the other two lunatics."

The Bear frowned. "What lunatics?"

David Peterson was flashing that awful smile again, now that he had regained the conversational upper hand. "Two days before our friend died, there were two guys spying on him. The Bear's widow says she caught them leaving the house right before she found her husband's body in the backyard."

"Who are they?"

"I have the address for one of them. He's ex-LAPD but now lives out in Port Hueneme. His wife's a genealogist, which is how they discovered our friend's identity." Peterson shook his head and smiled. "Kind of funny, isn't it? You can spend years, even decades, trying to track down someone's identity. Now any loser with a laptop can play Internet sleuth."

"Yeah," the Bear said. "Funny."

Inside, however, the Bear was *howling.* How dare they! The fact that a genealogist was on the case disturbed him greatly. Everything was moving fast now; there was very little time to play catch-up.

But the Bear gritted his teeth hard to control his rage, then took a deep breath. "Who's the other one?"

"Nobody knows. Maybe hired muscle. But now I'm thinking, maybe he's the guy running around pretending he's the Bear now."

Not the case, but it was fine that David thought that. For now. "Do you have the Port Hueneme address?"

The producer frowned. "Why do you want that?"

"I want to know who we're up against."

"We?"

"See, this is what I'm talking about. You've been keeping me at arm's length from this project the whole time."

"I told you I'd take care of you," David said. "Now is not the right time."

"Then let me take care of you," the Bear said. "Don't forget, my superpower is research. Let me dig around and find out who these people are. We can make them go away."

David Peterson the Two-Faced Producer stared at the Bear for the longest time, mulling it over, doing some kind of studio math in his head. Ultimately, he must have figured, *Why not?* Because it was never any skin off his back to have a writer go off and work for free. If the writer came back with nothing, then no great loss. But if he did come back with something useful, then it was the best non-investment you could ever make.

"I know one of them a little—she's the genealogist." A sly smile crept onto the producer's face. "You're going to love this. Her name is actually Jeanie."

"That *is* funny," the Bear said. "What's the address?"

"What are you going to do, stalk them?"

"Interesting you say that. Because there's something in my bag that I want to show you..."

"KILLER"

Downstairs in the hospital lobby, Jack could feel eyes on him. He scanned the crowd, looking for any familiar faces. Nothing jumped out at him, which should have been a good thing — because the face he was looking for happened to belong to a dead man.

Still, he couldn't shake the deep suspicion that he was being *watched*. The flesh on the back of his neck tingled, and his heart raced a little too fast. When someone reached out and touched his shoulder, God help him, Jack almost screamed.

"Jack, what are you doing down here?" Reese asked. She was annoyed, not concerned. "Louis wanted to head up and say hello to Matilda before he took you back to our place."

"That's the thing, Reese. I need a ride somewhere. I was hoping you'd stay with Matilda while Louis drove me."

Louis blinked, possibly roused from the tedium of his sad little life by the prospect of a new adventure. "What? Where do you want to go?"

"Uh . . . Port Hueneme."

"My husband," Reese said, "is not driving you to fucking Port Hueneme."

"Honey," Louis pleaded in a whisper, "this is a children's hospital."

Jack tried to project *I wouldn't ask if it wasn't desperately important.*

"What the fuck is so desperate in Port Hueneme?"

"Honey . . ."

Jack watched the wheels turning in Reese's mind. Not because she was seriously considering his request. She was most likely trying to come up with the most stinging insult possible. He decided to stop her cold the only way he knew.

"It's my employer," Jack explained. "If I don't meet with him this afternoon, the deal we have going will fall apart. That means no money in the foreseeable future. Do you understand?"

And...*click*. The gears in Reese's mind ceased turning. Reversed themselves. Found a new groove.

"Louis, drive Jack to Port Hueneme."

This clearly wasn't the adventure that Louis had hoped for. "I don't even know where that is."

"I can tell you on the way," Jack said.

"Shouldn't I say hello to Mattie first?"

"There really isn't time. We'll come straight back here when I'm done. You can visit with her then." Jack almost bit his tongue but figured a little sweetener couldn't hurt. "She'd love to spend more time with you."

This was not true. Matilda thought her uncle Louis was a serious weirdo.

But the flattery (and promise of money) sealed the deal for Reese. A minute later, Louis was leading the way back down to the bowels of the hospital, to the car that he and Reese shared—a gray 2009 Toyota Yaris. Jack wasn't looking forward to the hour drive out to Ventura County in this tin can. Riding in this subcompact nightmare back to Burbank was bad enough. And on top of everything else, he had Louis to deal with.

Jack used his drug dealer phone to try Hightower one more time—maybe the gods of crime would be merciful and the idiot would answer. But no.

"So what's out in Port Hueneme?" Louis asked as they merged onto the 101 North.

What, not *who*. This was Louis's suave attempt to pry some information out of Jack. He was curious about what kind of deal Jack might have cooked up with the ex-cop who'd helped spring him from prison. The problem with Louis was that he wasn't interested in the way a friend or relative might be. No, Louis was an aspiring screenwriter, and painfully obvious about wanting to collect gossipy tidbits here and there for scripts he'd never write.

"Nothing too exciting," Jack replied. "I'm basically a glorified gopher until I find another job somewhere."

"Is the old cop...Hightower, that's his name, right? Is he doing private detective work?"

Jack didn't know how to respond to that one. All his responses should have one objective: discourage further questions.

"More like consulting."

"Interesting! On cold cases? Do you think he'd ever want to talk to me? You know, for background research."

Fuck, this was going to be a long drive.

GENE JEANIE

"Hello, Jeanie Hightower," the producer said when he answered the phone. "I was just talking about you."

"You were?"

"Yeah. Does that surprise you? I had a colleague who might be interested in your services, so I passed your business card along. I hope you don't mind."

Jeanie paced her living room, phone pressed against her ear by her index finger, wondering what this all meant. She was certain Peterson wasn't promoting her family tree services among the Tinseltown elite. So either it was the usual bullshit, or David Peterson the producer had just been talking about her. But to whom? And why?

"I appreciate that," Jeanie said. "Not to press my luck, but I called because I have a slightly weird question to ask you."

"Weirder than last time?"

Jeanie gave him the fake laugh she thought he wanted to hear. Better to put him at ease before putting the screws to him. She had to play him just as carefully as he (may have) played her. If her hunch was right, this man was the only one in the position to know the truth.

"I know you're a California Bear aficionado, so I'm sure you've heard about the copycat attacks over the past couple of days."

Peterson laughed. "That's your question?"

"No. I'm still setting the table. You also may remember that I asked about Christopher A., one of several Bear suspects. The full name I had was Christopher Albin Dixon. And maybe this is just a wild coincidence, but Mr. Dixon passed away last week, rather suddenly."

There was a long pause. A game of conversational chicken. Peterson lost.

"Are you still laying out the silverware, Jeanie?"

"Just a few more pieces," Jeanie said. "If you were telling the truth, and Mr. Dixon was *not* the California Bear, then it seems like the subject of your documentary is out there making a comeback."

"Hmm. Interesting. Go on."

"But if you *were* fibbing a little to protect Mr. Dixon's identity, and he was in fact the California Bear, then someone is out there impersonating him. And my question, then, is simple. Is this the 'next-level' reenactment you were talking about last week?"

Jeanie expected a big belly laugh. There was dead silence on the line.

"David?"

"I don't have any answers for you, Jeanie," he finally said. "But I do have some advice. You might want to look a little closer at your household. Specifically, your husband. From what I understand, he's very obsessed with the California Bear. Maybe to a sociopathic degree."

"Who told you that?"

"Like I said, I'm not here to solve mysteries. That's not what I do. I would just strongly urge you to keep your eyes open. In this town, so few people are who they seem."

The call was disconnected before Jeanie had time to fully process the meaning behind David's previous statement. Look a little closer . . . at Cato? Did the producer really think her husband had snapped and was now going around town pretending to be the California Bear? How the fuck did this guy even *know* her husband?

A knock at the door snapped Jeanie from her reverie. She had no idea who might be visiting. Cato wouldn't knock, of course. And it couldn't be Peterson the producer — unless he had taken her call while standing outside on her front lawn. (Which would be creepy in the extreme.) Maybe her ex? No, couldn't be him either. He wouldn't risk running into

Cato. Maybe the mysterious cop who'd been watching her decided to forget the pretense and talk to her directly.

But it was none of the above. Instead, Jeanie opened the door to see Cato's ex-con, Jack Queen. Next to him was a stranger who looked like he needed a shower, a haircut, and a hug.

"I am very sorry to just drop in, Jeanie," the ex-con said. "But I couldn't reach your husband. Do you know where I can find him?"

She did but wasn't about to share that information with just anyone. "Who's this?" she asked, gesturing to the stranger.

"Oh, right. This is my brother-in-law, Louis. Uh, Louis, meet Jeanie Hightower, the wife of my... uh, business partner."

Brother-in-law Louis looked tired and annoyed. Jeanie could empathize completely. What she didn't understand was what these two men were doing on her front stoop. The weird conversation with David Peterson was still knocking around her brain. She was beginning to feel like her grip on reality was slipping away, and maybe she'd been missing something big this whole time.

"I hate to tell you," Jeanie finally said, "but you drove all the way up here for nothing. Cato's back in Santa Monica."

Jack deflated. "Does he have his phone? Because he's not returning my calls."

"I'm sure he has his phone. But he probably can't find the damn thing, the state he's in."

"Wonderful."

Brother-in-law Louis perked up. "Why? What's wrong with him?"

"Can I have a moment with you, Jack? In private? Excuse us, Louis."

Jeanie led Jack to the backyard, where they could talk. Unless the mysterious cop parked out front had bugged every square inch of her yard. The way things were going, anything was possible. That said, she hadn't seen the black Audi since calling in her favor the day before. Maybe her ex had done her a solid and scared the guy off?

"What's up, Jeanie?"

"I need a straight answer," Jeanie said.

"Of course. If I'm able to give it to you, I will."

"The man Cato believed was the California Bear..."

"Yeah?"

"You were there. Is he really dead?"

Jeanie watched Jack's eyes almost roll out of their sockets. "So you've been hearing about the new Bear attacks too."

"Shit. I was hoping it was just two coincidences in a row."

"My daughter, Matilda, doesn't believe in coincidences."

"Your daughter is a smart girl," Jeanie said.

"You don't know the half of it. She's spent the past week researching the history of the California Bear. I think it distracts her from what's going on around her."

"It's not going on *around* her, Jack. It's happening *to* her."

"You know what I mean."

"How is she?"

"Almost finished her first course of chemo. She's tougher than anyone I know. The wonderful yet heartbreaking thing about Matilda is that she's always worried about other people more than herself. She should be soaking up all the attention right now, but she's worried about *me*."

"Wait a minute... you told her what happened?"

Jack shook his head. "She figured it out almost instantly. Like I said, you don't know the half of it. She's thinking of things that never even occurred to me. What Matilda is saying is right. There's no way an imitator would just spontaneously start breaking into homes the same week the real Bear died. Unless that imitator knew his true identity. And if *he* knows the truth, then he probably knows about me and your husband."

Jeanie thought about her call with Peterson. "That makes a lot of sense."

"Or... the man who died in front of us wasn't the Bear at all, and the real Bear is out there somewhere, annoyed that someone else is getting credit for his work."

"I suspect this is why you're up here trying to find Cato," Jeanie said. "To figure out this mess and help put Matilda's mind at ease."

"Hers and mine. Matilda wants to see the case file."

"What does Matilda think is happening?"

"Either your husband identified the wrong guy, or there's a copycat. The first option is unlikely, because I'm very confident that old asshole who tortured us was the actual Bear."

"Yeah," Jeanie said. "Christopher Albin Dixon was definitely the Bear."

"How do *you* know? For sure?"

"Cato used me to confirm his suspicions. You know I do genealogical work, right? Well, the resident genius managed to steal a sample of Bear DNA from evidence lockup, then sent it to one of those commercial sites run by Mormons in a cave or whatever. I was able to match it to someone on his family tree. Once I started connecting branches, it was pretty much a lock."

What Jeanie didn't say was that she was using the same tricks to find out more about the mysterious Mrs. Bear—the serial killer's wife for thirty-plus years. A genetic sample wouldn't work, but filling in the details of her family tree was starting to paint a picture. Especially in terms of how the two may have crossed paths in the first place.

"So if Dixon was the Bear, for sure," Jack said, "then we're dealing with a copycat. Who could be anyone."

"Could be Cato for all we know."

"You're saying your husband is the new California Bear."

"I wouldn't put it past him, if it meant making a few bucks."

Jack laughed, and so did Jeanie, playing along...but now she wasn't so sure.

THE BEAR

Guess the trip to Port Hueneme was worth the gas after all.

But now the Reborn Bear had a choice to make. Stay here and wait for the known quantity—the ex-cop with the improbable name of Cato Hightower—to show up? Or follow these two knuckleheads on the chance that one of them was the mysterious second witness? The Bear would have liked to call David Peterson and have him ask Cassandra Dixon for a description of Mystery Man #2, but that would be pushing it. The Bear needed to keep David at arm's length until he wrapped up all these loose ends. (And then he was going to cut him into little pieces.)

But now, what he wouldn't give for a little wireless tracking device he could hide on the knuckleheads' Toyota and enjoy the best of both worlds. Remain here until "Cato Hightower" arrived home, use his claw on the ex-cop and his wife, then take care of the knuckleheads later today or tomorrow...

Whoops. Here they came now, out the front door. One of them—the taller of the two—looked like he could handle himself physically. Hard to pin down his ethnic background or even what he did for a living—which made it difficult to size him up in a fight. If it came down to it, the Bear would attack him first, claws out, with everything he had. There would be no toying with this guy. Go for the eyes or the throat or the guts (or all three in quick succession).

The other one—well, this was the type the Bear knew well. Slender, messy hair, aggressively white and bland. Probably fancied himself a screenwriter or some other kind of "artiste." Throw a rock anywhere in Los Angeles County and you'd hit someone just like him. And once you realized how much fun it was, you'd go looking for more rocks.

This very odd couple climbed into their shitty Toyota, with the asthmatic screenwriter climbing behind the wheel, and the thuggish bouncer dude (possibly?) easing himself into the passenger seat. Hard to understand the dynamic at play here. What was their connection to each other? How did they know the ex-cop who lived at this address? If it was just the bouncer dude, that would almost make sense—Hightower and his wife hiring some muscle to protect themselves. But then how did the asthmatic screenwriter fit in? Too many variables, all of which didn't even exist in the Bear's mind a few hours ago.

The Toyota's engine sputtered to life; the one unbroken taillight flashed pale red. The Bear lifted his finger, suspending it in the air. He had to decide. Yes, he could stay for the sure thing. But if they pulled away without the Bear knowing their deal, never to return, he'd regret it forever. *There could be no loose ends.* So he pressed the button that brought his car to near-silent life, then followed in their wake like a shark.

After some strange turns in the neighborhood—the Bear would swear these assholes were lost—the Toyota finally took the on-ramp to the 101 heading back to LA. Ah. They weren't local; like the Bear, they were just visiting from out of town. The Bear followed them back toward home.

"KILLER"

It was possible to make a left turn directly onto Entrada Drive — and Jack warned him that he needed to be in the leftmost lane — but Louis missed it anyway. Then Louis freaked out trying to figure out how to make a U-turn on the PCH (you can't) and didn't believe that the best way to turn around was to ascend to Ocean Avenue and then head back down to the PCH. By the time they were finally approaching the road-house again, Jack was ready to throttle his brother-in-law.

And then Louis complained there weren't any parking spaces in the micro-size lot behind Patrick's Roadhouse. By this point Jack didn't care about Louis's whining. He just needed to speak with Hightower and come up with some kind of plan.

"Why don't you just drop me off out front?" Jack asked. "I can find another way back to CHLA."

"I thought we could stop for lunch while we're here," Louis said. "I'm starving."

"Go for it. I have to meet with Hightower anyway."

"Why don't we all grab lunch?"

Good Lord no. "I don't think he's feeling too well, which is why he's down here." At this point, Jack was considering just opening the passenger door and stepping out while the Yaris was idled at a red light. Let Louis take the hint.

"I see a spot up the street!"

"Great," Jack said.

There was no shaking Louis, all the way back down the block and around the roadhouse and up the rickety wooden stairs that led to Hightower's room. Which reminded him: Was Hightower still footing the bill for Jack's former room, even though he hadn't set foot inside it in more than a week? Would Jack ultimately be responsible for that bill too?

"I really do need to meet with him in private," Jack told Louis.

"Yeah, cool, cool, man. I get it."

"He might be freaked out if you're standing here with me."

"I'll just say hello and head downstairs."

Louis: the man who could not take a hint.

Jack knocked. He heard the rumbling of a living creature inside, possibly human, knocking over furniture and kicking aside glass bottles on the way to the door. When it finally opened, Hightower blinked. The man was clearly drunk; Jack could smell the booze wafting from his pores.

"Finally," he said. "What took you so long?"

"Hey, Officer Hightower — it's Louis. You know, from the apartment in Toluca Lake? How are you doing?"

"What the fuck is *he* doing here?" Hightower asked.

"Louis gave me a lift here after we drove all the way up to Port Hueneme...where I thought you'd be."

"Didn't Jeanie tell you?"

"Yeah. She did. After we drove an hour to Port Hueneme."

"Whatever. Come in, grab a beer, don't grab a beer, whatever."

Louis was the first to take a step forward. Hightower held up a shaky hand.

"Not you."

Jack cringed inside, but only a little. "Louis, why don't you hang out downstairs, maybe get a bite. I won't be long." This was a lie. He had no idea how long this would take. After a moment of sulking, Louis waved goodbye and headed back down the wooden stairs. Jack stepped into the room and closed the door behind him. He immediately regretted this. The place smelled like a stoner's armpit.

"You hear about what's been going on?"

"Yeah."

"What are we going to do about it?"

"There's nothing to do. The Bear is dead. In fact, I can't get the image of his face out of my head . . . the idea that you could go, just like that. For eating a doughnut!"

"Forget about the doughnuts! There's a copycat out there right now trying to kill people."

"Not our problem."

"What do you fucking mean? *We created this problem*."

"Are you the copycat? I know I'm not, but maybe last weekend warped your brain a little. Is that what you're trying to tell me? Is this your confession?"

Jack had no idea if the man was serious, or drunk, or maybe both. "I'm not the copycat. Are you?"

"Nope. Glad we settled that."

"But it's up to us to find him."

"Good luck with that," Hightower said. "He could be anyone. He could be anywhere. Which is spooky when you think about it."

Jack sighed. "I can't believe I have to do this."

"Do what?"

"Dig down deep and try to give you a pep talk, spouting back some of the same damn shit you used on me when I first got out of prison. I don't think I have the patience for it."

"Then, don't bother. I'm having a beer."

THE BEAR

"Hey, man, this seat open?"

"Knock yourself out."

Go figure. The asthmatic screenwriter was poring over a menu and considering a snack. Probably avocado toast with a kale smoothie. But where was his bodyguard/bouncer/whoever? The Bear had temporarily lost sight of them once they reached Patrick's Roadhouse — the left turn onto Entrada Drive was a fickle one. For a few desperate minutes, the Bear assumed he'd made a fatal mistake and had lost them for good . . . only to spot the shitty Toyota squeezed into a street spot.

The Bear parked his own car, then stepped inside the restaurant, where he found the asthmatic hipster fuck perched on a stool at the short lunch counter, engrossed in a menu. But where was the other one? Maybe a little conversation would give him some answers.

"Thanks, man," the Bear said. "What looks good here?"

"No idea. It's my first time. Yours too?"

The Bear decided to lie. "Yeah, I decided to pull in at random. I pass this place all the time when I'm headed down the PCH, so I thought I'd give it a try. What brings you in?"

"My brother-in-law. He should be down in a few minutes."

The Bear nodded, satisfied with a small piece of the mystery solved. So they were brothers-in-law. Time to coax more answers out of this loser.

"Hey, I'm Ted, by the way," the Bear said. Okay, maybe that was a little too cute, but not as obvious as *Hey, I'm Yogi* or *Hey, I'm Fozzie* or what have you. "What's your name?"

"Louis," the asthmatic hipster fuck said. "Good to meet you."

"Yeah, same," the Bear said, idly wondering what it would be like to take one of the steak knives from the cup on the counter and drag it across Louis's throat. Would anyone try to stop him? Would anyone notice?

"I know everyone hates this question," Louis said, "but are you in the business?"

"What business is that?"

"You know . . . the only business in town."

"Corruption, exploitation, and bribery?"

Oh, did that make the asthmatic screenwriter howl in delight. No doubt a fake laugh, meant to strengthen the bonds of a burgeoning friendship. This guy thought he knew all the tricks.

"Well, some say show business is about all of those things," Louis said. "No, what I mean is . . . you look sort of familiar."

"I have one of those faces. I'm always reminding people of somebody's cousin, or the best friend of their second cousin's aunt, or what have you. But no, I'm not in the business. Are you? You look like . . . I don't know, maybe a screenwriter?"

"Trying to become one," Louis said. "I'm what they call pre-WGA."

"What's WGA stand for?"

"Boy, you really aren't in the business are you? It's the Writers Guild of America."

"Oh, okay."

Christ on a cracker . . . this screenwriter chump was too much fun! The new Bear decided he would honestly be sad when it came time to slice him into itty-bitty pieces.

"I have a few scripts out to producers right now," Louis continued, "and I'm helping a neighbor of mine revise a screenplay he wrote. He's a Serbian actor, pretty well-known in Europe, but between you and me . . ."

And from here Louis droned on about his hopes and dreams and ridiculous connections and the Bear glanced over at those steak knives in the cup. Except that wasn't the Bear's MO at all; not in public, anyway. Too complicated, and what would that accomplish?

No, the Bear started this dance. He would have to see it through until Louis's brother-in-law finally joined them.

Only then would the real fun begin.

"KILLER"

Hightower rooted around in his fridge and plucked two cans of Dos Equis from a shelf. The brass sculpture of the Weird Sisters had been placed in the tiny kitchenette, presumably to guard the alcohol supply. Or so that Hightower would have someone to talk to when he was super drunk and lonely.

He held a can of beer out to Jack, who was tempted for a moment. Fuck it. Maybe a beer would help him think. But no. He wasn't going to throw away two years of sobriety like this. And if he let Hightower lead this dance, they would be sitting here all afternoon getting hammered while the copycat Bear continued to run amok. Jack needed Cato focused if this was going to work.

"You have files here on the Bear, right?"

"Somewhere over by the bed. Or maybe the toilet. I don't know. Somewhere."

"There must be something we missed. Maybe the name of our copycat is somewhere in those files."

"Impossible." Hightower cracked open his can, thought it over for a moment, then cracked the other one open too. He proceeded to double-fist the beers. "I've been over every word and punctuation mark in those files. If there were a likely" — here the man let out a belch like a sonic boom — "excuse me, a likely candidate, I'd know about it."

"Matilda has a working theory."

"Great. Who's that?"

"Matilda? My daughter? The one currently fighting for her life?"

"Right, of course. I...uh, just mostly hear you referring to her as your daughter, not by her first name."

"You're unbelievable."

"What's her theory? Kids can be cute sometimes."

"She thinks there might be a conspiracy. She's been on all these message boards obsessed with the California Bear, and all kinds of people are trading all kinds of information, and techniques, and photos, and their own theories."

"A conspiracy..." Hightower repeated. This seemed to give him great pause.

"Not in the tin-foil-hat way, but in the literal definition of the word. Multiple people teaming up for a criminal enterprise."

"Goddamn it!"

Hightower's eyes widened. Whatever revelation had cut through his alcoholic fog was strong enough to make the man put down his beer. Both of them.

"What is it?"

"Jack, this is amazing! We're going to take the fight to this fucker's front door."

"You mean the fucker who could be anyone? Be anywhere? Where do we even start?"

"Leave that to me. Oh shit, this is exciting. In the meantime, wait for my call."

"Are you going to explain this to me at some point?"

By now Jack had come to understand something about Cato Hightower: he was the kind of guy who needed a partner. Not in a romantic sense—more in the Abbott and Costello, Stan and Ollie, Martin and Lewis kind of way. Left to his own devices, wounded, drunk, and lonely, he would have eventually withered away to nothing. But maybe Jeanie's visit, followed by Jack's own, had galvanized the deluded bastard? Maybe he simply needed to be...well, *needed.* Perhaps the man worked best as part of a team, and it took an idea from Jack to spark something inside him. Is it possible he had read Hightower wrong this whole time?

"A conspiracy," Hightower said, "means money. Nobody does anything unless there's a payday in it for them. We figure out how these bastards are getting rich from the Bear's name, then we can cut ourselves into the action too."

"You had me right up until that last part."

"Go. I need to check out of this dump. Keep your phone powered up, sound on. I may call you at a moment's notice."

"I'm going to be a little busy taking care of my sick daughter," Jack said carefully. "If you have a plan in mind, tell me now. Better still, let's plan it together."

"No time. Go, go, go!"

"Wait—Matilda asked to borrow your case files."

"Why?"

"She's really good at this kind of thing and thinks she can help."

"Does a ten-year-old even know how to read an incident report?"

"She's almost fifteen, *asshole,* and she's a genius."

"Whatever. Fine. Take the box. I have all I need up here." To accentuate the point, Hightower tapped his skull with a fat finger. The hollow sound it made did nothing to support his statement. But Jack was grateful he was able to score the files without an argument. He lifted the cardboard box—which contained only the highlights that Hightower had pilfered from Records—and made his way back down to the restaurant level.

Jack had expected to see Louis sulking and nursing a Diet Coke or something. Instead he was at the counter, engaged in a lively conversation with a chubby stranger.

"Hey, Louis—you ready to go, man?"

"Oh hey, Jack...this is Ted," Louis said. "Ted, this is the brother-in-law I was telling you about."

"Hey, brother-in-law Jack," the burly man said. "Glad to know you."

"Yeah, you too." Jesus, Louis could strike up a conversation with anybody. And at the most inopportune times. "We really need to hit the road. Did you order anything? Can you get it to go?"

"Where's the fire, Jack? Sit down and join us. Whatcha got under your arm there?"

This was the stranger speaking, and nothing annoyed Jack more than a total fucking rando inserting himself into other people's business.

"Just work. Come on, Louis, let's try to beat the traffic."

"On a Saturday afternoon? Relax. Is Hightower doing okay?"

Louis was literally unable to keep his mouth shut about anything.

"He's great. Pay your check. I'll be out by the car."

THE BEAR

Another interesting decision to be made.

Okay, so maybe "Cato Hightower" (the Bear still didn't believe that was an actual name someone would bestow on a child) was somewhere on the premises — most likely in one of the rooms above the restaurant. The Bear had had no idea people actually stayed here. He'd long assumed it was a kind of flophouse for coked-up executives to impress young inge-nues with "a trip to Santa Monica Beach." Why was Hightower staying here?

Never mind that for now. The Bear could easily figure out which room he was staying in, break down the door, and then maul the bastard.

Ah, but then he'd definitely lose brothers-in-law Jack and Louis, all without knowing their last names. Small talk hadn't progressed *that* far. Maybe the Bear would be able to figure out their identities from the clues Louis had unwittingly mentioned; maybe not. Los Angeles County was a big place, especially when you tack on Ventura County too.

Decisions, decisions . . .

Again, there was no real decision to make. The Bear could always circle back and kill Hightower here in his beachside hidey-hole or up at his pathetic little house in Port Hueneme. He wasn't worried about the ex-cop. The wild cards, however, greatly intrigued him. Who was this fucking guy?

THE GIRL DETECTIVE

So many Bear theories on the message board this afternoon, so little time to fully explore them all. The Girl Detective was not pleased and was super eager for her father to return. Hopefully with the case files...

Aside from the usual interruptions (well-meaning nurses like her bestie Meghan checking her temp, blood pressure, altitude, pitch, avionics, and so on) there was the Aunt Reese factor. She was, like the good nurses, well-meaning. But her constant check-ins ("Everything okay, honey?") and offers of board game play ("How about another round of Connect Four?") were seriously getting in the way of the Girl Detective's concentration. At one point she sent Aunt Reese on a very important cafeteria mission, and then — yeah, she was kind of a jerk for doing this — sent her back down again, insisting that she'd asked for some *other* kind of juice. Someday karma would get her for that, but whatever. She had urgent detective work!

Which meant going back to the message boards, which had gone insane with conjecture.

One web sleuth had an elaborate theory that the California Bear hadn't ever gone away; he'd just been hibernating, gathering his unholy powers. This line of thinking went religious very fast, so the Girl Detective felt no problem with skipping the rest...

But one sleuth took part of this idea and ran with it in a different direction. It was her old pal Carnivora83, who had reappeared after a brief silence.

Early this morning Carnivora83 posted a lengthy (even for him) diatribe where he tried to float the idea that the California Bear was larger than one man; it was a supernatural force of nature and could be transferred, quite literally, to another man. (The Girl Detective noted the gender bias there; was there no room for a Lady Bear?) This Bear manifests itself when a "corrective is needed." (Oh boy.) To make a long rant short, Carnivora83 likened the hedonism of the late 1970s and early 1980s to the hedonism of 2018, where humanity was patting itself on the back for never having it quite so good before. "A force of nature is required to descend upon humanity like a plague. Or in this case . . . a predator."

Other posters started talking about the announcement of the forthcoming *California Bear* streaming documentary, directed by award-winning cult director Lasca Foster. And that the recent attacks were merely a publicity stunt to bring the Bear and his story back to the mainstream. They did it with Zodiac, the anonymous posters argued, and they're about to do it with Charlie Manson (next year's *Once Upon a Time in Hollywood*) as well as the Son of Sam. There was a serial killer arms race going on; the weak would fall while the truly legendary killers would rise. The very idea made the Girl Detective sick to her stomach, even more than the chemo.

But the real research breakthrough came when her bestie, Violet, called with a long-awaited update on her *other* murder case.

"I went to the real estate office after school yesterday," she told the Girl Detective, "just like you said."

"And you pretended you were an intern for the insurance company?"

"I did."

"And were you . . . a *convincing* intern?"

"I kind of played it like myself. Just like you said, right?"

"That's my girl. What did you find out?"

"Well, it's a whole lot, and I'm not sure I understand it. I'll send you all the PDFs they gave me."

"Did you actually see him? Gregory Passarella?"

"See him?" Violet asked. "I talked to him. He kind of...like, *hit on me*. Which was gross and weird."

"Maybe you should let him take you out, see what he knows."

"What? Ew, Mattie, no."

"I was kidding. Unless, of course, you think it would be fun. Anyway, send me those PDFs as soon as you can. I'm dying of boredom over here."

"That's really not funny."

"Gallows humor, V. Sometimes, it's all I've got. Now, send those files."

While she waited, she heard Aunt Reese's voice in her head: *If you were ever considering a career in real estate, forget about it. The business is full of backstabbing pricks who would gleefully throw you in front of a speeding truck if it meant they'd make their commission.*

"KILLER"

They were barely off the PCH before Louis asked, "You going to tell me how it went with Hightower? Is everything okay?"

"Yeah, it was fine, he's just planning the next steps," Jack replied, knowing this statement didn't make much sense and practically begged for a follow-up question. But Jack was distracted. What the hell did Hightower have in mind? What should he be prepared for?

And was he completely losing his mind, or was a car following them as they drove along the 10 East?

The freeway was a mess as usual, even though it was a Saturday evening. Jack was judging by his view from the side-view mirror on the Yaris, which wasn't exactly generous in terms of field of vision. It was more a feeling—a paranoia that seemed to grow with every passing day. He'd spent all his free days thinking someone was watching him, hunting him—and being attacked by that random chick in the Sizzler parking lot hadn't helped. That was even before they'd accidentally (sort of) caused the death of the California Bear...

That must be it. Jack Queen, under the strain of pretty much everything, was finally having a crack-up. He was seeing monsters everywhere. Even monsters who should be dead.

"Next steps for what?" Louis asked.

"It's not important," Jack said.

"Then why the hell did we just waste the afternoon driving all the way out to Port Hueneme and then back to Santa Monica? What was so urgent?"

Jack realized he had to be a little blunt—cruel as that might feel—to stop this line of questioning. For Louis's own good.

"Did you ever think that maybe this was none of your fucking business, Louis? That I'm trying to put my life together, and that I don't need you snooping over my shoulder the entire time?"

"Right," Louis responded. "Your business. I forgot. I need to just shut up and drive you wherever you want to go because it's your *business.* We're just here to serve you, but God forbid we ask any questions."

"Oh, fuck you."

"No, fuck you, Jack! Do you realize what kind of financial strain we've been under for the past couple of years? I never wanted kids. Reese *certainly* never wanted kids. And we love Matilda, but she's not our child. And raising a kid is fucking expensive! Rent is going through the roof, everything is costing more, and we're just supposed to float along with a big fucking smile on our faces saying, sure, we're happy to help! Who gives a shit about our plans and dreams? Who cares! The famous Jack Queen gets to be drunk and do whatever he wants."

"My wife *died,* you insensitive asshole."

"I know, Jack. I lost a sister-in-law, and your daughter lost a mother. Where was your fucking head? That should have been your big wake-up call to get your life together, not let it fall apart."

The next few miles were driven in silence. They were cutting through downtown LA now, on the 110 on their way to the 5 North. Louis, ever the writer, probably felt he needed to put a double underline on their conversation, just to drive the point home.

"So yeah...forgive me if I'm looking over your shoulder. I'm just trying to make sure you're doing okay so maybe I can focus on *my life* again for a fucking change."

The rest of the trip was dead quiet. Jack, desperate for something else to occupy his mind, looked at the other cars on the freeway. Wondered what kinds of lives they were living. What troubles they had, if any. Maybe their biggest concern tonight was where to find sushi. Or where they might go for a romantic weekend getaway.

Louis decided not to come up to the oncology floor; he was too upset. As he pulled into the parking garage he called Reese, telling her that he'd be waiting downstairs in the lobby for her and *no,* he *didn't* want to talk about it. Not right now. It was as angry as Louis had ever sounded.

Jack grabbed the file box and took the elevator up to Matilda's floor, still shaken from the conversation. Make that: the *rant.* What bothered him wasn't Louis's tone, or what he'd said. It was that Louis was right.

THE BEAR

Children's Hospital Los Angeles might be the *last* place the new Bear expected to end up on this fine, hot Saturday evening. Why were the brothers-in-law headed here after a leisurely afternoon in Port Hueneme and Patrick's Roadhouse? The Bear was so, *so* glad he'd chosen to follow them. (Twice, in fact.)

The Bear stayed a few car lengths behind them as they drove into the hospital's subterranean parking levels. He hoped he wouldn't need to show some form of identification at this point, because that would not work at all. Too risky. Fortunately, no; he was simply required to take a little cardboard ticket.

The Bear followed the Yaris three levels down until they found a spot. He found a spot, too, not very far away. He kept his distance and watched them step into the elevator. He took a chance and caught the *next* car up to the lobby; Louis the asthmatic screenwriter would surely recognize him otherwise. When he reached the lobby, however, he was surprised to see only Louis the screenwriter waiting there; his brother-in-law, Jack, was nowhere to be found. Louis was on his cell phone spelling his last name to someone. *No, it's F-A-L-T-E-R, as in you know, faltering, and Meyer, as in Oscar Meyer . . .*

Thank you, Louis Faltermeyer.

Now who was Jack?

Some quick Googling led the Bear from "Louis Faltermeyer" to some pathetic screenwriting posts on social media ("My hot take: voice-overs are not cliché") to an actual news story—a hit-and-run incident from 2016. Seems some rich real estate asshole was run down by a jazz pianist named...oh wow. *Wow!* Jack "Killer" Queen. (Louis was quoted as saying how senseless and tragic this all was and simply wanted peace for his family.) Even better, the article mentioned that Jack had a twelve-year-old daughter, which would explain why he'd be visiting a children's hospital.

"Hey, David, it's me," the Bear spoke into his cell phone. "You're never going to believe who Cato Hightower's other guy is..."

GENE JEANIE

The knock at her door came after she reheated some protein (baked chicken) and tossed together a humble salad (mostly arugula) and poured a steaming mug of tea (Twinings Australian Afternoon). She should have known that such a healthy decision would summon trouble.

Namely, her wayward husband, on her front stoop, contrite and possibly even sobered up.

"Jeanie, I've fucked up something awful and need your help."

"Do tell."

"I'm serious. I'm going to need you if we're going to stop this son of a bitch. And maybe...you know, maybe get us paid along the way."

Unbelievable. Nothing would ever motivate her husband. Nothing except money.

"I'll help you," Jeanie said, "but only if you come clean about everything."

Cato blinked. "Everything? Like, *everything* everything?"

"Everything about the California Bear, you pain in the ass."

"Oh."

She opened the door all the way. "Come on. I have something to show you."

THE GIRL DETECTIVE

"Hello, Daughter," her father responded as he walked into her room with a stained bankers box tucked under his arm.

The Girl Detective fought the urge to pounce on her dad and rip the box away so she could giddily rifle through its contents. But better to play it cool for the moment. She didn't want to appear overly eager; that might freak him out.

"How was your trip up to Port Hueneme?"

"Hightower wasn't there, so we pretty much drove for nothing. I found him back at the same motel where we'd been staying. He's . . . kind of a mess."

"But he's going to get off his ass and help?"

"That's what he said."

The Girl Detective couldn't stand it any longer. "Are we finally going to talk about the box under your arm?"

Her father gingerly placed it on the chair next to her bed as if it were an explosive device on a hair trigger. "Promise me this stays super confidential. I mean, even the nurses can't see this. Pretty sure I'm breaking the law here, and I don't want you to be caught up in this nightmare too."

"Father, I am nothing if not discreet. Don't worry."

She was about to whip off the cardboard lid and go to town but noticed a haunted look on her father's face. Which was distinct from the haunted look he usually wore, especially while surrounded by doctors and nurses and medical gear.

"Everything okay, Padre?"

Her father sat down on the combination couch/bed beneath her windows.

"I think I'm losing my mind."

"Same."

"I don't mean it in the general sense," her father said. "I'm talking specifically. And I hate even bringing it up in front of you, but I promised to tell you the truth from now on. No secrets."

"Go on," she said softly, the murder box momentarily forgotten.

"I don't want to freak you out, but ever since I was released from prison, I feel like people have been following me. Watching me. Keeping tabs on me. Whatever. At first, I chalked it up to adjusting to life on the outside, but . . . I don't know."

"Let's assume for the moment that you're not crazy or merely adjusting," she replied. "What does this someone look like? Were you able to make out any details?"

"This is why I think I'm crazy. Sometimes it's a man with, like, a baby face. Sometimes it's, like, this dark-haired girl who looks like she should be in college. Maybe they're a tag team? Maybe part of the conspiracy?"

"Tell me more about this girl."

"She sucker punched me in the parking lot."

"Ouch," the Girl Detective said. "Is your parking lot feeling better now?"

"You know what I mean."

"And I meant *describe her,* as if I were drawing a police sketch."

As her father described her, something clicked into place for the Girl Detective. She'd have to check her notes to be sure, and maybe do a little Googling. But she was confident her hunch was correct. Not that she was ready to tell her father what she and Violet had discovered so far. That needed to wait until she was certain.

"You look beat," the Girl Detective said. "Have you had anything to eat today?"

Her father looked mystified, as if this were the strangest question in the world. As he searched his memory banks, she basically ordered him down to the cafeteria for some dinner, no arguments. After some well-meaning back-and-forth, Jack finally agreed but promised to be right back. The Girl Detective told him to take his time—and meant it.

She had a murder box to sort through.

THE BEAR

Apartment buildings were notoriously easy to break into — but this one practically invited the Bear in with a red carpet.

Trailing Louis the screenwriter wasn't terribly difficult either. Based on body language glimpsed through the back window of the Toyota Yaris, Louis and his girlfriend (or was it his wife?) argued most of the time, with the woman on the attack and Louis on the defensive as he navigated traffic up Los Feliz Boulevard. There was no chance they noticed the Bear following, even as he basically tailgated them along the looping ramp that would put them on the 5 North.

From there, the Yaris took the exit for the 134, and then left the freeway at Hollywood Way. Their apartment building was in that nebulous zone between Burbank and Toluca Lake. Parking wasn't even an issue. The Bear simply followed right behind them and chose an empty spot just a few spaces away.

The trickiest part was next — figuring out which apartment was theirs. But again, Louis and his partner made it easy. They ascended a flight of stairs to the open-air mail room to retrieve their stack of bills and supermarket flyers. The Bear simply noted which box was theirs on the grid; the moment they left, it was easy to peek at their apartment number: 305.

Back in his car, the Bear used his iPad to call up the building's site, which very helpfully provided detailed floor plans for each unit — as well as how much they paid in rent each month. (Too much for a concrete dump like this.) The way to their front door was obvious.

The Bear looked like a human being when he walked through the halls. But the moment he reached the stairwell that would take him to the roof, he pulled the furry mask over his head and slipped the glove over his left hand. This Bear was right-handed, but there was no changing that.

When he opened the door to the roof, he was fully and completely the California Bear 2.0—new and improved, with none of the baked-in weaknesses. He even slipped the foam headphones over the lumps of his ears and cranked up some seventies metal. The Bear guessed that his predecessor would be a Black Sabbath kind of monster.

The most obvious way into the apartment was across the tarred roof and down onto the balcony. Decorative wooden slats gave him purchase. He landed on the balcony without a sound.

The Bear tried the sliding glass door; locked.

But there was a window just off the balcony too. And it had been left unlocked. The Bear slid it open, parted a shade as carefully as possible, and slipped inside.

This was a girl's room. Teenager, most likely. Textbooks and posters of bands the Bear barely recognized (who the fuck were 21 Pilots?) and makeup and photos pinned to a strip of cork above her desk. The images showed other teenagers with one exception: a young girl posing on the Santa Monica Pier with two adults on a bright, sunny day. The woman he didn't recognize. But the man was Jack Queen.

Which meant the girl in this photo was Jack's daughter. Since the bed in this room was neatly made, and there were traces of dust on every visible surface, it stood to reason that Jack's daughter was the mysterious patient at Children's Hospital Los Angeles.

Now, that made things *very* interesting.

The Bear examined every element of the room, trying to build a composite image of the girl in his mind. There were many, many books beyond the texts typically assigned by your average high school. She was a reader. A writer, too, based on the stacks of notebooks and drawers full of manuscripts, all with the byline "Matilda Finnerty." He dragged his eyes through some of the text, expecting to be bored senseless by the banalities of teenage life. But no — this girl had a voice.

Stranger still, it was a voice he *recognized*. But from where?

The Bear was so absorbed in his examinations that he was truly caught by surprise when the lights snapped on. He spun around to see a woman wielding a baseball bat and screaming. He slipped off the headphones in time to hear.

"No — no fucking way!!"

And then she swung the bat.

The Bear lifted his gloved paw — pure reflex — and felt the full power of the bat strike his palm. His entire arm went numb. Oh, this would not do. The woman screamed again and prepared to swing. He recognized her. She was the woman from the photo. Matilda's mother and perhaps Jack's wife? Or would that be ex-wife? Whoever she was, she completely telegraphed her swing, enabling the Bear to push her with his human hand. She landed on her ass.

The Bear gave her his fiercest growl.

"What the fuck is that supposed to be? Are you actually *growling* at me, you sick fuck?"

"Do you know who I am?"

"You're going to be an asshole with a shattered skull if you don't get out of here!"

Ordinarily he would have slashed at her face for such an insult, but his clawed hand was still numb. Instead the Bear jumped back through the window.

She was at him again, faster than he'd expected, and landed quite a few blows on his legs as he pulled himself up to the roof. The woman was furious, screaming incoherently, taking out years of aggression on the Bear. This wasn't fair. What the hell did he do, except sneak into her house?

The pain and embarrassment, however, were well worth it. Because now he had the missing pieces he needed.

Especially now that he remembered where he'd heard that written voice before.

SUNDAY, JUNE 10, 2018

"KILLER"

Jack was barely awake before his burner phone vibrated on the little desk in the corner of Matilda's room. He reached over to silence it before it woke his daughter. Was this Hightower at long last? He'd been half-awake all night anticipating the man's call . . . which had never come. Jack had texted him, and even broken down and *called* him, just after midnight, but no response.

"You're not going to believe this."

This was not Hightower. This was his sister-in-law.

"What is it, Reese? What's wrong?"

"Some fucking asshole broke into our apartment last night!"

"What?"

"Are you not listening to me? Some asshole in a ski mask or something broke into Matilda's room. I don't know how long the fucker was in there, but I caught him in the act and beat the shit out of him with a baseball bat. You know, the one I keep under the bed for emergencies. Never thought I'd actually have to *use it* . . ."

Jack's blood froze as if someone had injected him with Freon. "Can you describe the mask?"

"What? Who cares what the mask looked like? He was probably some junkie looking for jewelry to sell. The asshole growled at me . . . do you believe that? Like he was some kind of wild animal. That's it. I'm telling Louis we're moving out of this place."

Reese had no idea who had broken into her apartment—but Jack certainly did. After a few more futile attempts to have her describe the attacker, Jack said he had to go, a nurse was here with an update. A lie, of course. By this time, Matilda was wide awake and had been tuning in to their conversation, putting together the missing pieces.

"I take it the Bear was in *my* room," she said.

"Sounds like it."

"Are Aunt Reese and Uncle Louis okay?"

"They're fine. Aunt Reese managed to scare him off with a bat."

Matilda processed everything with blinding speed. "This means the Bear knows everything. He must have followed you yesterday, all the way here to the hospital. And then when he couldn't follow you to the oncology floor, he decided to follow Louis home instead. Where he bided his time."

"This is not happening."

"But it is," Matilda said. "And hey, look on the bright side. You're not paranoid. You were being followed."

"Small comfort."

Matilda picked up her cell phone and dialed the number she'd dug up a few days ago.

"Hello?"

"Mrs. Hightower, hello. My name is Matilda Finnerty. I'm Jack Queen's daughter and I think we should talk."

"Lovely to meet you, Matilda," Jeanie said. "And I couldn't agree more."

GENE JEANIE

"Let's start over with the facts we know for certain," Matilda Finnerty said over the phone. "We know the Bear is dead."

"According to your father," Jeanie replied. "And, uh ... my husband."

"I trust my dad. Do you trust your husband?"

"Jury's out on that one," Jeanie said, "but he's ex–law enforcement. I think he can tell a dead body from someone who's just faking it."

"My dad said he felt for a pulse and there was none."

"So there's our fact. Christopher Albin Dixon, who was the serial killer known as the California Bear, backed up by genetics, is dead as Dillinger."

"Who?"

"Sometimes I forget how young you are," Jeanie said. "That's a compliment, by the way."

"I'm just messing with you. Of course I know who John Dillinger was. I even know what movie he saw right before the FBI turned him into Swiss cheese."

"*Manhattan Melodrama*? With William Powell and Myrna Loy?"

"That's the one. I wonder what was the last thing the Bear watched before he died—"

"The ceiling of his garage, if Cato is to be believed."

The girl laughed. "That's so ... *wrong*."

"I know. But back to the Bear."

"Second fact: someone else is out there right now pretending to be the Bear," Matilda said. "Either this is a wildly random coincidence..."

"Or someone wants the world to think the Bear is still out there, breaking into homes and terrorizing random people."

"I don't think it's a coincidence."

"Same here. I don't believe in them."

"Why the new Bear, then?" Matilda asked. "Why right now?"

The questions nagged at Jeanie. Who had said those *exact words* to her recently?

"There's only one motive that's ever made sense to me," Jeanie said. "Money."

"I don't think so," Matilda said.

"What, then?"

"I have some ideas about that. To quote an awful sequel, this time I think it's personal."

"If it's okay with you," Jeanie said, "we're going to come down to the hospital and talk all of this through. I think it's best if we're all together in the same room."

"Okay with me?" the Girl Detective asked. "I've been waiting for you to offer. I'm worried my father is in over his head."

"Well, my husband threw him into the deep end of the pool, so don't be too hard on him."

GENE JEANIE

"I still can't believe you got the kid involved," Cato complained. His hands were gripped tight on the wheel, as if trying to choke his car into submission.

"The *kid* is kind of brilliant. You should be thanking me."

"Jack's not going to be happy, I'll tell you that much."

"I think Jack would very much like to resolve all of this."

They were almost at the junction of the 134 and the 5. From there, they'd take the freeway down to Los Feliz Boulevard and then down Vermont to CHLA. Sunday morning is the one time in Los Angeles when you can pretty much drive anywhere and expect to arrive on time. Even with Cato behind the wheel.

"*Resolve*," Cato said with more than a hint of mockery. "Well, that's a fancy way of saying something completely ugly. We're dealing with maniacs here."

Jeanie's cell phone went off. She glanced at the screen. Oh fuck. Her ex. Timing, perfect as ever.

"Hey."

"Can you talk?"

"Not really."

"So just listen. A hit came back on your genetic sample. I hate to say this . . . it's one of ours."

"One of yours what?"

"The sample matched an active-duty cop. In fact, the same police officer who's been sitting outside your house. I don't know what you did to encourage a stalker..."

"What's the name?"

"Come on, Jean. I can't tell you that. But I'm not sitting on my hands either. I've already reached out to a buddy of mine in IA, and they're going to handle it."

"I need a name," Jeanie insisted. "It's very important."

"Jesus, Jeanie. You're killing me."

Cato finally tuned in to her conversation. "Hey, who is that you're talking to?"

"A client," Jeanie said, then turned her attention back to her ex on the phone. "I wouldn't ask if it weren't extremely important."

"Fine. His name is..."

"Hold on a sec." Jeanie pulled open the glove box in search of a pen and paper. Out popped a Glock pistol. She recognized it immediately: it was Cato's old service weapon. "What the fuck is this?"

"Are you talking to me?"

"No...never mind. Please, what's the name?"

"Cullen Gallagher. He used to hang around the same bars with Christopher Albin Dixon, the ex-cop they found dead last week. The big joke going around was that Dixon was secretly the California Bear, and Cullen was his little disciple. Everyone started calling him 'Cubby.' I don't know. I don't really know him, and I don't know why he's suddenly interested in you."

"I do," Jeanie said. "Thank you.

"Like I said, I have IA involved, so don't do anything else. I mean it."

"I promise, I'll steer clear of him."

Cato was getting even more annoyed. "Who the fuck is that on the phone?"

"Is that your husband? He sounds like an asshole."

"Apparently I have a type," Jeanie said, but before that landed with her ex, she thanked him and told him she'd be in touch soon.

"KILLER"

Jeanie brought Matilda doughnuts—two dozen. This cemented an instant bond with Matilda, who realized that Jeanie Hightower was a woman who not only paid careful attention to details but was thoughtful too. After Jeanie insisted that Hightower deliver the second dozen to the nurses' station ("Really? I thought we'd take some home with us"), they finally gathered around Matilda's bed to discuss the problem of the Bear.

"I have a kind of crazy idea," Jeanie said.

"What's that?" Jack asked.

"I'd like *you* to come with me to the Dixon house."

"No way," Jack said. "Matilda's going through a really rough time, and I'm not going to leave her alone."

"Matilda's right here," Matilda said, "and I'm the furthest thing from alone. Maybe you didn't notice, but I'm on the cancer wing of the children's hospital."

"Believe me, I know it's a big ask," Jeanie said. "But I need someone with me who knows the house and can tell me what to expect."

"Your husband has seen the house," Jack countered.

"Yeah," Hightower said, "but this husband here is still recovering from his last visit to Hell House. My arm still hurts like a motherfucker." The ex-cop seemed to catch himself, casting a glance at the hallway. "I know, I probably shouldn't say that in here."

"Either way," Jack said, "I'm sorry. No."

"I'm talking an hour or two, tops," Jeanie said. "We go there, we figure out what the hell is going on, and we nip this in the bud. Cato can stay here and guard Matilda."

"Oh, I'm sure she'd love that."

"Matilda is *still here.*"

"What? Girls love me."

"Topless girls made of brass love you," Jack said. "And that's because they have no choice. You bought them."

Jeanie turned to her husband. "You still have that stupid fucking thing?"

"I can't help it that you're a heathen who doesn't appreciate life's rich pageant."

"You're not using that expression the right way," Jack said.

"I thought you were a jazz pianist, not an art critic."

"Jack, listen to me," Jeanie said. "Matilda is the one who helped me figure this out. There's some kind of plot to bring the California Bear back to life, probably for some kind of movie or streaming series or whatever." Now she lowered her voice. "Clearly, this perp isn't the real Bear. And if it's about money, then his widow must be involved. All we have to do is look her in the eye, tell her that *we* know. She can either stop it in its tracks, or we go to the police. Easy as that."

Gene Jeanie had a way of making . . . well, total sense, unlike her husband. Fuck. This was the sensible thing to do. And he didn't trust Hightower to not fuck it up. That left it up to Jack and Jeanie.

"We'll have fun!" Hightower exclaimed, clearly relieved to be off the hook for this little expedition to a serial killer's lair. "Order some room service, put on a movie."

"There is no room service," Jack said. "And listen to me . . . you're not going to leave her side, you understand me? Not until I'm back."

"First of all," Hightower replied with more than a hint of condescension, "I won't leave her side. Second, this place is like Fort Knox. You can't get past the front desk without a parent badge. And unless this new California Bear happens to have a sick kid in this place, they ain't coming anywhere near us."

"For once," Jack said, "you have a good point."

"I mean, it's *you two* I'm worried about. What if you show up there, and the new Bear is all cozy with the widow? And this is all one big trap to lure you there?"

"Not *hel*-ping," Jeanie muttered.

"If I may speak," Matilda said finally. "I think it's an excellent idea. I am perfectly safe here. And I think if anyone is going to talk sense into Cassandra Dixon, it'll be the two of you. Though I still maintain it's about the fame, not the money."

"Cassandra Dixon is no fan of mine," Jack said. "If you all remember, I punched her in the face, knocking her unconscious next to the corpse of her husband."

"I'm sure she's not thrilled about the punch," Jeanie said. "But it'll help if she fears you a little. I'm the honey, you're the vinegar."

"And hey," Hightower said. "Nobody's perfect."

THE BEAR

If there was one thing the Reborn Bear knew, it was how hospitals worked. His mama, God rest her tortured soul, spent her entire life as a traveling nurse. Which meant she dragged her baby boy along with her, city to city, new school to new school, rootless, desperate at times, but always a new adventure! Or at least that was how she tried to sell it. And it was an adventure! Each new home meant a new set of bullies to deal with, arcane customs to navigate, and all kinds of ways to feel like a fish out of water. All throughout his childhood he wondered what it would be like if they didn't have to jump around all the time. Maybe if his father had been around, they could have stayed in one place—but his mama also said that his daddy was a traveling man, too, and maybe someday they'd cross paths again.

Yeah. Maybe.

But mama was gone now—bone cancer, early last year—leaving behind very little except a pile of credit card bills, her personal effects, and her nursing credentials. The last two seemed worthless until today.

"Joyce Sobczak?" the security guard at the front desk asked. "Yeah, I'm not seeing you on the rotation tonight."

"What else is new, right?" the Bear said, then sighed. "Is Shannon Morris in tonight? She's my contact here. I flew all the way from Denver, and I was really counting on these shifts."

The security guard gave the Bear a long look, then tapped a few keys. The Bear hoped his foundation wasn't running, or telltale beads of sweat escaping from under his wig. His mama's wig—the same one she wore during her treatment years. Transforming into a reasonable simulacrum of his mother hadn't been difficult, really. People always said he favored his mama. And he had a notoriously boyish face, which meant no one ever took him seriously.

All of that was about to change.

"No, she's not," the security guard said finally. "But go on in and check with Nurse Quigley. She'll help you sort things out."

The Bear thanked the guard and made his way into the hospital's inner sanctum. First order of business would be not Nurse Quigley but a restroom so he could rend these ridiculous garments from his body. There would be no need to completely wash off the makeup, however. Inside his mother's nurse's traveling kit was his version of the original California Bear's mask and clawed glove, painstakingly re-created with a combination of modern and vintage materials, guided by advice from Bear enthusiasts.

He couldn't wait to put them on again, in the dark, when the time was right.

THE GIRL DETECTIVE

"Okay, now we can have some fun," Hightower said.

"I'm sorry?" the Girl Detective asked.

"I'm starving! Let's put you in a wheelchair and hightail it down to the cafeteria. I hear the food's actually pretty good here."

"Are you serious?"

"Aren't you hungry? And besides, your meals are free, right? Are you allowed a plus one on your current plan?"

The Girl Detective immediately thought of a half dozen withering replies, many of them involving the idea of asking a cancer patient on chemo if they were hungry or not. But then she stopped herself. A trip to the cafeteria might be a great idea. Perhaps Hightower could help fill in some of the missing details of her *other* case—her father's hit-and-run conviction. A little ice cream would probably soften the big guy right up.

"The food *is* quite excellent," Matilda said. "Michelin rated, I hear. Let's go."

After arranging for a chair and getting her IV lines all squared away—Hightower seemed surprised it was such a production—they were finally off, headed down the long hallway to the double doors. As they passed by, the nurses at the station thanked Hightower again for the doughnuts.

And her favorite nurse, Meghan, walked over to her chair and whispered in her ear.

"You should hurry back," she said. "I'm hearing a rumor we've got a celebrity visitor this evening. A certain...*action hero* celebrity."

Celebrity visits, the Girl Detective had quickly learned, were one of the perks of having a children's hospital based near the entertainment industry. The visits happened constantly, and a B-list superhero or trending pop singer had a way of bringing a smile to the little ones' faces, she supposed. The Girl Detective would much rather a surprise visit from John E. Douglas or Patricia Cornwell.

"Really?" said Hightower, who was clearly eavesdropping. "A celebrity? Is it Chuck Norris? Or maybe Dolph Lundgren? Oh man, I've always wanted to meet him!"

The Girl Detective rolled her eyes. "You'll have to forgive my uncle Cato here, who hasn't seen an action movie since 1985. Who is it? I promise not to say a word."

Meghan mock-frowned at Hightower, then leaned in close to whisper the name into the Girl Detective's ear.

She pretended to be excited, but inside something troubled her. Seriously? *That* celebrity? She was sure all the little comic book nerds would be thrilled with the visit, but why did that particular name bother her so much?

GENE JEANIE

The lights were on at the serial killer's house. Well, at least somebody was home, and they didn't take a drive up to the Valley for nothing. Jeanie killed the ignition and was preparing to step out of the car when she noticed Jack wasn't moving.

"You okay over there?" she asked.

"I feel like I'm about to relive a nightmare," Jack said. "Whatever happens, we *don't* go into the shack behind the house."

"I'm sure it won't come to that," Jeanie said. "Come on. Let's get this over with."

Before they reached the front door, however, Jeanie realized someone was watching them. A brawny figure emerged from the shadowy path along the side of the house.

"Hold it right there."

As he stepped into the house security lights, Jeanie could see he was wearing the typical plainclothes detective gear: out-of-date shirt and tie, khakis, suit coat, service weapon in his shoulder holster. She'd been around enough cops over the years to know the type instantly—down to where this guy probably bought that unfashionable shirt and tie. But the recognition went even deeper.

"What do you want with Ms. Dixon?" the cop said. "She's been through a great shock."

"Good afternoon, Detective Gallagher," Jeanie said without missing a beat. The detective looked perplexed. Good. Even Jack Queen was surprised.

"You two *know* each other?"

Jeanie nodded. "You can say we've been intimate in the recent past."

"What?" Jack asked, clearly stunned. "Does Hightower know?"

And no, her husband didn't know. But Detective Cullen Gallagher certainly picked up on the reference. She knew his type. His genetic type. Even in this low light, she could see his cheeks redden.

"After you, Cubby," she said. Reluctantly the cop led the way to the front door. He rapped three times, and another male voice told him to come on in.

Cassandra Dixon was already seated at the dining room table with another familiar face. David Peterson, the producer. The ceiling and stationary fans were running at full blast, working hard to keep things temperate on this steamy June evening, but failing anyway.

"Hello, Mrs. Hightower," the producer said. "Good to see you again."

"Likewise," Jeanie said.

"Jeanie," Jack said, "what the hell is going on? Do you know *everybody* in this city?"

Cassandra said, "I remember *you,* you son of a bitch." Jack had nothing to say in response. He looked down at his feet, uncomfortable.

"Good evening, uh, ma'am."

Pleasantries dispensed with, Jeanie felt like it was time to get to the point. "We all need to have a come-to-Jesus talk."

"You here to share the gospel?" Peterson asked, wide smile on his face.

"We want you to stop what you're doing," Jeanie said, "or we will go to the police."

"Hey, lady," Cubby said, "I am the police."

"We'll get to *you* in a minute," Jeanie replied, shooting him such a withering glance that the little bastard acted as if someone had slapped a rolled-up newspaper across his nose. "Why don't you go find an underwear drawer somewhere and keep yourself occupied?"

"Jeanie," Peterson said, laughing. "Come on. You know *exactly* what we're doing. We're making a documentary."

"Yeah, with 'next-level' reenactments," Jeanie said. "You people are fucking sick."

Cassandra's eyes lit up with anger and she opened her mouth to reply, but Peterson patted her hand reassuringly.

"Cassie, honey, maybe if I explain what's going on, it will put their minds at ease. Here's the thing. The late Mr. Dixon was acting as our consultant. We wanted to re-create, to the best of our ability, the mental conditions that led to the Bear's original excursions. The idea is that Mr. Dixon would case the exact same homes he'd allegedly broken into back in the day, then tell us exactly how he'd break in today, down to the last detail."

"Frightening the hell out of innocent people all over again," Jack said.

"Look, that's just it. We wanted to do something along the lines of *The Blair Witch Project*. We rented those first two houses—the ones where Mr. Dixon *allegedly* claimed his first victims. And we hired up-and-coming talent to live there for a month. All the actors knew was that they were part of some kind of reality show where they'd be stalked and hunted in their homes...and at some point, there would be a home invasion. They were told to act naturally and react as they normally would. But nobody would get hurt."

"You were counting on a notorious serial killer to *behave himself?*" Jeanie asked.

"Mr. Dixon was merely a paid consultant. He would teach our lead actor, who would be portraying the Bear, *exactly* what to do. Body movements, his mindset, finding a home's vulnerabilities, how to terrorize. All that fun stuff. But at no point would anyone be in danger."

Peterson was right; this did make some kind of twisted sense to Jeanie. Call it *The Real Terrorized Housewives of Hollywood*. Then again, Peterson had lied to her about the identity of the Bear, and maybe he was lying now.

"Due to the unforeseen demise of Mr. Dixon," Peterson continued, "there's been a change in the focus of the streaming series. And I'm pretty excited about it, because frankly it should have been the focus all along."

"Let me guess," Jeanie said. "You have some other psycho running around pretending to be the California Bear to keep your deal."

Cassandra Dixon glared at Jeanie as if she could melt human flesh with invisible heat rays. Peterson squeezed her hand this time, as if to say, *Please let me handle this.*

"Funny you bring that up," Peterson said. "You want to know who this new Bear is? You might want to take a closer look at your husband, Cato. He's the right size, and he has a pretty strong motive to keep the California Bear alive. Think about it. Cato and Jack Queen over there were the ones trying to shake Mr. Dixon down for some of that deal money. When they pushed too hard, they realized their plan had just collapsed. If there's no Bear, there's no project, and if there's no project, there's no blackmail money."

"No offense," Jack said, "but Cato Hightower is neither ambitious enough nor athletic enough to start stalking people in Los Feliz."

"Well, that's kind of rude," Jeanie said, then caught herself. "But also . . . completely accurate."

"So who is it? Maybe it's your lead actor, gone psycho after consulting with Dixon for too long."

Cassandra was unable to bottle her rage any longer. "Your idiot husband and his hired muscle are the ones who fucked all of this up!"

"You've been married to a serial killer for nearly thirty years," Jeanie said. "Either you're an idiot for not noticing, or you did know and you're a horrible human being for covering it up."

"Oh, I knew," Cassandra said quietly.

"And you said nothing?"

"Cassie, honey, don't . . ."

"I knew from the very beginning. Because I was the California Bear's final victim."

THE GIRL DETECTIVE

By the time they reached the double security doors leading to the elevator banks, she had it. The actor's name. It was one of the lead contenders for the on-again, off-again California Bear movie that had been in development since...well, probably since 1984. Lots of actor names had been floated on the message boards, everyone from Schwarzenegger (back in the eighties) to Vince Vaughn (in the nineties) to Vincent D'Onofrio (in the aughts) to Dave Bautista (as recently as last week). Big, manly, burly men who could fill the role with sheer size and menace.

But for years the dark-horse candidate had been someone who'd started out as a whippet-thin actor, a performer who'd begun his career with cerebral and Oscar-bait roles before transforming himself into the master of stoner comedies, followed by yet another transformation into an unlikely action hero in comic book flicks, and lately, a transformation into a go-to heavy (pun intended) in Scorsese-style epics. Nobody took this particular actor seriously as a contender for a California Bear movie until he revealed in Deadline that he had been obsessed with the case since he was a kid.

This actor was the one who Meghan said would be visiting tonight. Kids would dig the Marvel factor; parents would be wowed by the Oscar-bait Scorsese stuff.

Only the Girl Detective knew the truth—that this was most likely the new Bear, because he didn't want his juiciest role in years to disappear. Why let an ex-cop and an ex-con stand in the way of a career-making turn?

And everyone else would think that Mr. Action Hero / Oscar Bait just had a free gap in his schedule and decided to make a few sick kids smile.

But this was it — this was how you slipped past hospital security. It was simple, really:

You can go anywhere if you're famous.

GENE JEANIE

Cassandra Dixon stared at her own kitchen table for a very long time before beginning.

"I was a desperately unhappy housewife in Glendale when the man known as the California Bear broke into my house, told me he was going to strip me naked, tie me up, and then cut me into little pieces. I told him, don't threaten me with a good time." Cassandra laughed with no hint of mirth whatsoever. "*That* threw him completely."

Jeanie couldn't help but notice that David Peterson's hand was no longer clasping Mrs. Dixon's. Instead, his hands were patiently folded on the table in front of him.

"I've gotten to know Christopher very well over the years," she continued, "and I know how much he gets off on pushing people's buttons. Scaring people was the only way he could get hard. And you know what? At the time, I meant it. I didn't care if he fucked me, then slit my throat, or vice versa. At least it would be an escape—an interesting way to die. People would talk about me. I'd live on, somehow."

"That's fucked up," Jack said. Jeanie kicked him. When someone is confessing their Great Truth, you don't interrupt.

"All of a sudden, Mr. Big Bad Bear couldn't leave my house fast enough. But I wouldn't let him. The tables were turned now. You see, when you're cowering in fear, there's no limit to his power. But you go after him, he gets all nervous and klutzy. Stumbles over his own big feet.

I managed to pull his stupid furry mask off and even steal his wallet before he finally smashed his way out the back door."

"He carried *his wallet* with him?" Jack asked. Jeanie kicked him again. Jack grunted.

"Christopher had been doing this for six years by this point and was growing both overly confident and sloppy. He would have been caught sooner rather than later. So in a weird way, I helped create his mysterious little legacy. The Bear wasn't caught. He didn't just stop. *I made him stop.*"

"How?" Jeanie asked. She also noticed that Cubby was looking like he was about to throw up. Clearly, this was news to him as well.

"I showed up at his house the next day—this very house, by the way—and made him an offer. Marry me or I go to the FBI. I had everything he touched in plastic bags. I had his wallet. I had his stupid fucking mask. Sure, it was my word against a cop's word, but once the Feds started digging, they wouldn't give up, and eventually they'd reveal it all. And he knew it. So yeah. He said yes. I left my husband that day. Poor idiot never knew what hit him. Romantic, isn't it."

She stared down at her fingers as they seemed to do battle with each other.

"So you see, while I was the California Bear's final victim, he was *my* victim. I didn't marry my best friend. I married my worst enemy. I've spent nearly thirty years making him pay."

There was a heavy beat of silence, befitting the heavy moment. Cubby seemed on the verge of passing out. Jack kept his mouth shut, even when the Bear's widow made one final jab.

"And it was all about to finally pay off, until your idiot husband ruined everything. I was going to be able to tell *my story.*"

"And turn a tidy profit in the meantime," Jeanie muttered.

David Peterson quickly jumped in. "Anyway...*that's* what we were here discussing when you decided to just drop in. Too many of these series are about the killer and the fetishization of murder. You rarely hear the victim's side of it. Cassandra's story is going to blow people's minds."

"She's not an innocent heroine, David," Jeanie said. "She hid a serial killer for nearly three decades."

"We're massaging that part a little. But here's the important thing. I think I have a solution here that will make everyone happy."

Peterson reached into his jacket pocket and pulled out a bone-white envelope.

"I spoke with our lead earlier today, and he's in total agreement. Jeanie, you're a super-capable researcher, and we could really use you on the project."

"Use me?" Jeanie repeated, incredulous.

"And, Jack...well, I don't think there's a budget line for a former jazz pianist, but I know I can find you some kind of gig on set. Maybe you can help with security. All you both have to do in return is sign this NDA and cash a very generous check."

Cullen "Cubby" Gallagher pulled the automatic weapon from his shoulder holster and trained it on Jack Queen. "Cassie, we're not giving these assholes a dime."

"Who's we?" Peterson exclaimed, angry for the first time. "Gallagher, shut the fuck up and put that thing away. Our lead is taking care of this."

"It's far too late for that," Cubby said. "I learned a lot from my mentor. Especially how to take care of loose ends."

And now he pointed his gun at Cassandra Dixon, the final girl, who lived with her monster for nearly three decades.

"How dare you," Cassandra said, her tone so cold that you could almost see her breath.

"No!" Cubby replied. "How dare *you*! He was a great man and you stopped his great work! You neutered him, you fucking bitch!"

THE BEAR

The name was correct: Matilda Finnerty, scrawled in marker on a little dry-erase board outside the room. But there was no one inside. No patient, no parent. The Bear could ask at the front desk, but he thought that might be too risky. Better to have no one connect him with this particular patient.

The Bear stepped inside the room, which was littered with stuffed animals and books and board games. One of the stuffed animals gave him pause. *Is that a rat? What kind of kid likes to play with a rat?* He walked over to the overbed table, which was also covered in junk — stress balls, fidget spinners, and little squishy animals that looked edible. (The Bear put one between his teeth and bit down gently. They weren't.) This was the room of a young girl fighting cancer, sure enough.

But wait...

The books. They were not your typical reading material. Truman Capote's *In Cold Blood.* A big fat paperback of locked-room mysteries. Old-timey stuff missing dust covers and with titles like *Trent's Own Case, The Red House Mystery,* and *Murder Can Be Fun.* Pretty dark for a little girl.

There was also a manila folder on the side table. The Bear pulled down the sleeve of his shirt to flip it open — fingerprints and all — and almost fell over in shock. Inside the folder were photocopied articles about *him.* Well, not him. His predecessor. They were mostly from the *Los Angeles Times* and *Los Angeles Herald Examiner.* They were immediately familiar because he had three-ring research binders full of the same clips. He knew many of them by heart.

This was not good.

Sure, there was a chance that the girl's father, this Jack Queen guy, left them around. But knowing the girl's taste in reading material made him think otherwise. She was helping him. Which meant she knew the secrets of his predecessor too. The Bear needed to find both father and daughter immediately.

He walked down the hall as fast as he could without calling undue attention to himself. A heavyset nurse stopped him anyway. "Can I help you find someone?"

"Oh...yes," the Bear said, praying she didn't notice the makeup on his face. "I'm looking for a patient named Matilda Finnerty. I'm friends with her father, Jack. I thought she'd be in her room, but..."

"I don't think Jack is here right now, and you just missed Matilda. She went down to the cafeteria with another family friend. You might catch them down there."

Fuck. Where was Jack Queen?

"Thank you so much. You're a lifesaver."

The Bear hurried—not too fast, not too slow—down the hall and through the security doors and to the connecting hall that would take him to the elevator bank. His prey was on the move, but it wasn't as if she could leave this place. The Bear would find her, even if it took all night.

THE GIRL DETECTIVE

"Oh shit."

"Oh shit what?" Hightower said.

"I think that was him. Out in the hall. I couldn't really tell because of the light."

"What? Him who?"

The descent of the elevator car made the Girl Detective a little nauseous. The slightest movements sometimes threw her entire equilibrium out of whack. Or maybe it was the raw fear of being pursued by a wealthy and unstoppable killer, with a not-so-bright ex-cop as her only protection.

"Did you fall down and give yourself a concussion, Hightower? The California Bear. The new Bear. He was standing at the end of the hallway just now. That means I was right, and he's coming after us."

"Are you sure?"

"Gee, I don't know. Let's go back upstairs and ask for his driver's license."

The elevator continued its slow descent to the ground floor. The Girl Detective gritted her teeth and tried to keep everything on the inside.

"You saw him for, like, a second," Hightower said. "I think your mind is playing tricks on you. Or you're hopped up on whatever pain meds they have you on."

"Your sensitivity and grace are an example for us all."

"Even if it is him, what's the big deal? We're in a busy hospital. He's not going to try to murder us in front of dozens of witnesses. Remember,

I've squared off against the original Bear, in real life, alone in his garage. He's dead, and I'm standing right here."

"That's not quite the way my dad tells it. And let me remind you that we're not facing off against the original Bear. This is a younger, stronger version. Who knows what kind of tricks he has up his sleeve? He could have a claw with poison tips. One scratch and your heart stops within sixty seconds."

"Are you sure you're only fifteen?"

"Fourteen, technically. And I'm not saying that's what it is. I'm saying we don't know what he has in mind. All we do know, for sure, is that a mentally disturbed human being felt confident enough to walk into this hospital and make his way up to my room. And I don't think it was to play a round of Connect Four."

"Fuck."

Ding.

Hightower pushed her out of the elevator car. The way he was panic breathing made her want to trade places with him. And this guy was supposed to be protecting her?

"Okay, you convinced me," Hightower said as he sped her down the hall to the main corridor. She wanted to tell him to slow down before a cop pulled them over. "I'll just take you out the front door."

"Nope. The guards will stop me. I can't leave until I'm formally discharged."

"Even if we're being chased by a psychopath?"

"Do you want to stop and explain the whole story? Go ahead. I'll just be over here in my wheelchair preparing to die."

"Shit! This is not good."

"Now you're getting it."

"KILLER"

Without warning Jack pushed Jeanie's chair across the floor, surprising her along with everyone else. He vaulted out of his own seat and slid on his ass across the floor until he reached the kitchen cabinets. He pounded a fist into the spring-loaded drawer, which popped open just like it had a week ago. Jack reached up for the automatic pistol.

That wasn't there. *Fuck.*

"If you're looking for the gun," Cubby said, "I did a sweep of the house after we lost Christopher. Like I said, no loose ends."

"You missed this," Jeanie said.

Jack missed it too—and at first all he heard was the screaming. And then his eyes found the black canister in Jeanie's hand. It was either the world's most powerful pepper spray, or they somehow found a way to put nuclear waste in aerosol form, based on the shrieks coming from the two of them.

The thing is, Jeanie Hightower had clearly been aiming at Cubby the Cop. But thanks to all the fans in the house, much of the crazy-hot spray blew directly into the faces of…*the Bear widow and David the producer.* And damn, did they howl.

Cubby, service weapon in hand, hesitated, unsure what to do. Shoot the canister out of Jeanie's hand? Proceed with the execution of his mentor's castrating wife, who was currently crying the high-octane pepper spray out of her eyes?

Jack used this momentary hesitation to scramble to his feet and rush toward Cubby, scooping up a kitchen chair along the way. He was not going to end up zip-tied in some fucking empty pool again. Cubby turned his weapon on Jack just as Jack whipped the chair in a small arc across the detective's outstretched arms and head. Wood splintered. Cubby fell to his knees, dropped his gun. Jack pounced on him and used the remnants of the chair to beat the living fuck out of him.

With his knee on the cop's neck, Jack said, "Check the drawers for zip ties."

Jeanie searched. Cubby made a few mumbled threats, but Jack only applied more pressure to his carotid artery. He didn't care if the cop's head popped off and rolled across the ground. Jack was already a killer. What was one more corpse on his rap sheet?

"Found them!"

As Jack secured all of their wrists and ankles — last weekend's experience with the California Bear had taught him exactly what to do — Jeanie pulled out her cell phone and quickly thumbed a number.

"Bob, it's Jean. Don't ask any questions, just listen to me. I want you to call your pals at IA. And I want you to send them to the address I'm about to give you."

THE GIRL DETECTIVE

"Here's what we do."

"What's that, kid?" Hightower asked.

"First," said the Girl Detective, "you stop with that *kid* stuff or I'm going to start calling you Meatball. Next, you find us two lab coats. It's almost shift change, so there's going to be a little confusion down here on the first floor. Then we fake like we're doctors for a few minutes, and hopefully that'll be enough to help us slip by the front desk and down to the parking garage."

"You can, like, walk and stuff?"

"I'm a little unsteady, but if I feel like I'm going to fall over, I'll just lean into you."

"What about your IV lines and all of that stuff?"

"I've watched my nurse pal Meghan cap the line. I know how to do it."

"Okay, that makes sense. You do look mature for your age. Sorry about the kid stuff."

"It's okay, Hightower. Now, go find us some coats."

The ex-cop hustled down the hallway, leaving the Girl Detective in her chair. Hopefully no one on the oncology floor had noticed she was gone quite yet. This was still technically dinnertime, so she could be down in the cafeteria or in the family visiting room. Boy, did she wish she were in the cafeteria instead of fleeing a celebrity who was pretending to be a serial killer from the 1970s.

The Girl Detective scanned the first floor while also trying to project a chill vibe. *Of course I should be down here; no need to ask me if I'm lost or need help.* She would feel a lot better once she was down in the parking structure. She realized she hadn't seen the parking levels yet—Aunt Reese and Uncle Louis had whisked her directly to the emergency room, and from there, she was shuttled all around the hospital until finally landing in oncology. Uncle Louis complained about how tight the parking was (and how expensive). But were there any good hiding places if it came down to it? She had no idea.

Oh shit.

There he was.

The Actor Bear hadn't seen her yet, but he was searching. The Girl Detective knew he was walking a tightrope too. He didn't want to be recognized and swarmed by well-meaning fans. She supposed this was the downside to being psychotic and famous—potential witnesses were everywhere.

On the flip side, however, who would believe that an all-American action hero and critical darling was here at a children's hospital on a mission to kill an ex-cop and a girl fighting cancer?

The Girl Detective tried to keep him in her peripheral vision. Looking directly at him would only tip him off. But he did look different. Heavier for one thing, and the lower half of his square-jawed face was shrouded in a thick Nick Offerman–style beard. She wasn't exactly a fan of his movies, but she knew her father liked them. Maybe that would help when it came down to it. Hey, Mr. Famous Actor, don't kill us! My dad loved you in *Brain Trust* and *Getaway Man* and *Bombshell*!

Speaking of her father, the Girl Detective also wondered how he was doing right about now as he entered the Bear's den...

Without warning, she felt herself glide backward, out of the lobby and into a corridor.

"Found us coats and scrubs," Hightower said, pivoting her as if he were helping her parallel park with the nearest wall. "Do you want me to turn my back or something?"

"They're coats and scrubs," she said. "I think I'll be able to disguise myself without scandalizing you."

"I don't have kids, so I don't know how any of this works."

"You are so damn weird."

"KILLER"

"Jack," mumbled a still-blind David Peterson. "Jack Queen, are you still here?"

"Shut the fuck up, asshole."

"No . . . listen to me. This is important."

"You can tell it to the police when they get here."

"By then it'll be too late. Come on, man, please listen to me. I know I fucked up but I'm trying to do the right thing here. That's all I ever wanted to do."

"Too late for what?"

"You have to go to your daughter. She's in serious trouble."

"What do you mean? How do you even know about my daughter?"

"That crazy motherfucker who thinks he's the California Bear is going after her."

"I think the new Bear is right here, unconscious on the floor. His name is Cubby Gallagher."

"No, you've got it all wrong. I thought so, too, but now I know who it *actually* is. I didn't want to believe it. It's the fucking kid. That's why he asked for Jeanie's address."

"What fucking kid?"

"This kid. Terry Sobczak. He's been pitching me a California Bear movie for years, claimed to be the world's foremost expert. And maybe he is. He's done a lot of great research and was a huge help on the project in the early years. Then he started pushing hard to write it, but he just wasn't ready for prime time. Lasca Foster thought he was a joke, so that made it a nonstarter right there. But the kid kept pushing and pushing, and I kept him at arm's length, figuring he could still be useful to us in some way. He was desperate to meet Cassie here, probably a fanboy thing . . . but again, that was a nonstarter. There was no way I was gonna let *that* happen."

"David, you are such an asshole," Cassie moaned.

"Why are you telling me about this kid?" Jack demanded. "What does he have to do with my daughter?"

"I think he's lost his mind," Peterson said. "The other day he showed me a California Bear mask that he'd made himself. And a few other things he said . . ."

"You're not answering my question."

"Jack, he knows your daughter is a patient at Children's Hospital. He was following you and your brother-in-law, Louis, around. He called me from the goddamned lobby! And I think he might be there now."

No.

All this time Jack had assumed that fucking Cubby was the one pretending to be the new California Bear. *But the new Bear was still out there . . . and hunting for Matilda.*

Jeanie threw Jack the keys to her husband's Honda. "I'll stay here with them."

"Thank you," he mumbled, scrambling for the front door.

"I'll call Cato . . . GO GO GO!"

THE GIRL DETECTIVE

"What are you doing!?"

The Girl Detective was already tired beyond the point of exhaustion. She should have known better. Just making the trip from her bed to the bathroom left her trembling and sweaty. Her body did not appreciate all this extra activity.

"Just one second," Hightower said. "I think this is the right trash can."

She looked around the corner . . . and saw him:

A tall, hulking form with a head like a werewolf. You would think the harsh fluorescent lighting of this underground parking garage would make the mask look silly. But somehow it had the effect of making him look even more surreal, like a character from a cheesy horror movie had stepped into the real world.

RIP my life, she thought. *The California Bear is headed straight for us.*

"Matilda," the Actor Bear called out. "Matilda Queen! Wait up!"

The Actor Bear knows my name. I'm dead. The Actor Bear knows my name. RIP me.

"Got it!" Hightower exclaimed.

The Girl Detective looked down in shock, forgetting for a moment that Hightower was even by her side. He held a gun in his hands. A gun he pulled from a trash can? Then in a nanosecond she realized how it probably got there.

"You brought a gun to a children's hospital?"

"My wife said the same thing! She's the one who made me leave it down here. But I stashed it in the can, just in case. I didn't want to be fumbling with keys at a crucial moment, you know?"

"A trash can is better?"

"And your father said I don't have a brain."

None of this made sense; maybe she was dreaming. Her brain was pumped full of drugs, and she had radioactive elements in her blood, and she spent most of her free time reading about serial killers, so that would make a lot of sense.

"Matilda Queen!"

But if this were a dream, the monster would get her name right.

Hightower stood up and pointed his weapon at the Bear. "Hands in the air, fuckwad!"

There was a horrible moment when Matilda thought she was about to watch a man's fake werewolf head blow apart. She felt dizzy and faint. Reaching out for the shoulder of a man holding a gun on someone probably wasn't the smartest move, but she had no choice. She latched on to his shoulder just as Hightower reached around her waist and pulled her close. His gun remained trained on the Actor Bear.

"Do it! Now!"

But instead, the man screamed and ripped the furry mask from his head.

"Don't!" the Actor Bear cried out. "Please!"

The ex-cop refused to lower his gun. "On the ground, arms and legs spread wide!"

"I just want to talk," the Actor Bear said, "to Matilda."

"I'm not going to say it again, you tubby psycho!"

Hightower had some balls on him, calling the Bear fat.

"Don't you know who I am? I didn't mean to scare you. I just wanted to talk. I thought you'd find it . . . kind of funny?"

"Oh God," the girl said, looking up. "Hightower. Listen to him."

"Are you okay to stand on your own?"

"Let me sit down on the curb here."

"I can't. I don't want to let him out of my sight."

"He's not going to hurt us," she said.

"How do you know?"

"She's right!" the Actor Bear cried out. "I'm not going to hurt you!"

"He's not going to hurt us because he's famous. And he just showed us his face. Besides, this isn't the real California Bear."

"Lots of celebrities kill people!" Hightower protested. "Look at Robert Blake! Phil Spector!"

The Actor Bear appeared visibly relieved, however, that the Girl Detective recognized him. "Can I reach into my pocket? I have something for Matilda's father. I thought he'd be here instead of you. He's who I really wanted to see."

"Hold on," Hightower said. "You were just chasing us through a goddamn hospital. Why should we trust you?"

"He wasn't chasing us," Matilda said quietly, but loud enough for the Bear to hear.

"She's right! I wasn't chasing you! Yes, I was *following* you, yes, but only until I could talk to you in private. May I reach into my pocket?"

Curiosity must have gotten the better of Hightower, because he lowered his gun a few inches. The Actor Bear reached into his jacket pocket and pulled out the fat cream-colored envelope. There was a bit of an awkward dance as the Actor Bear moved closer and Hightower lowered the Girl Detective to the edge of the curb.

"Throw it to her," Hightower said. The Actor Bear complied. She grunted a little as she reached for the envelope and dragged it across the ground with her fingers before picking it up.

"It's for your father, but you can open it."

She did. And she'd never seen a check quite so large. Then again, she was only fourteen going on fifteen and had a lot of living yet to do. But Jeanie was right. So many motives came down to money. And she finally understood the reason for the recent Actor Bear attacks.

"That's an NDA in there, along with a check," the Bear said. "Do you know what an NDA is?"

"Duh," she said.

"It's really simple," the Actor Bear explained. "Your father signs that, he can keep the check. I'm sure you all could use it. The producer and I really want your help on this project. It's been a dream of mine since I was a kid. About your age, in fact."

"What's an NDA?" Hightower asked. "And hey, lemme see that check."

She ignored the ex-cop. He could catch up later after the adults spoke. Though part of her was touched that he was willing to shoot a famous actor in the face to protect her.

"I really, really need this series to happen."

"I get it. But I can tell you right now, my dad is not going to sign this."

"Before you say something stupid," Hightower interjected, "let me see the check."

"You're Cato Hightower, right? Listen, man, Peterson has a check for you too. I think he's going to deliver it to your wife later tonight. Now, listen, honey . . ."

"Don't honey me. You broke into people's homes. You broke into my aunt and uncle's home—oh yeah, I *know* that was you."

"What are you talking about? We haven't filmed anything yet. I don't even *know* your aunt and uncle."

"But more importantly, you're planning on, what, making a big hit movie or streaming series so you can win some award or buy another Lamborghini? All while profiting from people's pain? Not cool, bro."

"Look, I know you're going through a lot. But I'm not going to stand here and be judged by a . . . kid."

"It's fine," she said. "You can go. I'll tell my dad you dropped by."

And then she ripped the NDA—and check—in half. And then in half again. Took all her remaining strength, but the Girl Detective thought the moment called for it. Poor Hightower scrambled to pick up the pieces. When he found the section of the check with the amount on it, she literally watched his soul leave his body.

The famous actor, who practically everyone on the planet knew, turned and departed his scene without another word.

"KILLER"

As Jack raced down the 101 back toward CHLA, he tried Matilda on her cell again. And again. And again. This wasn't right. He tried Jeanie on her cell to see if she was able to reach her husband.

"I'm sure she's okay," Jeanie said over the phone. "Cato is many things, but he's not going to let anyone near her."

"It's just strange that she's not answering," Jack said. He could feel himself trembling, as if there were fault lines in his bones, seismic alerts coursing through his nervous system. He was seeing flashes of color, too, that couldn't be explained by halos around the freeway lights. Was he having a panic attack? A stroke?

"Hold on . . . I have another call."

Jack was thrown into cell phone purgatory for a harrowing minute. Traffic slowed in front of him. Jack cursed and slammed on the brakes. Was there another, faster way down to CHLA? Was he wasting precious time on this fucking freeway? Jack only realized he'd been holding his breath when Jeanie came back on the line.

"Jack, I have Cato here."

"Hightower, it's me. Please put my daughter on."

"Relax, brother," he said. "She's okay. You may not be happy with her later, but I'll let her explain it to you. I've never seen a check with that many zeroes on it."

"What the fuck," Jack said, "are you talking about? Let me talk to Matilda. She hasn't been answering her phone."

"Don't worry, she's probably not back in her room yet."

"What do you mean? Where did she go?"

"Long story short, we had a run-in with the Bear. But it turned out to be a fake Bear, some action hero idiot. He was completely harmless."

"No, he's not…Jesus Christ, Hightower, get up there with her! I don't have time to explain it now, but there's someone in the hospital right now who wants to kill my daughter. It's some asshole named Terry Sobczak! I need you to find him and stop him!"

"And I'm trying to tell you, it was all a big misunderstanding. They were trying to pay us off, not kill us. Which to my mind is mission accomplished, right?"

Jack knew he was never going to convince this stubborn son of a bitch otherwise. He threw his burner phone into the passenger seat, hammered the accelerator, cut across three lanes of tight, speeding traffic, and took the next exit.

THE GIRL DETECTIVE

All she wanted to do was collapse on her bed and sleep for the next thirty-seven hours. She'd like to say it was the excitement of the chase through the hospital and the disguise routine and the bizarre encounter with the action hero guy down in the parking garage. But the Girl Detective knew the truth. She probably would have been just as exhausted if she'd visited the cafeteria for a snack. This chemo was no joke. And there was another treatment to look forward to later tonight.

The nurses gave her a little gentle chiding when they saw her return without a parent or guardian. She invented some excuse about her father needing to meet someone about work, saying that she'd insisted on returning herself. *Blame me, not him.* They didn't like it, but they accepted it.

So she could be forgiven for not noticing anything was amiss in her room when she finally staggered back into it. Her mind was laser focused on the bed and crawling under the covers. Her phone was on her overbed table, and she had a few missed calls from her father.

Only when she sat down on the edge of the bed did she notice the door to her room closing.

"Hello, Matilda," said a voice.

The Girl Detective tried to resist her own startle reflex, but alas. She hated showing signs of weakness, especially with an unknown adversary. But her brain was quicker than her reflexes; she knew who the shadowy figure in the corner must be.

"Hello, Carnivora83."

Now it was the stranger's turn to startle. "So, it was *you* on the message boards. GirlDetective03. I should have known. How did you know my handle?"

"You're the one I've liked for this all along. I presume you're either here to figure out what went wrong or try to kill me. Or maybe both?"

"Do you know who I am? In real life?"

"Your full name? No. But I have a couple of solid guesses on your last name."

"Go ahead. Let's see how much you've figured out."

"Just so you know," the Girl Detective said, "there's pretty much an army of nurses outside that door. One of them could walk in at any moment."

"Shift change is in twenty minutes," the Bear said. "My mother used to work at hospitals. I'm very familiar with how they operate. How do you think I made my way inside this place? Nobody is coming in here until 7:05 at the earliest. Spoiler alert: I won't need that long."

"I can push a button on the edge of my bed and summon one."

"I know how that works too. And even if you could reach the button before I stopped you, I'd still have all the time I needed."

"To do what?"

She couldn't make out the Bear's features, but the shadow of his stocky body suggested a shrug. The man was being awfully nonchalant about making a death threat. She needed to throw him off-balance.

"And now I know your last name, by the way," she said. "You just gave it away."

"Did I?"

"Your mother the nurse. There were only two Bear attacks involving rape in 1983. One of them was Alannah Guthrie, a librarian in San Luis Obispo. The other was a nurse named Joyce Sobczak."

"Go on."

"Which would make you Terry Sobczak, the only child of Joyce. Father unknown. But you believe your father was the original California Bear."

Terry Sobczak sighed. It was a sigh born of not frustration or disappointment, but relief. As if someone finally, *finally* understood. Someone *saw* him.

"You figured all of that out from my posts?"

Well, duh, no, not exactly. She had a little help from Hightower's stolen files. And the final piece didn't fall into place for the Girl Detective until this very moment. Something about being in the same room with the new Bear, feeling his powerfully toxic abandoned-child energy. Once she viewed his posts through that lens, it was almost obvious. This was not a web sleuth trying to jealously protect his sad little piece of true crime turf. This was a stunted human being trying to protect — and at the same time understand — his absentee father. This was an impulse she could understand, if not perhaps to this twisted degree.

"I know everything," the Girl Detective said. "So does my father. And his bestie, who happens to be a police officer. Whatever you have in mind, it won't help. How about we just talk about it?"

The hulking form took a step forward. The light was still very dim, but she could see he was wearing a furry mask, just like his father before him.

"Sorry to be the — well, forgive the pun — *bearer* of bad tidings. But your father is most likely dead by now, along with Hightower's wife. Cubby Gallagher's a vengeful son of a bitch. He won't forgive them for murdering my father. And the cop, who is retired by the way, is no threat to me. He's pathetic."

"Do you consider me easy to kill?"

The Bear laughed. "Surely you're joking. You're just a kid, and you're fighting cancer. You're precocious, I'll give you that. You're not exactly my greatest adversary. More a nagging little detail I need to sort out before I move on."

"It's not easy to kill a human being without leaving a trace of yourself behind. I'm just wondering how you're going to do it."

"Precocious... and morbid."

Precocious? This Terry guy sounded like he spent long, passionate nights with a thesaurus. While she kept him talking, her left hand crawled toward the CALL NURSE button wrapped around the side arm of her bed.

"Guilty as charged," she said.

"It's rare but not unheard of for a chemotherapy patient to succumb to a blood clot or heart failure. Let's just leave it at that."

"And you expect me to just sit here while you mess with my IV lines? Without fighting back? You're crazier than your psycho father."

"I doubt you have the strength to stand up right now, let alone fight back. And without someone advocating for you, the chances of the police investigating your death as a homicide are exceedingly slim."

"Fair enough," the Girl Detective said. "But what next? What happens after you kill us all? What's the big plan, Bear Man?"

"I'm not going to make the classic mistake of standing here and explaining my plot to you while you stall for time," the Bear said. "I'm keenly aware of how much time I have left in this room."

"This may be true. But I have one advantage you don't."

The Bear took a step forward. "What's that?"

"A father who is still very much alive."

"KILLER"

Jack "Killer" Queen put his entire shoulder into the door, knocking it open, which in turn knocked the California Bear down to the sheet-vinyl flooring.

The big guy was faster than he looked. He flipped over onto his back, sat up, and lashed out with a clawed glove just as Jack was reaching for him. The sharpened claws cut through Jack's shirt and the flesh of his right forearm.

Jack didn't care. He snapped a punch into the Bear's masked face. The Bear swatted back. Missed. Jack punched him again, and again...

Running down the hallway to Matilda's room had felt like it took forever — especially when he saw a bulky figure in there, slowing inching toward her bed. And through the partially obscured window, the combination of terror and forced bravery on her face.

Now that he had this motherfucker within reach, Jack was not going to stop until the California Bear was warm goo on the floor.

He heard the shouting of nurses and an alarm going off, but he didn't care. Jack punched the Bear in the throat and heard him gag. Jack ripped the mask off the Bear's head and used his fist like a jackhammer against the man's naked face. Which, weirdly, was painted with makeup. This confused him for a moment but didn't stop him from delivering more punches. Jack felt hands on him — maybe nurses, maybe Hightower, he had no idea. He didn't care. He was lost in this fever dream of vengeance.

Was this what he felt when he mowed down his wife's killer? Would he forget this too?

The Bear was desperate to escape but couldn't. Jack wouldn't let him. Blood spattered all over his pudgy cheeks. His dark, beady eyes were wide with panic.

Good. You should feel afraid, you son of a bitch, because these are your last few seconds on earth.

But one thing cut through his red, red rage and swollen fists and the screaming in his brain.

"No! Dad, no!"

It was Matilda, reaching out for him, from the side of her bed.

Jack looked over at her. She was terrified, but not for herself.

"This isn't you," she said. *"You're no killer."*

INDEPENDENCE DAY 2018

JEANIE HIGHTOWER

Having a house full of people was kind of wonderful.

Well, not *full,* exactly. Only the seven of them. Sweet Matilda, her best friend, Violet, her aunt and uncle, her father. And Cato, naturally, who was manning the grill with Jack Queen trying to take command. Something about not wanting to eat hopelessly charred hamburgers drowning in cheap, oversweet barbecue sauce.

"And stop squeezing down the patties!" Jack complained. "You're going to dry them out!"

"I don't want a cum shot of grease spurting into my mouth whenever I take a bite. Maybe that's your kink, but not mine."

"Give me the spatula."

"You can have my spatula when you pry my dead fingers from the handle."

"I can make that happen."

Jeanie tuned out the boys (always the boys bickering) and wandered across the yard. They were all gathered outside. The weather was hot but nice, and the interior of their house was still very much a mess. Cato had refused to help her clean up ("What's wrong with it?") so Jeanie made the executive decision to give the neighborhood kid fifty bucks to tidy up their lawn and have their Fourth of July party back here.

"How are we doing, ladies?" Jeanie asked her youngest guests.

"I'm Gucci," Matilda said, while her best friend just smiled shyly.

Jeanie was still surprised she was here. Matilda had only checked out of the hospital three days ago, after two agonizing weeks of waiting for her blood numbers to reach an acceptable level. When she said yes, Jeanie was thrilled and worried for her in equal measure.

"Lunch should be ready just as soon as my husband and your father stop arguing," Jeanie said.

"We're gonna starve, is what you're saying."

After they shared a laugh, Jeanie hesitated. "I don't know if you're up for hearing this, but I found out some more news about our friend..."

"Terry Sobczak, also known as the California Bear 2.0? Let me guess. He wasn't actually the son of Christopher Albin Dixon, also known as the OG California Bear."

"No, he wasn't," Jeanie said with a smile. "I compared the Dixon sample I already had with Sobczak's family tree. Turns out he has a great-aunt in Philadelphia who's really into genealogy. She uploaded a sample of her DNA, and there was no match."

"Why did Terry think he was the son of the Bear?"

Jeanie shrugged. "There's no doubt his mother, Joyce, was a victim of the Bear. But maybe she was already pregnant and didn't want to reveal the child's real father?"

"Or she became pregnant soon after, and...well, same?"

"We'll never know, because Joyce Sobczak died of bone cancer."

"I'm very sorry to hear that," Matilda said. "It was early last year, wasn't it?"

"How did you know?"

"That's when Terry Sobczak's online posts intensified. He must have gone off the deep end when he lost one parent, which sent him looking for the other."

"Even if he happened to be a rapist-murderer," Jeanie replied.

"I guess we can't pick our parents."

All three of them—Violet included—looked at one another for a moment before breaking out in laughter. You had to laugh at the awful things in life. Otherwise, you'd go insane.

"I have something else to discuss with you," Jeanie said. "A question, really."

"Okay...?"

"I know you're in the middle of all kinds of insanity. But my genealogy business is growing a lot faster than I expected, and I could use a smart researcher to help me fill in the gaps."

"Do you want me to help you sort through résumés?"

Jeanie smiled and shook her head. "No. I want to *hire* you."

"What?" Matilda appeared to be truly perplexed. "You know I'm only fifteen, right? I mean, not even. Not for another two weeks."

"I know how old you are, and the excellent work you do. This is a paying job, by the way. We can do hourly, or a weekly stipend, whatever you prefer. I'd love to consider you my in-house private investigator."

Jeanie wasn't exactly sure why, but these words brought a broad smile to the girl's face. One she quickly realized was showing. She tucked it away.

"I still have my English paper to write," Matilda said. "You know, the one about how my mother was killed."

"Of course. But after you finish that paper?"

"Well... I'm probably going to need to ask my dad."

"Fair enough. Just think it over. But I'd love to have you on my team."

To Jeanie, it was a no-brainer. And perhaps Jack Queen would consider it charity—but that was the furthest thing from the truth. Jeanie needed the help, and she couldn't think of a more qualified candidate. Plus, she hated the idea of this girl drifting away. She felt like family now.

Someone gasped. Jeanie scanned the guests in her yard. Cato and Jack were still arguing over the grill, Matilda and Violet were next to her, and Reese and Louis were gawking at the house as if they were property inspectors. That is, until Reese saw what Jeanie was seeing now: a stranger walking into their yard from the side gate.

A stranger in bright-red lipstick and a black leather jacket, holding a gun.

"KILLER"

Okay — the girl who'd assaulted him outside the Sizzler wasn't a hallucination. That, he supposed, should provide some small relief.

However, this meant the girl was real and holding an actual gun, which was pointed directly at Jack.

Once again, the world took on the texture of a living nightmare. He felt unhinged from his physical body. This must be an afterlife of constant guilt, of constant punishment. After all they'd been through with the two California Bears... was this how his life was meant to end? Shot to death by a random girl who had somehow tracked him all the way to Port Hueneme?

The battle with the Bears, however, had changed them all. Hightower reached under his noisy Hawaiian shirt and pulled a snub-nosed revolver from a leather holster clipped to the wilting waist of his jeans. He pointed it back at the mystery girl. Likewise, Jeanie quietly pulled her canister of weapons-grade pepper spray from her pocket and aimed it at her too — though she was nowhere within range. Perhaps she was counting on the girl not knowing that. Even Louis, to his credit, stealthily moved his own body in front of Reese. Just in case.

Hightower spoke first. "Don't do anything stupid, honey."

"Fuck you, Hightower. And don't you fucking dare call me *honey*."

The man made a confused blink, as if that would somehow jog his memory. "Uh, do I know you?"

A mirthless laugh escaped the girl's mouth. "Oh, of course you don't know me. Why would you? That just speaks volumes, you fucking asshole."

Hightower turned to his wife and gave her a look that more or less said: *I swear to God, I have no idea what this is about, and if I should, I was too drunk to remember.*

"Who *are* you?" Jeanie asked. Jack was grateful for that question, because at the moment he was desperate to know the same thing, only he was having trouble forming words with his mouth.

"My name is Laura Church," the girl with the gun said. "My father was Julian Church. Jack Queen murdered him."

Finally, this made sense. Not just to Jack, but to everyone gathered as well. The name Julian Church hadn't been spoken among them. Ever. It was still too raw, even all these years later. But not a day had gone by without Jack thinking about that name, and the person it used to belong to. The man who killed his wife. The man he killed.

"You're a little behind on the news, darling," Hightower exclaimed. "My man was exonerated."

Now Laura turned her gun on Hightower, who flinched. Jack also snapped back into reality. If he didn't do something, this was going to spiral into a bloody nightmare. He couldn't let that happen. Not with Matilda just a few feet away.

"What do you want?" Jack asked.

Laura Church kept the gun on Hightower but locked eyes with Jack.

"I want you to tell the truth. I don't care about technicalities. I don't care about your exoneration. I don't care about paint chips or fucking paint-chip experts. I just want to know what really happened to my father."

"I swear to God," Jack said, "I do not remember."

"Really? Do you want something to jog your memory?"

"I had a few drinks at the Smoke House in Burbank. I was supposed to meet a friend, but he ghosted on me—a meeting ran late or something. The very next thing I remember was waking up in the driver's seat of my car..."

"Hold on, now," Hightower said. "Jack—don't say another fucking word. We're in murky legal territory here, and all I know is, this psycho is trespassing."

"Oh, *I'm* the psycho?" Laura asked.

"And let's not forget . . . your dear old dad killed my pal's wife. Who was young Matilda's mother."

This crushed Jack more than anything—the look on his daughter's face at this brutal reminder. She was stoic. Too stoic, he thought. He knew this hit her hard. Part of him wanted Laura Church to just fucking shoot him and get it over with. But not in front of his daughter. Maybe she'd agree to take her revenge down by the beach, where the ocean could pull him out and away from everyone he'd hurt.

"My father was also *exonerated* for that accident," Laura said. "And then your best buddy here went around town stalking him anyway. Until one night, when he got drunk enough to work up the courage to run him over in a fucking garage. *Run over my wife? I'll run you over.* It's plain as fucking day! So if you're asking me what I want, Jack? I want you to go back to jail."

A calm, quiet voice spoke.

"My father didn't do it," Matilda said, "and I can prove it."

MATILDA QUEEN, GIRL DETECTIVE

All eyes were on her now, of course, like the end of some drawing room mystery. She loved those moments in films and books. Of course, they were usually set in some posh English estate, not a tiny backyard in Port Hueneme, California. But these were modern times; the Girl Detective would have to learn to be flexible.

"May I explain?" she asked. "And, Laura, in the meantime, would you lower that weapon a little?"

Laura, gobsmacked, complied.

"Everyone was focused on the paint-chip evidence," Matilda continued. "While it's true that the expert was an unreliable drunk, and some evidence got mixed up *somehow...*"

She shot Hightower a look here, subtle enough for him to know she had his number.

"...that wasn't the real issue. The issue was who was behind the wheel of the car. And I can prove it wasn't my father, Jack Queen."

"Matilda," her father said, a haunted look on his face. "What are you doing?"

"Something any decent defense attorney would have done two years ago. Painted the full picture, with or without your cooperation."

With Violet's legwork, the Girl Detective had been able to dig up interviews with witnesses at the Smoke House — where her father had been drinking on the night in question. Yes, he'd had too much. But as a jazz piano player, he had a high tolerance. Two gin martinis with sidecars—the items on her father's bill—wouldn't be enough to render him completely unconscious. But the individual who happened to be sitting next to her father had *four* martinis on his bill.

"Holy shit," Jack mumbled. "I remember that now. He listened to my sad story and insisted on buying me a drink. Why couldn't I remember that until now?"

"My theory?" Matilda asked. "You wanted to kill Julian Church *so bad*... you just assumed you had gone and done it. Which is why you didn't press your defense attorney to do more digging. You barely mounted a defense at all. Which is what they were counting on..."

"They?" Laura asked. "Who's *they?*"

"Your father's business partners. One of them is Gregory Passarella. He was the man sitting at the bar next to my father at the Smoke House. And the same man who several witnesses remember escorting my father out to his car before placing him in the back seat... with Passarella behind the wheel."

"Uncle Greg?" Laura asked, but it wasn't really a question. More a query to herself, half not believing, half running through memories in her mind.

"I don't know exactly why 'Uncle Greg' would want to kill his business partner," Matilda continued. "I haven't nailed all of that down yet. But I have a few educated guesses. The easiest is that the hit-and-run accident that killed my mother brought a lot of shame to their firm, despite the exoneration. Julian Church had serious addiction problems—that much I know. Maybe this was a step too far for good old Uncle Greg."

The devastated look on her father's face was heartbreaking, and the Girl Detective almost considered taking a little breather to just give the old man a hug. But she needed to finish—to bring this awful mess to some kind of conclusion.

"But what I do know," Matilda said, "and can *prove,* is that Gregory Passarella was behind the wheel when my father's car drove to the Burbank Town Center and ran down Julian Church... who, by the way, was staggering out of Barney's Beanery and waiting for an Uber when he was killed."

"Holy shit," Jeanie mumbled. "Matilda, honey...how did you learn all of this?"

"I had a lot of hours to kill at the children's hospital."

"No, I'm serious. How could you possibly know all of this?"

"You'd be surprised by how many doors open when you...um, impersonate an insurance investigator. And Violet is very skilled at pretending she's a college intern about to be drawn and quartered unless she brings her big, bad boss man exactly what he wants."

"High school drama class," Violet said quietly by way of explanation. When she realized everyone was staring at her, she shrugged. "We did a lot of improv."

Everybody, that is, except Laura Church, who appeared to be as lost as Matilda's father. "I'm going to need to see this proof," she finally said to Matilda.

"I've got an even better idea," Jeanie said. "Put the gun away, have some food, and then we can discuss next steps."

"What do you mean, next steps?"

"A few minutes ago, I became a professional private detective," Matilda Queen said. "And you're my first client."

JEANIE HIGHTOWER

After the guns were tucked away, and halting, awkward apologies made (all around)—as well as equally awkward introductions—Jeanie turned to her husband. "Nice work, genius."

"I'm not even sure I follow half of that," Hightower said.

"Yeah, no shit. But I do. That kid is a prodigy. So glad I hired her."

"Hey, I never claimed to be a good detective."

"At least you're good with a gun."

"You don't know that. I still haven't had the chance to fire the damned thing... and, wait, what do you mean you *hired* her? For what?"

"My business," Jeanie said. "Correction: *our* business."

"You're a genealogist. I'm retired. I'm not going to spend the best years of my life digging through baptism records in some dusty fucking church."

"That's not what we're going to be doing."

"What, then?"

"Catching the people who think they've gotten away with it."

Hightower smiled. "Did you know that Arthur Conan Doyle once said it's every man's business to see justice done?"

JACK QUEEN

Close to sunset they walked down to the ocean together, just father and daughter. She was weak and tired but insisted on it. The ocean was the thing that excited Matilda the most when they first moved to Los Angeles all those years ago, before life took a crazy left turn. Maybe they weren't trapped in some Alternate Universe of Awful.

Well, there was still some awful. The day before, July 3, they had met with the oncologists at Children's Hospital. Matilda had responded well to the chemo, but that wouldn't be enough. Not for this fight. They still believed the only way to save her would be with a bone marrow transplant. They said very little to each other on the ride home to Toluca Lake and upon arrival retreated to their own corners (Matilda on her phone, Jack on a laptop borrowed from Louis) and proceeded to Google-terrify themselves. When they finally did talk about it, they agreed to table it until after the Fourth of July. They had just been through a month of hell; no need to dive back in so quickly. But it was on their minds.

Jack tried hard not to let it intrude on this particular moment, however. The sun was slipping down behind the horizon, casting deep pinks and purples everywhere. Matilda smiled, her face lifted for both the final rays and the biting sea wind, her arms stretched wide and — in typical Matilda Finnerty Queen fashion — completely unafraid.

AFTERWORD

California Bear was meant to be my jab at the true crime industry, where huge profits are reaped from people's worst nightmares. I watched a lot of those streaming series with some degree of admiration. They look slick and are smartly produced. But I also sit there and think: *My God, I am being entertained by someone's worst possible day.* And there are a lot of amateur sleuths out there making strange connections that have no relation to reality. A lot of times, they make things worse.

We live in a time where so much goes unpunished; the wicked and corrupt have free rein. (And that's just in American politics.) I like the idea of a bunch of scrappy people out there trying to right some wrongs.

I should also explain the very personal motivation behind this novel. In April 2018, I read an *LA Times* piece about an ex-cop who overturned the wrongful conviction of a man who spent forty years in prison for two murders he did not commit. The former felon, it turned out, went on to live with the ex-cop and his wife at their beach house. I wondered: Wow, what was it like to finally sit down and have a beer with the man who sprung you from prison? And then I wondered: Wait . . . what if it turned out that the killer *actually did it*?

That was April 29, 2018. (I just checked my notes.)

Exactly one month later, in late May 2018, my daughter, Evie, was diagnosed with leukemia. It was a tremendous shock to our family, but we rallied around her. My wife and I swore she would never be alone in the hospital, so we took turns spending the night with her. There, late at night in Children's Hospital Los Angeles, I starting writing the early chapters of *California Bear* as an escape hatch. I wanted some degree of control over the world, even a fictional one.

And the character of Matilda Finnerty was pure Evie, facing the unknown with incredible strength and humor and grace. Evie has always been a muse to me, and I thought this new character would be a natural follow-up to the heroes of *Canary* (Sarie Holland) and *Revolver* (Audrey Walczak). This felt like the third chapter of my "daughter trilogy."

We lost our daughter in October 2018. And for a while, I wasn't sure I'd be able to finish this novel, or any other.

But when I returned to work on it, I realized that the Girl Detective was there waiting for me to keep going. It was nice to hear her voice again. I may not have control over what happens in the real world, but I sure as hell can make sure Matilda's brain and heart continue to live on in an old-school mystery—a genre Evie dearly loved. They can be an escape hatch, maybe, from this increasingly absurd world.

June 2023

THE GIRL DETECTIVE'S
HONOR ROLL

Matilda Queen would like to thank the following individuals for their assistance in compiling the case history of the so-called "California Bear." When pressed for more details, Miss Queen responded: "They know what they did."

Farhad Amid

Linda Arends

Lou Boxer

John Carpenter

Sandy King Carpenter

Kim Cooper

Ainsley Davies

Arthur Conan Doyle

Chris Farnsworth

Katherine Fausset

Danielle Finnegan

Joe Gangemi

Eileen G. Ghetti

Allan "Knight Moves" Guthrie

Donald Kanewski

Peter Katz

Joshua Kendall

Barry King

Robert Kulb

Chris Morgan

Terry Morgan

Shannon Morris-King

Marie Mundaca

Kevin Nicklaus

Helen O'Hare

Patton Oswalt

David Peterson

Scott Reynolds

Sam Secor

Richard Schave

Tim Scully

Brent Spiner

Ben H. Winters

And on the very top of the honor roll, forever: Meredith, Parker and Evie.

ABOUT THE AUTHOR

Duane Swierczynski is the *New York Times* Bestselling and two-time Edgar-nominated author of ten novels including *Revolver, Canary* and *Expiration Date,* as well as the graphic novels *Breakneck* and *Redhead.* Along with James Patterson, Duane co-wrote *Lion & Lamb* and co-created the Audible Originals *The Guilty,* starring John Lithgow and Bryce Dallas Howard, and *Zero Tolerance,* starring Hilary Swank. He's also written over 250 comic books including *Cable, Deadpool, The Immortal Iron Fist, Punisher, Birds of Prey, Bloodshot* and *Star Wars: Rogue One.* His first short story collection, *Lush and other tales of Boozy Mayhem,* was recently published by Cimarron Street Books. A native Philadelphian, Duane now lives in Southern California with his family. Learn more at gleefulmayhem.com.